**As an evil traitor threatens
to destroy the top-secret SPEAR agency,
A YEAR OF LOVING DANGEROUSLY
continues....**

Jeff Kirby
A green-eyed M.D. and a man
very much in love with his wife…

*Though he'd married Tish Buckner in haste,
this M.D. in training took his vows very seriously.
Especially now that his bride
was struggling for her life!*

Tish Buckner
A stubborn strength in her dark brown eyes
was outdone only by her passion

*She never dreamed she and Jeff had a chance,
yet her heart could not refuse his sudden proposal.
But had her dangerous undercover work
jeopardized her future with Jeff?*

Del Rogers
An amber-eyed agent
who is determined to get his man

*After seeing the havoc the deadly traitor called
Simon had caused for his colleagues,
Del is prepared to do anything to take down
the man who hopes to take down SPEAR....*

Dear Reader,

Once again, we've rounded up six exciting romances to keep you reading all month, starting with the latest installment in Marilyn Pappano's HEARTBREAK CANYON miniseries. *The Sheriff's Surrender* is a reunion romance with lots of suspense, lots of passion—lots of *emotion*—to keep you turning the pages. Don't miss it.

And for all of you who've gotten hooked on A YEAR OF LOVING DANGEROUSLY, we've got *The Way We Wed*. Pat Warren does a great job telling this tale of a secret marriage between two SPEAR agents who couldn't be more different— or more right for each other. Merline Lovelace is back with *Twice in a Lifetime,* the latest saga in MEN OF THE BAR H. How she keeps coming up with such fabulous books, I'll never know—but I *do* know we're all glad she does. Return to the WIDE OPEN SPACES of Alberta, Canada, with Judith Duncan in *If Wishes Were Horses....* This is the kind of book that will have you tied up in emotional knots, so keep the tissues handy. Cheryl Biggs returns with *Hart's Last Stand,* a suspenseful romance that will keep you turning the pages at a furious clip. Finally, don't miss the debut of a fine new voice, Wendy Rosnau. *A Younger Woman* is one of those irresistible stories, and it's bound to establish her as a reader favorite right out of the starting gate.

Enjoy them all, then come back next month for more of the best and most exciting romance reading around—only in Silhouette Intimate Moments.

Yours,

Leslie J. Wainger
Executive Senior Editor

Please address questions and book requests to:
Silhouette Reader Service
U.S.: 3010 Walden Ave., P.O. Box 1325, Buffalo, NY 14269
Canadian: P.O. Box 609, Fort Erie, Ont. L2A 5X3

Pat Warren
The Way We Wed

Silhouette®

INTIMATE MOMENTS™
Published by Silhouette Books
America's Publisher of Contemporary Romance

Special thanks and acknowledgment are given
to Pat Warren for her contribution to the
A YEAR OF LOVING DANGEROUSLY series.

This book is dedicated to my neighbor,
Judy Eddy, whose energy and sense of humor
make her a joy to be around.

 SILHOUETTE BOOKS

ISBN 0-373-27140-9

THE WAY WE WED

Copyright © 2001 by Harlequin Books S.A.

Visit Silhouette at www.eHarlequin.com

Printed in U.S.A.

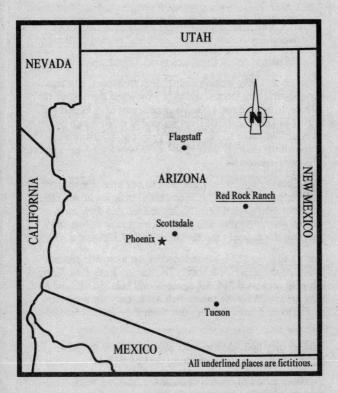

All underlined places are fictitious.

A note from popular writer Pat Warren, author of over thirty novels for Silhouette and Harlequin Books

Dear Reader,

As much as I love writing and reading romances, I'm also very drawn to mysteries, which is why when the editors at Silhouette offered me a chance to be a part of A YEAR OF LOVING DANGEROUSLY, I jumped at it. To watch a love story unfold between two special people is heartwarming. Then to see all the dangers their jobs—their very lives—are involved in is pure excitement.

Tish Buckner turned her back on a life of privilege to work with the agents of SPEAR because she believes in what they stand for. She's intelligent, highly trained and dedicated, as well as very beautiful. She has no intention of falling in love, yet from the moment she lays eyes on Jeff Kirby, she's his.

Jeff's had a hard life—abandoned by his alcoholic parents, living on the streets, constantly on the run. Until East Kirby, a highly respected SPEAR agent, found him and showed him how to care. When he meets Tish, he's ready for love. Now all he has to do is convince her that what they feel is real and lasting.

And all they both have to do is stay alive amid terrorist bombings and an evil man out to destroy SPEAR.

I've been a part of several continuities, starting with Harlequin's TYLER series a while back, then Silhouette's first MONTANA MAVERICKS and also the more recent MONTANA MAVERICKS series. It's a privilege and a challenge to join so many talented authors in telling a thrilling love story with a mystery threaded throughout all twelve books. I hope you enjoy reading about Tish and Jeff's romance as much as I enjoyed writing it for you.

Pat Warren

Chapter 1

Condor Mountain Resort and Spa

The late afternoon sun was quite hot along the Pacific Coast of Southern California even in mid-April. Jeff Kirby felt his shirt sticking to his back as well as the dampness of his jogging shorts, but he ignored both. Running on the hard-packed sand of the beach at the foot of Condor Mountain Resort and Spa was something he looked forward to each time he returned. His shoes hit the ground with staccato precision, spraying clumps of wet sand as he made his way north alongside the frothy waves. Some distance out, seagulls artfully dived into the sea in search of a late lunch.

Glancing at a cloudless blue sky, Jeff felt glad to be alive, grateful for each day. A near-death experience will do that to a person, he decided. He'd come a shade too close for comfort last year and didn't ever want to repeat the ordeal. Yet he was increasingly aware that the work he did, the job he'd chosen, would ultimately put him in danger more often than not. He knew that, yet chose to stay, and his reasons were many and varied. They included his dad, the exciting challenge and the assurance that he was contributing, doing some good in some small way.

Jeff's adoptive father, Easton Kirby, had once been one of the top field agents for SPEAR, a secret government agency that dated back to the Civil War and was rumored to have been founded by no less than Abraham Lincoln himself. But a devastating personal incident had all but turned East into a recluse, a man haunted by his own demons, one who holed up in his room at Condor and withdrew from all who cared about him.

Until the night he'd encountered a fourteen-year-old boy who'd run away from the latest in a series of foster homes, a boy as damaged and needy as East was. That boy's name was Jeff.

They'd both been the walking wounded back then, but each had managed to overcome a disturbing past, to bond with one another and learn to care, to trust again. After a slow healing time, East, who'd been twenty-five ten years ago, only eleven years older than Jeff, had adopted the boy and taken over the running of Condor Mountain Resort as a civilian employee. Only occasionally these days did either of them speak of those past terrible years.

Through most of his teen years and later, Jeff had met or heard about several agents—men and women—who'd been badly hurt in the line of duty, some physically, some emotionally. A few had even died. But with the arrogance of youth, he'd felt certain none of those things would happen to him. He'd quickly shot up to a height of six feet, lean and muscled from training sessions and working out regularly. He'd felt confident, invincible, ready to take on the world.

Until the day he'd been kidnapped, buried alive and left to die.

Slowing his steps, Jeff came to a stop, breathing deeply. He bent over, bracing his hands on his knees, letting his body cool. That episode had changed him forever.

Finally he straightened, squinting into the sun, swiping the dampness from his face. It was after he'd been rescued that he'd learned from Alicia, the woman Easton eventually married, how the kidnapping had affected his adoptive father. East had left the comfort and safety of Condor Resort and spearheaded the operation that had saved Jeff's life. That was the second time Easton had rescued Jeff. His gratitude and love for the man knew no bounds.

A curious gull executed a graceful landing close to where Jeff stood, cocking his head at the human intruder before taking off overhead. Jeff watched the bird circling for a minute, envying his freedom of movement, then started on his run back to the only real home he'd ever known. He ran more slowly this time, appreciating the pull and strain of his muscles. He'd recently returned from Australia where he'd received more field training for his medevac specialty before the summer session began. He'd doubled up on his courses and attended med school year-round, and he'd just finished his first year of residency with two more to go before becoming a full-time doctor and SPEAR agent.

Jeff frowned as his thoughts drifted to another matter, one equally if not more important to him: Tish Buckner. Skirting a moss-covered rock, he wondered why the course of love never ran smoothly. Certainly East and Alicia—or Ally as she liked to be called—had had some difficult times and it was no different with almost everyone he knew. Falling in love was only the beginning, Jeff decided. It was the happily-ever-after part that was a problem.

He'd met Tish last year at Red Rock Ranch in northern Arizona where he'd gone to recuperate after his ordeal, and he'd fallen for her fast and hard. She was a SPEAR agent who'd come to take a refresher course on her vacation because she wasn't the type for lazing about. But their road to happiness had been filled with stumbling blocks right from the start and, sadly, they'd gone their separate ways. Running across her in Australia a few weeks ago had been a lucky break, but they'd had too little private time. He'd pretty well convinced her they should try again when the call had come in that Tish was needed along with several other SPEAR agents. A traitor known as Simon, who'd been orchestrating all sorts of treasonous acts against the country and framing Jonah, the head of SPEAR, had been traced to New York. Tish had quickly boarded a helicopter to follow him. But she'd promised to meet with Jeff to talk more as soon as her assignment ended.

This time he'd make her see that they belonged together, Jeff vowed, as his steps brought him back to the foot of the majestic resort where he paused. As always, this view from below captured his imagination. The first time East had walked with him along the beach and they'd paused at the steps leading up, forty-four to be exact, Jeff had said the place looked like pictures of castles he'd seen in books. He never had figured out how they'd managed to put up such a magnificent building that was five stories from the beach side, yet appeared to be only four from the front entrance. As boy and man, the arrangement had intrigued him.

It was part of the Monarch Hotel chain owned and operated as one of SPEAR's legitimate business enterprises. The lobby floor of Condor offered moneyed guests a luxurious retreat with a magnificent view and a cosmopolitan atmosphere with a renowned chef holding court in both restaurants. Floors two, three and four offered suites of varying sizes, all beautifully appointed. But the penthouse floor was where East and Alicia had their quarters plus there were private rooms reserved for agents who might need a little R and R, some downtime. East saw to it that they got what they needed and went back to the field refreshed. Jeff's room was also located on the fourth floor.

At the sound of a barking sea lion, Jeff turned to watch the slick seal sun himself on a spit of land that zigzagged into the sea. Some Californians didn't care for this rocky, often treacherous section of beach, but Jeff loved it. There was majesty here and power and, ultimately, peace. He stood for a minute more gazing at the relentless waves pounding at the shore, then began the steep climb.

He was nearly to the landing that led to the stone stairs of the terrace dining room where waiters were setting the tables for the evening meal when he spotted his dad standing by the waist-high railing. As always, Jeff was aware that there was a certain presence about East that people recognized immediately. Perhaps it was his height, a couple of inches taller than Jeff's six feet, or his powerful build that suggested he might be a professional athlete. There was a hint of mystery about East that attracted women and intrigued men. He was definitely a formidable man, but Jeff had experienced the kindness and compassion beneath the tough exterior of those chiseled features.

Now, as Jeff hurried up the last few steps, he couldn't help wondering what had put that very serious look on his father's face. From the beginning, they'd shared a remarkable intuition about one another that was usually right.

Jeff felt a worried frown form as he stepped onto the terrace. "What's wrong?" he asked East.

"Let's go to my quarters and I'll tell you." East made his way through the tables, nodding to the maître'd who was arranging dinner menus.

Jeff followed him across the rustic lobby past the guest elevators and stopped in front of the one at the far end, their private car to the fourth floor. As East inserted his special key to gain access, Jeff felt a shiver skitter down his spine which had nothing to do with the air-conditioning cooling his sweaty body. Dad had taught him patience as a teenager—which went against his nature—and also that they were never to discuss SPEAR business in front of outsiders. Stepping into the elevator and turning to face the doors that silently slid shut, his thoughts ran through several possibilities, but he couldn't seem to settle on any one thing. The most probable choice was that SPEAR needed him at some other location where his medevac training, incomplete though it was, would be useful.

Stepping out on the penthouse floor, East again used his key to enter his quarters and walked directly to the kitchen where he handed Jeff a clean towel before pouring him a tall glass of orange juice.

Jeff knew his dad was not one to be rushed, that he would say what needed to be said in his own way. So he drank the juice and wiped his face, then draped the towel around his neck as his anxiety built. East was openly studying him, as if gauging how best to deliver bad news. Finally Jeff could stand it no longer. "What is it?"

"There's been an accident. In New York." The ever present shadows in East's brown eyes seemed to darken to near black. "Several agents were checking out a warehouse where Simon was reportedly stockpiling weapons. A bomb went off."

Jeff felt the blood drain from his face as his hands tightened on the glass he was holding. "Tish?" He managed to get her name out, his voice strained. *Oh, God! Not now, please.*

"She's in the hospital, unconscious." East reached over, placed a hand on his son's shoulder and squeezed hard.

"The prognosis?" Jeff asked as a terrible weight took up residence in his chest.

East shook his head. "No one knows."

Jeff was not a man who could wait for answers. He had to take action, to find out for himself. He set down the glass and picked up the phone on the kitchen counter. "What hospital?"

East handed him a notepad where he'd jotted down the phone number, knowing his son would want to call. "Metropolitan General in Manhattan."

It took Jeff some time to get through to the right floor, the right nurse's station. Tish was in surgery, he was told, her injuries quite serious, but the nurse wouldn't elaborate. Trying to stay in control of his emotions, Jeff scrubbed a hand across his face. "I've got to go there," he told East as he hung up.

His dad handed him a sheet of paper. "You're booked on the red-eye out of Los Angeles International Airport. Get ready and I'll drive you to the airport."

Jeff saw the concern in East's eyes and it was almost his undoing. He took a step closer and felt his father's arms close around him in a comforting hug. "I can't lose her, Dad. Not again."

"You won't, son. Go to her, let her know you're there. It could make all the difference." East stepped back, then let him go.

Jeff hurried to his room, his mind racing, his heart heavy.

"Why can't we get this guy?" Jeff asked, frustration evident in every word. Seated beside East in his fortified ATV as his dad expertly maneuvered the steep, winding roads of the mountainous area where Condor was located, he wanted to lash out at something, someone. "SPEAR agents have been chasing this traitor all over the globe for months and no one's come close to capturing or killing him. How long are we expected to keep this up, until all our best people are maimed or dead?"

In direct contrast, Easton's voice was calm, reasonable, reassuring. "I understand how you feel. Actually, several agents have come close to capturing Simon, but..."

"Close only counts in horseshoes and hand grenades," Jeff muttered, then realized what he'd just said. A hand grenade was similar to a bomb and a bomb was what had put Tish in the hospital.

"It's hard to be patient when someone you care for is involved," East continued in the same quiet tone and Jeff was reminded of all that his father had gone through when he'd been held captive. "You've been with SPEAR quite a while now, Jeff. You're aware how treacherous and devious this man is. But we have to keep trying until we get him. It's a matter of national importance."

Jeff let out a shuddering breath. "I know and I'm sorry. I'm just so damn worried. I don't even know if she made it through the surgery."

"Use your cell phone. It's been several hours. Call the hospital again."

Jeff pulled out his cell, the special phone all SPEAR agents carried. The system was established by orbiting satellites, not dependent on normal cells, so he could talk to anyone on the planet at any time. The signal also was digitalized and encoded so no one else could unscramble the conversation.

When he finished his call and disconnected, he drew in a deep, calming breath. "She made it through surgery and she's in recovery. She'll be transferred to the intensive care unit from there. But it's still touch-and-go." He turned toward East. "Did you talk with the hospital earlier?"

"Yes, while you were showering. I let them know who you were and that you were to have top clearance for visitation. They didn't much like it, but then hospital personnel usually don't like outside interference, even from government agents. However, they promised to cooperate." East entered the freeway and headed for LAX.

They drove in silence for several miles, each lost in his own troubled thoughts. Finally, Jeff spoke, a sudden rush of emotion clogging his throat. "I thought, after Australia, that we'd have a chance, but we didn't have enough time."

A muscle clenched in East's jaw. "When there's a crisis, there's never enough time."

"And there's always a crisis somewhere." Jeff sounded defeated, which wasn't like him. Normally, he was upbeat, hopeful. But this wasn't a normal circumstance.

"You can always quit SPEAR," East suggested, then held his breath.

Jeff took a moment to consider that. "You know as well as I do that if I were a quitter, I wouldn't be here at all."

His father sent him a look of understanding, of love and gratitude. "Nor would I, son."

Minutes later, East pulled up at the boarding terminal and stopped. He shoved the gearshift into Park as Jeff climbed out and grabbed his leather overnight bag. East walked around the vehicle, stopped in front of his son and gazed into his eyes. The look held and seemed to say volumes. "Keep me informed, will you?"

"I will. Give my love to Ally and the baby. I'm sorry I didn't get a chance to say goodbye." East and Alicia's baby girl, Annie, had been born three days ago; mother and child were still in the hospital.

"She'll understand," East assured him.

Jeff hugged his father tightly for several long seconds, then picked up his bag and walked toward the double doors, not looking back. He didn't want his dad to see the moisture in his eyes.

The first-class ticket East had arranged got Jeff a comfortable aisle seat on the big jumbo jet in the second row. After takeoff, he stretched out his long legs and accepted a cup of black coffee from the flight attendant, but refused the snack she offered. He didn't need food. He needed a miracle.

A bomb blast. Good Lord, how could anyone survive such a thing? Myriad questions whirled around in his brain. How close had Tish been to the blast? How extensive were her injuries? What had she been operated on for? What was her revised prognosis? The nurse he'd spoken with had said, ''It's still touch-and-go.'' What exactly did that mean?

Jeff had two more years of medical training left, planning to specialize in trauma injuries, the choice SPEAR felt would be most beneficial to the organization. Well, a bomb injury certainly qualified as a trauma. Yet he had no idea what kind of injuries she'd sustained.

Just a few weeks ago in Australia, he'd treated SPEAR agent Lise Meldrum for a gunshot wound to the shoulder. Simple things like that didn't throw him. But bomb injuries? Most doctors never even run across such a thing in a lifetime of practice. But then, most doctors don't work for secret government agencies.

The coffee was hot and strong. Jeff drank half a cup before leaning his head back and shutting his eyes. He knew he couldn't sleep so he might as well enjoy the caffeine. Who could sleep when his imagination had him picturing all sorts of terribly traumatic injuries? Behind closed eyelids, scenes past and present, along with future possibilities, vied for his attention.

Actually, on second thought, Lise's injury hadn't exactly been cut-and-dried. The bullet had exited through the other side, but had come perilously close to the pulmonary artery causing a great deal of bleeding. Lise also had difficulty breathing because the passage to her lungs was involved. A grateful Russell Devane, another SPEAR agent who'd fallen in love with Lise, had thanked Jeff profusely for saving her life. The doctor at the hospital where they'd finally taken Lise also had praised his work.

But that was still small potatoes compared with bomb injuries, he was certain. He'd heard through the grapevine that Russell and Lise were getting married. Not for the first time, he wondered if it was possible in this crazy business to be happily married? East and Ally seemed content, but they were only on the fringes of SPEAR now, managing Condor.

Restless, he leaned toward the window and gazed out into the dark night. It was dark with not a cloud visible. Jeff reached for the phone on the seat back in front of him and dialed the New York hospital. After much transferring about, he finally was able to talk with the recovery room nurse. But all he learned was that Tish was resting comfortably considering the circumstances.

What the hell did that mean?

Disconnecting, Jeff vowed that when he became a full-fledged doctor, he would never be vague with relatives of his patients. If only they knew what they put people through, they'd be more forthcoming. Maybe.

Sitting back, he drained his coffee cup and again closed his eyes. The overhead cabin lights had been dimmed and the half dozen other passengers in first class appeared to be settling down for some shut-eye. If he couldn't sleep, at least he could rest his body, Jeff decided, and pushed his seat back as far as it would go. He tried closing his eyes and emptying his mind, but it didn't work. Awake or asleep, he pictured Tish, her lovely smile, her wonderful laugh.

Sighing, he let himself remember the summer day last year that he'd seen her for the first time....

Red Rock Ranch, previous summer

Jeff leaned against the corral fence, one booted foot propped on the bottom rung, lazily watching the horses on a hot August afternoon. Red Rock Ranch in northern Arizona was the perfect place for him to recuperate after his ordeal in Idaho, or so East had said. His dad had told him to do as little or as much as he wanted, not to push himself, to let his psyche heal.

However, Jeff had arrived only yesterday and he'd already discovered that he wasn't very good at doing nothing.

Red Rock was another of SPEAR's legitimate businesses, a working cattle ranch that also provided adventure vacations for monied tourists. But more importantly, it was a SPEAR training site ideally situated in the rugged mountains surrounding the ranch. It was beautiful country with its freshwater streams, the isolated location that brought about pitch-black nights, the silence broken only by the animals nearby.

And there were plenty of them, two thousand head of Brahman-cross cows, twenty bulls and a couple dozen horses. The nearest town was two hours away on a rough dirt road scarcely navigable without an ATV. There were several of those around, too, and even an ultralight aircraft the manager used to fly out each morning over the 120 acres to check the water supply, fences and livestock. It was a huge operation and Jeff had learned to respect the dozen or so ranch hands who kept things running smoothly.

He eased his hat back farther on his blond head and glanced up to watch a hawk chase a low-flying quail. He'd only visited Red Rock once before in his late teens, but the manager, Slim Huxley, remembered him well. That summer, Slim had taught him to ride a horse, how to spot fresh mountain lion tracks and the best way to round up cattle to herd them to a different pasture, and a whole lot more. East had commented when Jeff had returned to Condor that fall that he'd sent away a boy and gotten back a man, for Jeff had filled out and muscled up.

Suddenly the lazy afternoon quiet was broken by the sound of a galloping horse coming closer. Jeff turned his head in the direction of the open pastureland off to the left.

She was some distance away yet, astride a chestnut mare, her short dark hair flying about her face. With the pounding of each hoof, red dust sprayed from the dry rocky soil beneath the short, tough grass. Luckily there were no trees in her path for she was riding at a pretty good clip, heading for the barn right behind him. Straightening, he watched her approach.

Now he could tell she was as one with the horse, leaning forward over the thick neck, grasping handfuls of coarse mane. She was a small woman, yet she seemed totally unafraid of the huge beast. Fascinated, Jeff wondered who she was, this woman who rode so confidently. He was aware there were about twenty tourists staying at the ranch just now, but none that he'd seen ride like that.

The mare sensed the ride was nearly over and seemed reluctant to stop even though they were nearing the barn. Finally, the big horse gave in and moved into a canter, then a walk. Moments later, both mare and rider came to a halt near him. The woman swung out of the saddle with a move so graceful that he knew she'd done it many times before.

Jeff studied her in silence, taking his time to admire. She was small and feminine-looking despite the outsize man's shirt and snug jeans she wore. Her wind-tossed hair was a rich brown, glossy, curling forward at her chin. Her face was flushed from her ride, a lovely olive complexion hinting at a Mediterranean heritage, her features fine-boned. Her mouth had a full lower lip that immediately had him wondering how it would feel to kiss her.

Jeff leaned against the fence and waited for her to notice him.

"Good girl," the woman told the mare as she stroked the horse's hide. The horse bobbed her big head up and down, then stretched to nuzzle the rider. The woman let out a husky laugh, then swung about and spotted Jeff for the first time. She shook back her hair while her chocolate-brown eyes slowly took inventory of him from his black Stetson to his leather boots, lingering just a heartbeat too long on his midsection.

Suddenly she smiled and Jeff felt his heart do a somersault.

"You must be new," she said in a voice as husky as her laugh. She stepped closer, held out her hand. "I'm Tish Buckner."

He straightened, took her hand, slender but capable, and felt a jolt skitter up his spine. Her fingers trembled in his grasp and he knew she felt something, too. He watched nerves dance in her surprised gaze, saw her try to conceal her reaction.

"Jeff Kirby," he said, relieved that his voice hadn't cracked since he felt like a pubescent teenager meeting his first girl. He could easily stand here holding her hand and staring into those fathomless brown eyes forever, he decided. Lord, but she was beautiful.

"Nice to meet you," Tish replied, then tugged her hand free of his, but kept her eyes on his face. She studied him a moment longer, then raised her firm chin that hinted at a stubborn streak and handed him the mare's reins. "Would you cool her down, please? Her name's Belladonna and she belongs in stall 10."

It took a moment for Jeff to realize she thought he was one of the ranch hands. Amusement bubbled up inside him, but he struggled not to react to her somewhat haughty, lady-of-the-manor attitude. A natural mistake, he supposed, seeing as how he was hanging around the corral wearing worn jeans, a denim work shirt and scuffed boots.

"Yes, ma'am," he said, smiling down at her. He was half a foot taller at the very least. He had a sudden urge to reach over and touch her shiny hair, to watch the heat move into those big eyes. Or would they turn cool and frosty? he wondered. He decided to find out.

Moving one step closer, Jeff raised his hand and tucked a loose strand of her hair behind her ear, then let his fingers linger in the softness. He watched the sun get caught in her eyes and fleck the brown with gold as she narrowed them at him, then stepped back.

"If you value your hand, you won't do that again," Tish said, her voice suddenly cold as a mountain stream.

So she was skittish, like a newborn filly. She didn't seem like the average city-bred tourist who came to Red Rock for a ranch vacation, Jeff thought. She was too good a horsewoman and definitely not interested in a flirtation with a cowboy. No rings on her fingers, he noticed, so she probably wasn't attached. If she was a SPEAR agent, he hadn't heard of her. His gaze slid to her mouth, that full lip that seemed to invite a man to explore. No, he definitely hadn't met her before. He'd have remembered that mouth. He'd love to question her, but he decided it might be more fun to allow her to think he was a hired hand. For now.

Jeff dropped his hand, gave her a lazy smile. "No offense meant, ma'am. I guess you don't like to be touched." It was his turn to narrow his gaze, as if sizing her up. "But maybe you just need to be touched by the right man."

Now there was fire in her eyes as she stiffened. Without another word, she turned and caressed the mare's flank, noticeably angry when she saw that her hand wasn't steady. "See you tomorrow, baby," she whispered to Belladonna. Turning, Tish walked away, her back ramrod straight, her shoulders obviously tense.

Jeff watched her go until she was out of sight, then led the mare to the side pasture to walk her awhile before wiping her down after that vigorous run. "Sure wish you could talk, Belladonna," Jeff commented. "I'd love to hear all about that lady."

Red Rock Ranch consisted of several outbuildings including separate barns for milking cows and newborn calves, others for insemination and birthing as well as horse stables. There was also a large bunkhouse where the ranch hands lived and an adjacent mess hall that had its own cook. The tourists vacationed in a luxurious three-story building that offered spectacular views from deluxe suites. Their dining room took up nearly half of the lower floor.

SPEAR agents stayed in the two-story main house with large, homey rooms with private baths on the top floor. On the lower level was a rustic lobby with slate flooring, a conference room, the manager's office and a great room with a huge stone fireplace, comfortable furniture, a large-screen television and a full wall of bookcases filled to over-flowing.

There was also the dining room which could easily rival that of a five-star hotel. Breakfast was served from five to ten, lunch from twelve to two and dinner was a leisurely affair available from six on into the evening. In between, snacks could be had by phoning the kitchen and would be delivered to the agent's room, provided Elsa Winchester, the cook, liked you. All others had best stay out of her way, for she ran her kitchen with an autocratic hand.

Jeff deliberately hadn't gone down for the evening meal. The first reason was that Elsa was a terrific cook. Too terrific. He'd had a big breakfast and a mammoth lunch, at Elsa's insistence, since she remembered him from his earlier visit and still thought of him as a growing boy. If he added a huge dinner, he'd be taking in as many calories as the cowhands who spent twelve or fourteen hours using up energy while he was doing precious little to work off gigantic meals. The last thing he wanted was to balloon up, so he decided to drop by around the time he figured most of the agents would be either finished or having coffee.

The second reason was that he'd mosied over to the tourist quarters and discovered that Tish Buckner wasn't staying there. Next he'd cornered the clerk at the front desk of the main house for the real lowdown. Naomi Star had red hair, thick glasses, an infectious smile and knew everyone and everything that went on at the ranch. Jeff had turned on the charm and Naomi had revealed that Tish wasn't married, was a very private person and, that as far as she knew, Tish was at Red Rock on vacation.

Armed with that knowledge, Jeff sauntered into the dining room around seven just as the sun was streaking the sky outside the cathedral-style windows with gold and orange and magenta strokes before it disappeared behind the mountains. He was in luck for Tish was there, seated between Slim Huxley, the ranch manager, and John Winters, a fortyish, dark-haired agent Jeff had only just met yesterday. The three other chairs at the table were vacant. Of the dozen tables in the room, only two others were occupied.

Tish was deep in conversation with Slim and didn't notice Jeff's arrival. Jeff walked to the side board, poured himself a cup of steaming coffee and slowly carried it over to Tish's table.

Slim was the first to spot him and smiled a welcome. "Join us, won't you, Jeff?" He glanced toward the swinging kitchen doors. "I know Elsa wouldn't mind getting you something to eat." Slim was nearly fifty with laugh lines around his eyes permanently etched into his tan face, a tall man with thinning sandy hair who never gained a pound no matter how much he ate.

"Thanks, Slim, but I'm not hungry." Jeff pulled out a chair, sat down and greeted John before swinging his gaze to Tish. He saw that she looked puzzled and just a little suspicious.

"I don't know if you've met Tish Buckner, Jeff," Slim continued, "one of our agents who just arrived for a little R and R. Tish, this is Jeff Kirby. Or should I say *Dr.* Kirby?"

"Hello." He smiled at Tish, waiting for her reaction.

"We met this afternoon," Tish began, acknowledging him with a wry smile. "He's the cowboy I asked to cool down my horse after a run." The smile spread to her eyes, which were a shade of coffee brown this evening.

So she could laugh at herself, Jeff thought, pleased. By turning the joke on herself, she'd defrayed the embarrassment.

"You're kidding!" Slim commented, grinning. "You thought he was a ranch hand?" He laughed out loud while John just smiled. "You'll have to tell that one to East, Jeff."

Sipping his coffee, Jeff watched her face, could almost hear the wheels turning in her mind. She was wearing a yellow silk blouse tucked into khaki slacks tonight and looked better than anything he'd seen on the dessert table.

"You're related to Easton Kirby?" she asked, curiosity obviously getting the best of her.

"He's my father," Jeff said, then watched confusion wrinkle her brow as she did the math. He was aware that he looked older than twenty-four, but even if he hadn't, it would be unlikely that East fathered him. "My adoptive father."

Tish nodded. "I met East some years ago at Condor. He's a wonderful man."

"Damn right he is," John Winters added, rising. "Saved my life back when we worked together years ago." He reached in his shirt pocket, pulled out a pack of cigarettes. "'Scuse me, I'm going outside to grab a smoke."

Was he the only one feeling the vibes across the table? Jeff wondered as he studied Tish. No, he could tell she felt something, too, the way she'd been looking at him from beneath thick lowered lashes. She dropped her gaze and picked up her cup to drink, then noticed it was empty.

"Can I get you a refill?" Jeff asked, pushing his chair back.

"No, thanks." She rose, smiling at Slim. "I think I'll turn in. Five o'clock comes around real fast."

Slim leaned back in his chair. "I told you, Tish, you don't need to get moving that early."

"You promised me a ride in your plane tomorrow morning. I'll be ready."

"Okay, then," Slim said. "Meet me at the hangar 'bout six."

"Will do. Good night." She stepped aside as Slim got up and walked toward the side door in the direction of his office, then she raised her eyes to Jeff. "Glad to have met you."

"Same here. I'll walk you to your room."

A slight frown came and went on her forehead. "That's not necessary, but thanks."

"Sure it is," he insisted, falling in step with her as she left the dining room. "Don't you know there are mountain lions in these parts?"

She ignored that and briskly walked to the elevators in an attempt to discourage him, but Jeff's long strides had no trouble keeping up. The doors of the car closed, locking them into a forced intimacy.

Instead of facing the front, Jeff faced her. "So, where are you from?"

"The East Coast."

"Where in the East?"

"New York." It was apparent that his closeness made her feel uncomfortable, as if he were invading her space. When he raised a hand as if to touch her, she swatted it aside, turning to glare at him. "Didn't you think I meant what I said earlier about that hand of yours?"

Jeff shrugged, then gave her his best boyish grin. "I like to live dangerously."

"I wouldn't if I were you. There's not much call for a one-handed doctor." The elevator doors slid open and she stepped around him and out, marching to her room.

Jeff followed and almost bumped into her when she stopped abruptly at her door. "Look at that, we're neighbors. I'm right across the hall."

"How fortunate for me. If I need a doctor, I'll be sure to call." She slid her card key in, pushed open the door. "Good night, Dr. Kirby."

His hand on her wrist, gentle but firm, stopped her. "Wait just a minute, Tish. Why are you running off like this? It's only seven-thirty." He could feel her pulse go into overtime beneath his thumb as he held her loosely, his eyes on hers as he noticed that she didn't pull away. "Why don't we go for a walk? The stars in an Arizona sky night are fantastic."

Tish let out a long sigh. "Look, we should get something said between us right now. I'm not interested and…"

He stepped closer, so close he could inhale her fragrance. She smelled like wildflowers he'd once picked on a hillside. "Do you want me to show you just how interested I think you are?" Before she could respond, he dropped her wrist and reached up to glide two fingers along her cheek and down the silk of her throat, and watched her eyes darken, her breathing go shallow. Having made his point, he stepped back so she wouldn't feel as if he had her penned in.

She didn't move, looking as if she were stunned at her own reaction. Finally, she eased inside and, without a word, quietly closed the door.

Jeff knew she was still there, on the other side of the door, probably leaning against it. You're interested, Tish, and so am I, he thought, then walked to his own room.

Chapter 2

The man across the plane aisle was snoring loud enough to wake the dead, Jeff thought as he sat up, jolted from his mind meanderings. He shifted in his seat, trying to get comfortable. Apparently the flight attendant, a tall blonde somewhere in her thirties, noticed Jeff's restlessness and walked over.

"Would you care to change your seat, sir?" she whispered, glancing toward the snoring passenger.

"Thanks, but I'm not sleeping anyway." He handed her his cup from the tray table. "A little more coffee would be great."

"Certainly." Silently, she made her way to the galley, returning minutes later with a steaming cupful. "Can I get you anything else? A pillow or blanket?"

Jeff shook his head and smiled his appreciation before tasting the hot brew. As someone in the medical field, he knew he shouldn't drink so much coffee, but during the long hours at the hospital, at times the caffeine was all that kept him going. That and thoughts of Tish.

Leaning back again, Jeff closed his eyes, thinking back again to that fateful week they'd met in Arizona....

From that first evening on, he couldn't keep his eyes off her. From the next table over at meals or pausing along the corral fence to study her as she worked a horse or gazing across the campfire one evening as several of the agents and guests gathered to sing songs with the majestic mountains in the background. He kept watch and smiled at her occasionally, but rarely spoke and never moved close enough to touch her. Though he wanted to...badly.

For her part, Tish kept him in her sights as well, sometimes openly staring, periodically tossing a glance over her shoulder as she walked away, her eyes occasionally searching a room for him. Now and again, he'd catch her gaze locked to his face, her expression thoughtful and contemplative. She made no move to come nearer, though she seemed on the brink of doing so.

He liked the way she carried herself, straight and proud, her demeanor that of a tall woman though she was no more than five- four or five. He liked the way the setting sun would get caught in the brown of her hair and turn it auburn. He liked the way her smile got all warm and fuzzy when she talked with the two children of a tourist couple.

She'd even arranged to give the older child, Luke, a boy of about twelve, riding lessons. He was gangly and awkward but, in no time, Tish had him smiling and almost confident astride one of the gentle mares. Afterward, he'd thanked her and started back toward his mother, then he'd impulsively run back for a fierce hug. Jeff had seen the surprised look of pleasure on Tish's face before she'd turned aside.

Then there was that hot afternoon, about a week after they'd met, the day the new calves were branded. It was a miserable job that called for agility, strength and a certain hardening of the heart when the calves bawled and struggled and fought. Branding was not Jeff's favorite job. He'd been told by East to do only the things he wanted to do while healing and regaining his strength, but he hadn't turned down the job boss when he'd all but challenged him to help out. Jeff knew he was the youngest agent there, mostly inexperienced and unseasoned. He also guessed that the cowhands were out to test him, to see what he was made of.

Four hours into it and Jeff was ready to drop. Muscles he didn't know he had hurt like hell, sweat was pouring into his eyes and only half the day was over. Mac was the job boss, the one releasing the calves from the chute, aiming them over to Jeff and three others in the corral with the branding irons. Mac was a mean one, short, bandy-legged and prematurely bald so he never took off his hat, and he had the temperament of a jailhouse guard. No one liked him, including Jeff.

That day, Mac was mainly picking on Teddy, a new hand who couldn't have been shaving long, looking no older than nineteen. Mac kept yelling criticisms that the kid wasn't fast enough, strong enough, good enough. The dressing down in front of half a dozen cowboys hanging on the fence finally took its toll on the kid and he looked near tears. That's when Mac moved in for the kill, shouting that Teddy was useless, finally grabbing the branding iron from him, looking for all the world like he was going to press the fire-hot metal end onto Teddy's tender flesh before he tossed it aside with a disgusted grunt.

To this day, Jeff didn't know what came over him. Certainly, he was no hero and no match for Mac who outweighed him by a good thirty pounds. But during the years he'd been a runaway he'd run into his fair share of bullies and hated them all. Standing behind Mac, he dropped his own iron and yelled to get his attention.

Mac's thick neck scarcely moved as he turned his head toward Jeff. "What'd you say?"

"I said leave him alone," Jeff answered, his eyes angry, his stance challenging, feet apart.

Mac smiled and it wasn't pretty. Then he took a step toward Jeff. "And who's going to make me?"

"I am," Jeff answered, and let loose with a right to the man's gut followed by a left to his jaw that sent him sprawling, narrowly missing the fire where the branding irons were heated. Mac scrambled to his feet, fire in his eyes. He came charging at Jeff like a bull, but Jeff was younger and faster, so he moved aside in time. Furious now, Mac spun around and smacked a thick fist into Jeff's shoulder, but Jeff held his ground.

The cowhands yelled encouragement but Jeff just wanted to end it. He waited until Mac came thundering close again, then let loose with a sucker punch to his already injured jaw. Mac went down like a felled tree. He tried to get up, flailing his arms halfheartedly, lifted his head, then fell back, out cold.

Jeff yanked off his gloves. "I'm through for today," he said, and walked out of the corral. The boy he'd rescued was too stunned and probably too frightened to move, but the guys along the fence cheered and those nearest him patted his shoulder as he made his way to the barn. He was hot, tired and disgusted with himself.

He'd done exactly what East had repeatedly warned him not to do, settled something with his fists instead of his brain. He'd been young those years he'd lived on the run and the only way he'd survived was to be a street fighter out of necessity when bigger runaways had tried to take advantage. But he'd given that up ten years ago, or so he'd thought until Mac had gone too far.

Nearing the barn, Jeff heard running footsteps, then felt a tap on his shoulder and turned to see Teddy, looking awkward and shy. His crooked smile would have made an orthodontist's hands twitch.

"Thanks," he muttered, his face reddening.

Nodding, Jeff walked on and almost didn't notice Tish standing in the doorway, in her eyes a new respect. Still, he marched on by, knowing he'd made a formidable enemy in Mac.

He went straight to his room, took a long, hot shower, then lay down on his bed, trying to rest his overtaxed muscles and his throbbing right hand. Ever since his ordeal of being buried alive, of not knowing if he'd ever see daylight again, he'd noticed that he had a much shorter fuse. He was grateful to be alive and wondered why others didn't see what he saw, that each day was a gift. The petty arguments, the anger, the need to best someone smaller and younger, all of it made him see red. Jeff sighed, thinking he'd have to work on these sudden temper flare-ups or he'd become just like the bullies he disliked.

Feeling restless, he got up and tried watching television, but nothing held his interest. He flipped through a couple of magazines, but he didn't feel like reading. Pacing, he thought of Tish Buckner and wondered why she showed signs of interest, yet only from a distance. And he wondered how he could change that.

Jeff hadn't done a lot of dating, mostly because living at Condor with East when he'd been a teenager didn't give him much opportunity. Except for school kids, the only people he'd spent time with had been SPEAR agents much older than he. And East had kept him on a fast track of learning, year-round classes to make up for studies he'd missed as a runaway, then college and finally med school where he spent the few free hours he had falling facedown on the bed, dead to the world with exhaustion.

Sure, there'd been a few women; after all, he wasn't a monk. Enough so that he recognized that certain look in a woman's eyes when she was sizing up a man, considering possibilities, wondering, imagining. That special male-female connection that is difficult to explain but is unmistakable to the parties involved.

And Tish Buckner was definitely sending out those signals.

Maybe he'd try getting her alone after dinner tonight, ask her to go for a walk, get to know her. Checking the time, Jeff saw that it was nearing six. He went back to the bathroom and took pains getting ready, combing his thick blond hair just so, choosing pressed chinos and a navy shirt, loafers instead of cowboy boots.

Patting shaving lotion on his face, he studied his image and spoke to the mirror. "That's as good as it gets, folks," then smiled at his flight of fancy. Was Tish causing him to talk to himself? he wondered as he grabbed his leather jacket and left his room.

She was already in the dining room, seated at Slim's table for six as usual. Reggie Miller, a fortyish agent who thought of himself as God's gift to women, was regaling two female agents and Tish with tales of his days as a lumberjack in the Pacific Northwest as Jeff took the last chair after filling his plate at the buffet table. There were greetings all around, though Reggie barely stopped in his recitation to nod toward him.

Apparently Reggie's story had been quite funny since there was hearty laughter when he finished. Jeff concentrated on his food with occasional glances at Tish, biding his time.

"I heard about what you did at the branding," Slim said in a quiet aside to Jeff. "I guess you loosened a couple of Mac's teeth." The normally taciturn manager grinned. "Wish I'd have seen that."

"It's about time someone punched out his lights,"

Marge Collins on the other side of Jeff commented. "But I'd watch my back, Jeff. He's a mean one."

"I think Jeff can handle himself," Tish said softly, her eyes on him.

"Then again, could've been a lucky punch," Reggie said, anxious to turn the attention back to himself. "I did some boxing awhile back. That old one-two punch comes from street fighting, right, sonny?" he asked, his cool gaze on Jeff.

Every time he'd been around Reggie, the man had called him sonny even though he knew his name. It was a subtle put-down, but Jeff wasn't about to rise to the bait tonight. One fight a day was more than enough. "Call it what you want, it worked."

Reggie couldn't think of a clever comeback, so he changed the subject to the ride up into the high country scheduled for the next day to deliver salt to the cows in the far pasture. "We could go together, Tish. It's real pretty up there this time of year."

Jeff heard her say something noncommittal before he turned to answer a question Slim had asked. The conversation shifted to other topics as they finished their meal. Finally, Reggie left the table to get his dessert and Jeff saw his chance. Sliding back his chair, he rose and walked around the table to Tish's side.

"It's a nice night," he began, standing behind her chair, inhaling the fresh scent of her hair. "I was wondering if you'd like to go for a walk."

"I'd like to, Jeff, but…"

"But she's promised to take me on in a game of chess," Reggie said as he returned with a generous slice of pie. "I don't suppose you play, eh, sonny?"

For the second time that day, Jeff wanted to hit a man, and he wasn't very happy about it. "Some other time then,'' he said more curtly than he'd intended, and left the dining room.

He needed fresh air, Jeff decided, to be outside where he could walk off his anger and this pent-up energy. Detouring through the kitchen, he stopped to praise Elsa's barbecued brisket while he snitched a couple of small carrots and apples. He stuffed them in the pockets of his jacket, gave the cook a quick hug and escaped.

Finally outdoors, he stood on the back porch, breathing in the fresh mountain air. He walked out toward the barns, then stopped, closed his eyes and listened. Here, away from the people and buildings, it was so different. The world was alive with sound—the muted gurgle of water rushing over stones in the nearby creek, the flutter of wings as a night bird flew by, crickets singing and small, furry creatures darting about in the underbrush. A distant owl sent up a protest as Jeff slapped at a mosquito.

He slipped on his jacket and strolled. From the barns came the sounds of a horse whinnying, probably a stallion picking up the scent of a mare.

Walking briskly, he headed for the stables, circling the entire structure before going inside. The horses were housed in a long aluminum building with stalls on either side and cement flooring on the center aisle plus overhead track lighting, now on dim as Jeff pushed open the sliding door. Thoroughly modern, all of Red Rock's barns were electronically monitored by the ranch manager or his assistant so that it wasn't necessary to have a person on hand to check on the animals at night. But the ranchers often wandered in to inspect their mounts or to tend to a sick cow or newborn calf.

Tonight, the horse stable appeared to be empty of humans, Jeff noted as he strolled down the center aisle. As he passed the stalls, he noticed ears twitch as the horses turned their big heads toward him, acknowledging his presence. One or two snuffle-guffed or snorted and from the far end came a short whinny. The combined scent of leather and animal hide wasn't altogether unpleasant, he thought as he sauntered along, whispering a soft greeting to this one and that.

Snowflake, a two-year-old spirited white mare he'd ridden yesterday, bobbed her big head at him, inviting attention. "Okay, girl," he said softly, "I see you." He caressed her nose as she nuzzled him, sniffing out the treats in his pocket. Laughing, he gave her one of the carrots and walked on.

He spoke to a few more mares, reading their names from the metal plate attached to each stall door. Pausing at Belladonna's stall, he greeted the big chestnut. "She gave you quite a workout again, eh, girl? Yeah, I saw you both and you looked like you were loving it." He stroked her nose while the mare poked her way around toward his pocket. Funny how horses could ferret out a treat in moments.

"Has she been down here to see you tonight, Bella?" Jeff asked as he gave her an apple. "Or is she playing chess with that creep, all the while thinking of me?" He chuckled at that thought as he watched the mare's big teeth make quick work of the apple. "Yeah, right." With a last pat, he moved on down, heading for the males at the far end.

Domino, the black stallion he'd ridden earlier today, was restlessly pawing the floor of his stall. He let out a sharp whinny when he spotted Jeff and shook his proud head, ruffling his thick mane. "Yeah, I know how you feel, boy."

Jeff wandered closer and saw the big horse settle down as he gave him an apple, though he was sure food wasn't the stallion's biggest problem. His back to the section he'd come from, he leaned on the door of the empty stall next to Domino's. "Got a girlfriend down there you'd like a little time with?" he asked the stallion, male to male. "Is she playing hard to get?" Domino bobbed his big head as if in answer to his question. "Females! They're like that, aren't they, boy?"

Finished with the apple, Domino stuck his head over the half door, looking for more treats, able to smell them. "Greedy, aren't you?" But Jeff gave him a carrot nonetheless.

Sighing, he gazed out the high window on the far wall, seeing the stars filling the night sky. "Not a good night to be alone, right, Domino?"

He shook his head, trying to figure things out. "All I wanted was to take a walk with her. Was that so much to ask? If I was smart, I'd walk away and forget her. But I keep seeing those big eyes, how the corners crinkled up when she poked fun at herself the other night, the way they warmed when she talked about liking Dad. Her skin is so soft, you know, and her hair makes a man want to bury his fingers in it. Then there's her mouth and, well, hell! There's just something about Tish Buckner that—"

Jeff heard a sound behind him and swung around.

She was standing on the opposite side two stalls down, one elbow propped on the door. She was wearing black slacks and a white silk blouse. She'd slipped on a rust-colored suede jacket against the desert night's chill. Even in the dim light, he could see those steady brown eyes watching him, her expression unreadable.

He covered up his surprise by coughing into his fist. "I believe you've interrupted a private conversation, lady." And he wondered just how much of his ramblings she'd heard.

Her lips twitched just the tiniest bit. "I apologize. I should leave you two guys alone."

He waved a forgiving hand. "That's all right." He turned to Domino who practically had his nose buried in Jeff's pocket. "Do you mind if she stays?" he asked as he gave the stallion another carrot. "No? Okay then." He swung back to Tish. "You can stay."

"That's very kind of you both." Still trying to hide a smile, she moved a bit closer. "Having a man-to-man conversation, are you? Or should I say, man-to-horse?"

Jeff leaned back on the empty stall across from her, propping his elbows on the half door. "More like man-to-stallion." He gestured with his head in the direction of the mares. "They wouldn't understand because they're the problem. Females, that is."

Looking as if she were enjoying this, she seemed to relax. "What sort of problem are you and Domino having with females? Maybe I can help. After all, I am a female."

"Oh, yes, you are. I definitely noticed that." He glanced at Domino who was noisily finishing his carrot. "You don't mind if I bring her in on this, do you?" The stallion snorted. "I'll take that as a yes."

Jeff stepped across the cement walk, seemingly pondering a serious problem, and stopped alongside Tish. "Well, you see, Domino's got this mare he's interested in and he'd kind of like to play it out, get to know her, see where they could take it, you know? But she's backing off, pretending she's not interested, even though we think she is. Tell me, how would you handle that?"

Tish shoved her hands into the pockets of her jacket as she looked down at the floor littered with hay. "That's a tough one. Did it occur to either of you that perhaps she's really *not* interested and simply doesn't want to hurt his feelings by just blurting it out?"

"No," Jeff answered immediately. "We know she's interested. Men know these things." His smile was cocky now, challenging.

"I see." Just that quickly, her eyes turned serious. "Maybe she is interested, a little, but she has a very good reason for not pursuing things. Maybe she's very intent on her job and thinks it's a mistake to get involved with a fellow worker.'' Tish paused, then raised her eyes to his. ''And maybe she's simply not good at relationships and prefers to stay...unencumbered.''

''Unencumbered.'' Jeff seemed to consider that. ''Good word, but shucks, lady, I think what Domino had in mind was less an encumbrance and more like a thing. You know, a fling.''

Tish raised her dark brows. ''A fling? Well, gentlemen, you should know that most females, human or horse, aren't all that enthusiastic about flings. At least not mature females who are involved in serious careers.''

''Sooo,'' Jeff drew out the word as he edged closer to her. ''You don't want another relationship or a fling. Hell, lady, no wonder we males can't figure you women out.'' In a move too fast for her to dodge, he took hold of the front of her blouse and tugged her up against his chest. ''Maybe this will help you make up your mind.'' And his mouth closed over hers.

Shocked by his own boldness, Jeff knew he couldn't back down now. He'd never done more than shake hands with another agent, yet here he was tussling with one after meeting her mere days ago. His only excuse was that since the first moment he'd seen Tish Buckner, he'd been able to think about little else.

He'd been expecting her temper, perhaps a struggle, even possibly a kick in the shins followed by a hard slap. After all, she'd warned him twice to keep his hands to himself. Instead, she stiffened for several long seconds, holding herself rigid. Jeff ignored that and tried to coax her lips to respond while his hands at her back kneaded and caressed. Just when he was about to give up and give her this round, her lips began to move, to answer.

She opened to him, allowing his tongue entry to the secrets of her mouth, while her arms raised and enfolded him.

White-hot passion exploded in a flash of heat, its intensity so unexpected that he nearly lost his footing. Her mouth was so soft, so giving and he drank from her like a desert walker who'd just found water. Her body was small and firm, and suddenly straining to get closer, the sweet friction driving him crazy.

Shaken, Jeff drew back, breathing hard.

Tish stared up at him, her eyes luminous in the dim lighting, looking as if she were fighting some internal demons, and losing the battle. She drew in a deep breath, yet it didn't seem to calm her. Then, in an act that mimicked his, she grabbed his shirt front and pulled him to her, kissing him with an urgency that set his blood to boiling. There was no surrender in her kiss, but rather an acknowledgment of a need that perfectly matched his. She held him close, lost in passion newly awakened.

Just that quickly, Jeff began to fall over the edge and into love. How long had he subconsciously wanted and waited for such a woman? he wondered in the sluggish part of his brain still able to think. The scent and feel and taste of her wiped out the memory of every other woman he'd ever touched. His hands were trapped in the thickness of her hair as her sweet feminine fragrance wrapped around him. How could he have known she'd taste like all his wild dreams, exotic yet romantic at the same time? How could he have guessed she was the other half of him, just waiting to be found?

This time it was Tish who drew away, taking a step back, lowering her head and trying to regain control. Jeff ran a hand through his hair, unnerved to find it unsteady. He'd been wanting to kiss her, hoping to interest her, but even in his reckless dreams, he hadn't expected either of them to react quite so fervently.

He saw Tish shake her head as if to clear her mind. He

thought he ought to say something, though he wasn't sure what that should be.

"Look, I…"

"No," she said, "let me." Eyes downcast, she seemed to search for the right words. "I—I obviously didn't expect that to happen or that I'd—I'd—"

"Feel so much?" he offered.

Slowly, she lifted her eyes to his. "Yes, exactly. All the more reason why I need to keep my distance from you. I don't have time for whatever it is you have in mind. SPEAR is very important to me and—"

"It's important to me, too. But the attraction we feel for one another has nothing to do with SPEAR."

As if she hadn't heard, she went on. "SPEAR keeps me focused, grounded, and I need that. I don't need a fling or a thing."

Jeff decided to backtrack a bit, thinking perhaps he'd rushed her. "Why don't we aim for friendship and see where that takes us?" Although he knew he was already light-years past a mere friendship.

Tish studied his face, then shook her head. "No, friendship isn't what you have in mind. I can see it in your eyes. I've noticed for days now that you've been watching me and I know what you're thinking."

Caught between amusement and curiosity, he stepped closer. "Just what is it you think I want?"

She was quiet, thoughtful, then raised her chin. "More. More than I have to give."

Jeff thought that over for a few seconds. "Someone hurt you badly, didn't they?" he asked softly.

She crossed her arms over her chest. "Bad enough."

"So you're not going to let anyone get close enough to do it again. Is that about it?" When she didn't reply, he had his answer. Again he invaded her space just enough so she had to look up at him. ''What makes you think I'd hurt you, Tish?''

She gave him a long look. ''Because you're someone I could care for. Only people we care for can truly hurt us.''

Jeff wanted to ask who had hurt her, what had happened, but he didn't want her to close up and back away. She'd admitted she could care for him. He'd work from there. There'd be time for questions later.

He disentangled her arms and took her hands on his. ''I won't hurt you. I swear. Let me prove it to you.''

She closed her eyes, as if fighting her own needs. ''Please, Jeff. This can't go anywhere.''

He smiled then, hoping to lighten her mood. ''Honey, it already has.''

She took a deep breath, drawing courage. ''No, I'm serious. I can't get involved.''

His heart lurched. This didn't sound like good news. ''Are you going to tell me you're married?'' Naomi Star at the front desk had said Tish was single, but she could have been mistaken. The man who'd hurt her, was she still involved with him?

She stared into his eyes as the seconds ticked by. ''Would it make a difference if I were?''

He didn't answer her. Instead, he shifted her closer. ''You couldn't be happily married and kiss me like you just did.'' But he waited, his breath backing up in his throat.

''You're right about that and no, I'm not married,'' she said at last.

Jeff visibly relaxed. ''Then what? What's wrong?''

She found the middle button of his shirt fascinating as she tried to tell him. ''After you left, I talked privately to Slim and asked him a couple of questions about you. I wanted to know some things and—''

''I thought you were going to play chess with Wonder Boy.''

"I begged off from that."

"Good move." He squeezed her arms. "I don't mind if you talked with Slim. I have nothing to hide. Did he say something that upset you?"

"Not really upset me, it's just that he told me you've got a couple of years of residency to go yet and I'm sent all over the world by SPEAR. I don't think long distance relationships work well and I'm committed to my work."

"I'm committed to SPEAR, too. I don't see what that has to do with anything." Domino chose that moment to give out with a loud whinny. "See, he doesn't either."

"No, wait, Jeff, I—"

"No, Tish, you wait." He leaned down, his face inches from hers. "When I kissed you just now, when you kissed me back, tell me *honestly* how you felt, and remember, Domino's listening."

Her features changed, lightened, as she remembered and a gentle blush warmed her face. "Honestly?" She looked hesitant, then apparently decided to tell him the truth. "I felt like the top of my head was going to take off, like I was walking into a hot, white flame, like nothing I've ever felt before."

Jeff smiled. "So did I, and that's something neither of us can fake. That's all we need to know, how we feel now. The future will work out somehow. Let's try friendship, companionship, doing fun things together. And let's stop worrying so much." He bent his head, needing to kiss her again, but her hand on his chest held him at bay.

"You're going way too fast for me. We've just met and—"

"And we just kissed," he said, interrupting her protests. "And nothing, *nothing* will ever be the same again. For either of us."

She released an exasperated sigh. "You're an incurable romantic, I see. Life isn't that simple. We don't all live happily ever after because we're attracted to someone. I should know. I vowed two years ago that I'd never buy into that impossible dream again. Apparently you haven't had to face life's harsher realities yet.''

It wasn't the way he'd intended to tell her, if at all. His difficult youth and more recent ordeal were, in fact, things he rarely mentioned. But apparently she thought he was the fair-haired prince born with a silver spoon who'd led a charmed life. He had to let her know.

''I suppose you're right,'' he said, stepping back. ''I probably haven't had too many harsh realities. Unless you'd call being born to two alcoholics who did me a big favor by abandoning me at age ten, although living on the streets for four years wasn't exactly a day at the beach. Then there was a more recent incident where a couple of Simon's men kidnapped me, buried me alive and left me to die there. Other than that, my life's been a breeze.''

The shocked look on her face made him wish he hadn't been quite so flip. But he wanted her to stop thinking of him as some pampered, privileged person.

''Oh, God, Jeff. Abandoned. Buried alive. I had no idea.''

''And I didn't want to bring it up, but I need you to realize that we all have *stuff* in our past that makes us who we are. I'm well aware life isn't simple and that we can't all live happily ever after. But when someone comes along who touches us, I think it's a mistake not to pursue that. Do you see where I'm coming from?''

She looked as if she wanted to ask more questions, but then seemed to decide now wasn't the time. ''Yes, I do.''

He shifted her closer back into his arms. ''Good because you can run from me, but you can't hide.''

Finally, her smile was genuine. ''I don't want to run or hide from you. But I would like to ask you something.''

''Anything,'' he said and meant it.

"Would you kiss me like that again?"

"Oh, lady," Jeff murmured as he lowered his mouth to hers.

They hung around the horse barn a while longer, lingering over kisses that set their blood heating. Only the night clerk was awake downstairs when they'd finally made their way into the main building, the lights on low. His arm around her shoulders, Jeff walked Tish to her room, where they both paused in the dim hallway.

"I don't want to let you go," Jeff whispered, his hands on her waist, his lips nuzzling her neck.

Tish seemed to be struggling, wanting to be with him yet feeling she shouldn't begin something she couldn't finish. "Me, either," she finally admitted.

He eased back and studied her fine features now that his eyes had adjusted to the near darkness. "You seem afraid. Why?"

"Because I'm getting in too deep too quickly, something I promised myself I'd never do again."

"Do you want to talk about it?" Maybe if she told him about the person who'd hurt her, she'd feel better. They could go into her room, talk in the sitting area, though it might tax his resolve to not touch her.

"No," she said quickly. Then more softly, "No. Maybe one day, but not now." She raised a hand to touch his hair, then trailed her fingertips along his cheeks and chin. Leaning back, her gaze stayed on his face. "You have the most incredible green eyes. It's the first thing I noticed about you."

"Not my manly physique?"

She smiled. "That's not bad, either, but, no, your eyes. They're such a vibrant shade in the daylight, then they turn to emerald at night. I admit that I'm jealous."

"You needn't be. Your eyes could be any color and still be beautiful."

Her expression turned shy. "I wasn't fishing."

"I know. Still, I have to tell you, it wasn't your eyes I noticed first."

Suddenly wary, she looked up. "All right, tell me what."

"The way you rode that mare, like the two of you were one. You impressed me and everyone else watching. Where'd you learn to ride like that?" It seemed to Jeff that a shadow crossed over her features, then was gone just as quickly.

"Upstate New York where I was raised. My family belonged to a country club and a hunt club. By the time I was ten, I was competing."

"Ah, the blue bloods. I suppose you went to Ivy League schools. Must be nice, dear old Dad having tons of money." This time he couldn't mistake the frosty look that she struggled to hide.

She turned within his arms, dug out her key and unlocked her door. "I should say good night."

He'd hit a nerve, Jeff decided. Something else to delve into another day. The past clings to all of us, he knew.

"Not without a good-night kiss," he said, turning her back, placing her arms on his shoulders and taking her mouth.

If her mouth had cooled, it took but moments for it to heat up again beneath his seeking lips. Jeff molded her small frame to his with his big hands at her back. He felt his senses surge at the feel of that soft female body against his. He wanted nothing more than to shove open her door, follow her inside and slowly strip off all her clothes before moving to her big double bed.

But alas, SPEAR frowned on its agents cohabiting openly. So, although it cost him, he reluctantly stepped back. "See you tomorrow?" he asked, his voice husky.

She nodded vaguely and drifted inside.

Jeff heard the lock click, then turned to enter his own room across the hall. An ice-cold shower might be in order, he decided.

Chapter 3

Jeff awoke with a start, surprised he'd fallen asleep at all. Feeling stiff, he unfastened his seat belt and got up, glancing around the first-class section of the plane. The lights were on dim and the other five passengers all appeared to be in dreamland. The man across the aisle was still snoring, but not as loudly. A mother and daughter in the last row were cuddled together, snoozing. And a young couple who appeared to be newlyweds snuggled under a blanket, the woman's head on her companion's shoulder.

Stretching his cramped muscles, Jeff's gaze stayed on the young couple, envying their togetherness. He and Tish had had so little time together to just be with one another. So many things had interfered—his hospital duties, SPEAR obligations, everyday things that kept them apart. Small wonder their relationship had been rocky.

Walking to the front, Jeff nodded to the flight attendant and went into the small compact lavatory. He splashed cold water on his face then dried off with a paper towel. He debated about shaving, then decided that could wait. Checking his watch, he saw they had two more hours left before landing. Impatience ate at him, but there was nothing he could do to hurry things along.

Resuming his seat, he glanced out the window and saw it was still dark out. A man of action, he'd always hated waiting. Not knowing how Tish was doing added to his unease. He picked up the phone to call the hospital again, then tucked it away, deciding that he didn't want to irritate the staff by calling too frequently.

Finally settling back, he let his mind roam, remembering those early weeks with Tish, hoping the memory of their good times would sustain him during this time of uncertainty....

From that first kiss in the barn that summer evening at the Red Rock Ranch, Jeff had known Tish was the woman for him. He didn't know how he knew; he simply did. Not a day since had he questioned that fact. He'd simply accepted it. She was the one.

But he'd known better than to let her see the depth of his feelings. She was skittish, wary, cautious in everything she said to him, in her reactions to him. He'd have to go slowly, he told himself. But the need to make her his had burned within him, coloring every aspect of their budding relationship. It had taken all of his control to rein in his needs and put hers first.

The morning after their first kiss in the barn, he awakened early. He was anxious for the day to begin, so he could see her, touch her, talk with her. Only when he'd gone down to breakfast, even though it was not yet seven, Slim was the only one in the dining room.

Sipping his coffee, Jeff sat down. "Where is everyone this morning?" he asked, trying to be casual.

"They left early, a couple of our agents going with a

few hands to round up strays that wandered away from the herd. I spotted several from the plane yesterday when I went up, so I asked for volunteers.'' Slim dipped the last of his toast into the remaining egg yolk and popped it into his mouth.

Jeff thought that over, kicking himself mentally for not rising earlier. "Who were the agents?" he asked, fully expecting Tish to be among them. Something had been mentioned about the ride last night at dinner, but he hadn't paid much attention.

"Mmm, let's see. John and Tanya are the only agents. Oh, and Tish. They were going with Derek, Jim and Pete, the cowhands familiar with that range. Kind of a rugged area." Slim used his napkin to wipe along the edges of his mustache.

Why hadn't Tish mentioned this trip to him last night? Jeff wondered. Had she decided they needed a little distance after their heated encounter? Or had the trip slipped her mind? She might also have gone on impulse. He drank more coffee, studying Slim and wondering how to find out what he wanted to know without arousing too much suspicion.

"Just for the day, you mean?" Jeff asked.

Slim finished his coffee before answering. "Three or four days, I'd imagine. It would take six or seven hours of riding just to reach the winter range." His weathered brow furrowed as he looked at Jeff. "Why do you want to know?"

He shrugged, trying to look nonchalant. "Just curious. Not much going on here." He glanced out the window, saw it was a sunny day, though probably cool. "Too nice to stay indoors, eh?"

Behind his hand cupping his mouth, Slim grinned. "I can tell you how to get where they're going. *If* you're interested, that is."

Jeff tried to look as if the idea had just occurred to him. "Well, if you think they'll need another hand."

"Couldn't hurt. You can carry a message to Justin. He's the cowboy who's been up there three weeks now. I just got a call from his wife and you can tell him her checkup went well, baby's fine and definitely not due for another three weeks. He'll be relieved next week and home in plenty of time for the birthing."

Jeff knew that only one cowhand was assigned to keep watch on the herd in the mountainous region and that the men took turns on a rotating basis, usually four weeks at a time. "Will do." Delivering the message would give him an excuse for showing up.

Slim took a small notebook out of his pocket and began drawing a map with a stubby pencil. "Good. I know he's worried about that baby. It's his first." Slim labeled several trails. "This is the route to the winter pasture. Won't be long and we'll be herding them back down here. Another couple weeks. You'll recall the passage once you start out 'cause landmarks haven't changed all that much since you spent time here." He tore out the sheet and handed it to Jeff. "Go get her, son."

He should have known he couldn't hide anything from Slim. Looking sheepish, Jeff took the map and stuffed it in his shirt pocket.

"Stop in the kitchen and have Elsa fix you up some food. And be sure to take your bedroll and a blanket. Gets mighty cold up there at night."

"Thanks again, Slim."

The way to the winter range was scenic at the beginning, Jeff thought as he rode Domino along the riverbed through desert country with plenty of browse and grass. But the way soon became treacherous with the trail narrowing to a path only a surefooted horse could follow. Domino was that kind of stallion, having lived all his life on Red Rock so he was familiar with every trail, bramble and bush.

Riding him, Jeff felt secure that the horse knew the way even if he hadn't had Slim's map. He hurried the big stallion as best he could on the rugged terrain, well aware that the others had a two-hour head start on him. Then again, they probably hadn't been hard riding since there was no rush to reach the high country. The hands might even have taken off ahead, letting the three agents follow at their leisure. At least, Jeff hoped that was the case so he could catch up with them more easily.

Leaving the creek bed, he saw fresh mountain lion tracks and hoped the big cat was off somewhere sleeping since they did most of their prowling at night. Nevertheless, his rifle was securely in place by his saddlebags. The sky was a deep blue with hardly a cloud visible and there was a nip to the morning air. The temperature had been about fifty at the ranch but had cooled as he climbed.

On open land at last, he urged Domino to speed up as he passed a butte with a huge pile of rocks on top. Red rocks which gave the area and the ranch its name, the soil rich with minerals. The wind had picked up and had Jeff securing his hat on his head. He stopped after another hour to let the stallion have a drink from a creek and to rest a bit while he chewed on some beef jerky, having missed breakfast in his haste to get going. Perhaps it was his imagination, but Jeff could swear he heard the muted bawling of calves not far ahead, the sound carried on the wind. He drank some water, then reined the big horse around and set off again.

They rode another hour, Jeff pacing the stallion so as not to wear him out too soon. Finally, Domino snorted and bobbed his big head as he sniffed the air.

"What do you smell, boy?" Jeff asked, stroking his long

neck. "I'll bet there are mares up ahead." With his knees, he urged Domino on.

Another half an hour and the whinny of horses could be heard clearly, for the mares had picked up the stallion's scent. The gentle mooing of cattle drifted to Jeff as well. Even though he'd been climbing steadily, the sun had warmed the temperature to near sixty, he estimated. Checking Slim's map, he saw that he was close.

A few minutes later, he rounded a bend and saw three horses tethered to a juniper tree that provided spotty shade for the agents sprawled beneath having their lunch. John Winters was the first to look up.

"Hey, Jeff. I didn't know you were joining us." Seated on the ground alongside his hat, John squinted up as Jeff swung down off Domino.

"Last minute decision," Jeff said, walking Domino over to a second tree upwind from the mares and tying him to a strong limb.

Walking toward the three of them, he greeted Tanya and then looked over at Tish. She was studying him, trying to figure out his real motive in following them here, he was certain. He sat down opposite her and took an apple out of his jacket pocket. "Slim wanted me to deliver a message to Justin about his wife."

"Mmm-hmm," John said, a knowing grin on his face. He gathered their trash and moved toward his horse, stuffing crumpled paper into his saddlebag. "We're about ready to head out. You need to rest awhile?" he asked Jeff.

Chewing on his apple, Jeff shook his head. "No, I'm all set." He watched Tanya stroll over to her mare before turning to Tish. "How are you this morning?"

"Why are you here?" she asked so softly he had to bend closer to catch her words. "And don't give me that nonsense about a message for Justin."

Feigning indignation, Jeff gave her a wide-eyed stare. "Why else?"

Her shrewd dark eyes stayed on his. "You're not as innocent as you pretend. I think you have ulterior motives, a hidden agenda."

He splayed a hand over his heart. "You wound me." But his eyes danced mischievously.

Shaking her head, she rose. "You're too much, Jeff Kirby."

He was up and beside her in the next heartbeat. "Would you believe the truth," he whispered, "that four or five days without you around was more than I could handle?"

Stepping back, she again shook her head. "No, I wouldn't."

"You're a hard sell, Tish Buckner," he commented.

"You have no idea how hard," she answered, then turned to walk toward Belladonna.

Untying Domino, Jeff smiled to himself. And she had no idea how persistent he could be.

By the time they got to the winter grazing pasture where the cowboys had made camp, the sun was low in the sky. Pete and Derek had already found and rescued a calf stuck in a narrow canyon but Jim wasn't back yet from scouring the area. The new arrivals took care of their horses first before asking the seasoned hands what they could do to help.

"We'll split up tomorrow morning," Pete said, taking charge as the most experienced, "two by two, each taking a section and roping any lost calves or cows, bringing them back to the herd. Justin's down the canyon aways, heading here. If someone would like to get dinner going, I'm sure Justin would appreciate something other than jerky and beans."

Derek studied the sky. "I don't think we have to pitch

tents tonight. Doesn't look like we'll have rain anytime soon." He angled his chin toward a grassy shaded area. "You can set your bedrolls over there."

They all worked well together, and in no time, they had wood gathered and a fire going. Jeff positioned the big black pot over the simmering blaze as the two women spooned in precooked stew that Elsa had packed for them. Tanya dug out tin plates and utensils while Tish cut thick slices of fresh brown bread that was one of Elsa's specialties.

If Tish noticed that Jeff spread his bedroll next to hers, she didn't let on. Soon Jim returned from his search-and-rescue effort empty-handed and Justin arrived from doing a perimeter check, glad for the company. And pleased to meet Jeff who'd just informed him that his wife was doing well.

"Thanks," he said, his perpetually sunburned face creasing in a smile. His fair skin and blond head didn't fare well with constant exposure to the sun, even wearing a wide-brimmed hat.

"Did your wife have an ultrasound?" Jeff asked as they all sat down around the campfire. "Do you know if you're having a boy or a girl?"

"Nah, she didn't want to. Me, I'd like to know, but Marianne said it's more fun if you're surprised." Justin tossed his cigarette butt into the fire. "Really though, I don't care as long as the baby's healthy and Marianne's okay."

"Medicine's come a long way," Jeff pointed out. "Problems in childbirth are less common these days."

"Good, because I'd like to have lots more. Maybe four more. Five sons, my own basketball team." He grinned. "I haven't mentioned this to Marianne yet."

"You might want to hold off on that," Tanya told him, "at least until she's recovered from this first one."

"Ah, but what if you have five girls?" Tish teased him. "Five prom dresses, five weddings to put on."

"Oh, save me," Justin said, laughing. He saw the stew was hot enough and was the first to ladle a healthy portion onto his plate. "Man, you guys don't know how great this smells. Three weeks up here alone with cows, eating dried fruit, beans and jerky, and you begin to fantasize. Not about women, about a big steak with all the trimmings."

"He's been up here too long," Jim commented and everyone laughed.

Listening to the ebb and flow of conversation, Jeff sat on the edge of the circle. He wasn't one of the cowhands and as someone still fairly inactive in SPEAR even though he was a part of the team, he felt like he didn't quite belong to either group. It had often been like that for him; growing up in a household where drunken behavior was the norm, he hadn't felt as if he belonged to a real family unit. All he'd dreamed about was escaping. Which he had as soon as he'd been old enough.

Living on the streets, he never felt safe, either, never confided in others, never made friends because getting close to someone was inviting trouble. Runaways could turn on you for a slice of bread when they were starving, or a dollar when they needed cheap wine or a fix. He'd never been part of a real family, or a group of like individuals until East had taken him home. Even after that, it had taken Jeff months, years to trust, to relax, to feel safe with anyone except East.

Now, here with his fellow agents and experienced men who worked the herd at Red Rock, he felt a kinship, but still he didn't feel as if he were a part of either specialized group. Listening to the way the men joked with one another with Tanya joining in, Jeff wondered if he would ever belong.

Finishing his plate, he glanced at Tish and saw that she,

too, seemed on the perimeter of the group, observing and listening but seldom joining in. He wondered if their apartness was something they had in common, or if he was reading something into her behavior that wasn't there. Maybe she was just shy or perhaps self-conscious because he was there and last night they'd shared a couple of powerful kisses. For him, a life-altering happening. But for her, had it been just one of those things?

He needed to find out, which was one reason he'd followed her up into the red rock high country.

Everyone helped to tidy up, no chauvinism here. After all, the women helped with the cattle so it was only fitting that the men help with food preparation and clean up. There was no pampering on ranches or with ranch chores.

After dinner, Justin talked Pete and John into a card game. Jim joined them while Tanya walked downstream to bathe, though she stayed within sight of the campfire. Tish sat near the fire, gazing off into space, seemingly lost in thought. Jeff was feeling pensive and perhaps a little embarrassed about racing up the mountain after a woman. Especially since that woman had probably left in the first place because she needed some space, some time to think about this sudden overpowering attraction.

So he lit one of the small cigars he rarely smoked and wandered upstream in the opposite direction from where Tanya went. If Tish needed to be alone, he'd let her be.

There was a moon out, not quite full but lending a good deal of light that reflected on the shimmering water as he walked. The small stream gurgled and dribbled over rocks small and large, the sound pleasant and appealing. Thinking of his hospital work in California and even East's place on Condor Mountain, this red rock country was like being in another world. One that was peaceful, where the needs of animals superseded those of man. Mindful of the possibility of wild animals in the area, he knew it was also a dangerous place, but he didn't feel threatened. In fact, he felt safe.

Maybe feeling safe had more to do with the people a person was with rather than the environment, Jeff decided.

He drew on the slim cigar, enjoying the pungent taste in his mouth. Reaching a fairly smooth rock, he sat down facing the stream and gazed up at the stars. He supposed there were just as many stars in the night sky over a busy metropolitan city as there were out here, yet there seemed more in the wilderness. An illusion probably.

He'd always thought that once he finished working for SPEAR, he'd like to settle near the sea. Yet this mountainous region held almost as much appeal. Perhaps he could find a place that offered both. Provided he lived to see that day.

Jeff wasn't a melodramatic man or a pessimist. He was just a realist. Someone aware of the danger yet knowing that a man had to do what he had to do in order to look at himself each morning in his shaving mirror and not be disgusted with what he saw.

"A dollar for your thoughts," a soft voice behind him said. When Jeff turned, he saw Tish and smiled. "I figure a penny, with inflation, should be at least a dollar by now."

He moved over, making room for her on the rock. "My thoughts are kind of scattered tonight. How about yours?"

She sat down, her hip grazing his out of necessity since the space was limited. "I'm just taking in the beauty of nature out here. When you spend most of your life in an urban setting, you don't realize how peaceful, how quiet and lovely a desolate area like this can be."

The mooing of a cow broke into their thoughts just then as the scent of the big animals drifted upstream. "I've never seen so many cattle at one time in my entire life," Tish commented. She'd walked out among them for a while after they'd first arrived. "Some of them have such sweet faces. I'll never look at a hamburger the same again."

He smiled at her. "I hear they make lousy house pets."

"Oh, silly, I didn't mean that. But they have such sad eyes."

"I don't suppose you've ever visited the Chicago slaughter houses."

"No! And I don't ever want to."

"Still, you're not a vegetarian?" He'd seen her eat her fair share of the beef stew tonight.

"No, I'm a head-in-the-sand carnivore who doesn't want to think about those poor animals losing their lives so we can enjoy a meal."

Jeff shrugged. "Survival of the fittest." He glanced up toward an outcropping of rocks. "Take the mountain lion. He harbors no such thoughts. He'd pounce down on us, we'd be dinner for him and he wouldn't give his conscience a second thought."

Nervously, she glanced over her shoulder. "There really are mountain lions up here?"

"Could be. This is their territory and man is invading it. I suppose that's why he feels its his right to devour us if the opportunity presents itself." Jeff dropped his cigar and ground it out with his booted foot.

Tish got up. "Maybe we should go back with the others closer to the fire."

He took her hand, pulled her effortlessly onto his lap, which had been his motive in bringing up the mountain lion in the first place. "Don't worry. You're safe with me."

In the pale moonlight, she studied his face. "Safe is a relative term."

"Yes, well, I won't devour you, but I might nibble a little around the edges." And he bent to do just that along the silken line of her throat. He felt a shiver take her and wondered if it was from the chilly night air or his ministrations. "Mmm, you taste almost as good as you smell."

She was silent, but she shifted slightly to give him better access.

Emboldened by the fact that she'd sought him out while the others were occupied, he nuzzled more, then with two fingers on her chin, he turned her face toward his and captured her mouth. The kiss was light, gentle, yet arousing. Her lips played with his, teasing, tempting. Her tongue darted into his mouth, then withdrew playfully. Jeff wasn't certain how much more of this he could easily handle with her snug on his lap.

Needing to distract himself, he eased back and ran his fingers through her hair as it curled around her ear. "You have beautiful hair, did you know that?"

Tish frowned. "No. It's just brown hair. Nothing special."

"That's where you're wrong. I'd always thought people with brown hair got short shrift, too. Blondes are described in all manner of flattering terms, fussed over and envied. Those with black hair are described as ebony or jet or raven. But brown hair, I thought, was just, well, brown."

"Exactly."

"Ah, but not yours." His fingers moved deeper now, threading through the thickness, lightly massaging her skull. "In the sunlight, I can see half a dozen shades of brown from russet to mahogany and auburn to brandy to chocolate. In the moonlight, there are amber streaks in it. Fantastic hair and you don't even seem aware of how great you look."

"Look, Kirby, flattery will get you absolutely nowhere." But he could see her head drop forward as his fingers worked their magic on her scalp.

"So you say. Flattery is good if it's honest. And mine is."

Tish shifted so she was facing him. Smiling, she plunged both her hands into the thickness of his hair and studied his eyes in the moonlight. Suddenly, the smile began to slip and her look softened. Slowly, she moved her head closer and pressed her mouth to his in an openmouthed kiss that all but stole his breath away.

His senses swimming, Jeff came up for air. He was a little too old for these necking sessions that went nowhere. "You know, I'll bet no one would notice or care if we moved our sleeping bags over here away from the rest."

Her hazy eyes seemed to clear instantly. "I don't think that's a good idea. I don't relish being the talk of Red Rock Ranch." She got off his lap and moved several steps away, looking just as shaken as he felt.

Jeff rose, too, his jeans uncomfortably snug as he walked to the stream. He picked up a rock and skimmed it across the surface, thinking maybe they needed to talk. Turning, he saw that she had her arms wrapped tightly around herself, her face turned up to study the stars. He wanted to pull her back into his arms, to ask her why she'd sought him out twice now only to cool down quickly. He thought that perhaps something in her past was keeping her from acting on her feelings.

Go slowly, he told himself as he moved closer but didn't touch her. "I seem to be getting some mixed signals here, Tish. Or is it my imagination?"

Sighing, she finally looked at him. "No, it's not your imagination. I…well, I don't have to tell you that I'm attracted to you, Jeff. I like talking with you, being with you. But I'm very wary of things that happen too fast. I had that once, that swift, fierce attraction that seems to erase all your good sense. And it ended badly. I don't want that again."

Still not touching her, he stepped closer so he could see her features more clearly in the moonlight. Her eyes looked genuinely troubled. "It doesn't have to be like that. We can go slowly...."

"Can we? The moment you touch me, I can't think of anything but how much I want you."

There it was, her confirmation of how she felt. "It's that way for me, too. But I told you, I won't hurt you."

"Maybe not purposely, but—"

"I'm not him, Tish. I'm not the man who hurt you."

Her luminous eyes met his and he saw her lips tremble ever so slightly. "Are you ready to tell me what happened?"

She walked back to the rock, sat down on the patchy grass and leaned her back against the cool stone. She waited until he joined her, taking her time, as if she were trying to find the right words. "I was in college in the East. A good school because, as you guessed, my parents had money. I didn't know why but I was already rebelling against the good life, as my father called it. The privileged life that wealth can buy you."

So very different from how he'd grown up, Jeff thought. Yet he knew that there were people who'd been born into wealth who developed a strong social conscience. He let her tell her story without interruption.

"But Eric had no such problems. That was his name, Eric Townsend. We met in a political science class. He was having trouble with it and asked me for help. He was in school on an athletic scholarship—basketball—and had to keep his grades up or he'd lose his funding. So I agreed to tutor him."

Tish picked up a stone and began stroking it with unsteady fingers. "Are you sure you want to hear this?" she asked.

"Yes," Jeff answered as he slipped his arm around her, mostly to let her share his body heat since the night air had become quite chilly. But he held her loosely, allowing her to sort out her thoughts.

"We studied together, but by the second day, he started making moves on me. I tried to keep him focused on his upcoming test, but he was very persistent and I was mostly inexperienced. I gave in and we became lovers." Her voice was low, as if the words had been difficult to say out loud.

"We did get some studying in and his grades improved. I went to all his games and we spent most of our free time together, though we each had our own dorm rooms. I was twenty-one and thought I was madly in love, though something kept me from saying the words out loud. Not Eric, though. He told me over and over how much he loved me, what a great future we'd have together after graduation. He even asked me to marry him and, God help me, I was considering it. And he kept pestering me to take him home for Christmas break, that he wanted to meet my family. I thought that was rushing things a bit, but I finally agreed. We were going to drive to my house after our final classes on Friday. I finished early and went to wait for him in his room."

Tish threw away the stone and crossed her arms over her chest, her expression bleak. "I shouldn't have snooped, I know, but there were all these papers on his desk. I think I told myself I'd just straighten things up a bit. But one paper caught my eye. My father's name was on it."

Jeff tightened his arm around her, fairly certain he knew what was coming next.

"I couldn't believe it. He had my father's financial report, his company's end-of-year statement, his stock portfolio, his bank accounts, his total assets down to the penny. Don't ask me how he got all that information, although he was one of the early whiz kids with computers."

"It's not that difficult if you know how," Jeff said quietly.

"I suppose not. Anyhow, I was just staring at the papers when he walked in, all smiles, ready to go meet my family."

"How'd he react when he saw that you knew what he'd been up to?"

"Oh, he denied he'd done it with anything terrible in mind, like marrying me for my father's money since I'm an only child. He was just curious, he told me. No harm done, although maybe my father could put in a good word and get him a job at his firm. What was wrong with that? Eric wanted to know."

"And what was your reaction?"

"I simply walked away and told him I never wanted to see him again. Naturally, he didn't drop it, kept calling, writing, showing up, swearing he loved me. Love via Dun & Bradstreet. Wonderful. If that's love, you can keep it. I went home, finished my classes by mail and never saw Eric again."

Jeff wanted to punch the SOB for hurting her and wanted to reassure her that one encounter with a jerk didn't mean all men were the same. "You had a bad experience with a heel, Tish. He claimed he loved you, but he was really after your father's money and influence. I hope you don't think I'm interested in you because of your father's money."

She turned her head toward him. "No, not at all. I'm saying I'm distrustful of anything that happens fast, and acknowledging you have strong feelings for a person you met a week ago is fast in my book. All that happened a long time ago, Jeff, but it was a terrible thing to go through, falling for a man, actually considering marrying him, and then finding out that all he wanted was my family's money. Eric left a few scars on me. Under the same circumstances, I think you'd be cautious, too."

"I'm sure you're right. But I have no ulterior motives. I also think that sometimes people fall for each other quickly and other times it takes awhile. As for us, I think you should know that I'm having a lot of trouble keeping my hands off you. I don't have a hidden agenda here. I'm being up front with you.''

She couldn't help but smile. ''I'm being honest, too. I don't know what it is, chemistry or something. But all I have to do is look at you and my heart starts to pound.''

He shifted her into his arms, placing one hand over her heart. ''I see what you mean.'' His hand started to wander, to encircle her breast, but she stopped it with her own.

''Let's take it slow, Jeff. Maybe you're right, that people can fall for each other very fast. But frankly, when a man says he has feelings for me, I have trouble believing him. Words are cheap. It's actions that count.'' Her eyes grew dark, serious. ''I've had to learn that bitter lesson the hard way.''

There was more, Jeff thought, not just the Eric incident. But she appeared all talked out for tonight. There'd be time enough later. He'd find out because it was important for him to know just what he was up against.

He let out an exaggerated sigh. ''All right, I'll try to keep the brakes on.'' He bent his head and kissed her, but kept it light.

Walking her back to the campfire, he wondered just how much time she'd need.

Patience had never been his strong suit, Jeff readily acknowledged, though East had tried to teach him to go slowly, to consider all angles, to not plunge in without thinking things through. Still, he didn't want to wait. He knew Tish was the woman for him and he had great difficulty giving her time.

Work was one answer, and work they did the next day and the day after that. Pete paired them off into twos and they'd ridden out, looking for strays. With no small amount of maneuvering, Jeff had managed to align himself with Tish, but they'd had little personal time. The graze land was vast, the cows restless and the calves born over the long winter distrustful and given to loud bawling if anyone came near.

Jeff again had to admire Tish's ability on horseback, the way she'd scamper up a rocky cliffside, following the cry of a calf, then signal him. He'd ride up, lasso the little wanderer and between the two of them, they'd manage to free the animal and drive it back to join the herd. It was tedious work and the weather was muggy, low clouds trapping the moisture in the valley. By the end of the day, all of them were hot, tired, hungry and grumpy.

On the second afternoon, the sky began to darken and heavy rain clouds moved in. Jeff and Tish were several miles out, chasing a stubborn cow that had managed to evade the rope. It took the two of them nearly a full hour to finally herd her back toward the others, and by that time, the rain had started. As they hurried toward camp, it began to pour, making the hilly path a bit more treacherous.

At one point, Belladonna almost lost her footing, but quickly regained it as Tish talked calmly to the mare, soothing her. Just ahead, Jeff slowed his mount and swung around in his saddle to make sure horse and rider were okay. He pulled his hat lower on his head as Tish came out into the clearing and drew up alongside him where he waited astride Domino.

"That was a little too close," he shouted above the sound of the rain pounding down.

"We're okay," she answered, steadying the reins.

"Follow me then," he said, taking the lead. In the ten minutes it took to reach camp, they were both thoroughly soaked. Jeff noticed that they were the last two to come in and that the others were already raising the tents.

Swinging off Domino, he led him to the makeshift cover

the men had rigged up for the horses, tethering him on the far side since he was the only male. He saw that Tish was seeing to Belladonna as well, both of them aware that, especially out on the range, you had to take care of your horse so that when you needed him, your mount would take care of you.

By the time Domino was fed, watered and put up for the night, Jeff decided he was wet clear through to his underwear. Hurrying over to where the others were anchoring the poles of the small tents, he helped them finish up.

"Not enough tents," Derek told him. "We're caught short because rain wasn't predicted. We'll have to double up. Take that one down there."

"Right." Jeff noticed that everyone was hurrying to get out of the rain, so he carried his saddlebag containing his dry clothes to the far tent. He opened the flap and saw that Tish was already inside sitting on her bedroll. A small battery-powered lantern was beside her. He paused, uncertain

"Uh, they tell me we're short of tents. The others have already staked a claim and this is the last one available."

Her expression didn't change. "Fine. Come in and close the flap." Not looking at him, she dug a towel out of her bag and began drying her hair.

Jeff did as he was told, closed the flap and, on his hands and knees, spread his bedroll alongside hers. He sat down and slipped off his boots, then pulled his towel from his saddlebag and began drying off. But it was near impossible with his clothes drenched.

"Look, I hope I don't offend you, but I've got to get out of these wet things."

"Me, too. Turn your back and I'll do the same."

Feeling a shade silly, Jeff turned, pulled dry underwear and a shirt from his satchel, then went up on his knees to struggle out of his wet clothes. As tall as he was, it wasn't easy, his head grazing the top of the tent with each move ment. He was worried the stakes might loosen in the wet ground. Toweling off as he set aside each sopping article, he heard a muttered oath from Tish as she struggled to peal wet denim down her damp legs.

"Need some help?" he asked once he had on dry briefs and a flannel shirt.

Tish peeked over her shoulder and saw he was much further along and decently covered. "I could use a little, yes."

Jeff swiveled on his bottom and placed all the wet clothes in a pile in the far corner of the tent before turning to her. She had on a dry T-shirt under an open flannel shirt but her wet jeans were bunched around her calves. First he pulled off her damp socks, then took hold of the bottom seam of the pantleg and inched one down, then the other. Finally he yanked them off and tossed them into the wet pile.

"Thanks." He noticed her gaze got lost for a moment studying the way his damp blond hair curled at his ears, a lock falling onto his forehead. She swallowed hard. "Listen, could you turn around for another minute or two?"

"Sure." Jeff swung about, wondering if she knew how clearly her chilled breasts under that skimpy cotton shirt could be seen. Next he wondered how he was going to get to sleep even after lights out with the mental picture of her straining nipples in the forefront of his mind. He listened to the rustle of clothing until she finally told him she was all set.

Slowly, he turned and saw she was pulling on a pair of socks. He decided that was a fine idea and dug out his last clean pair. "I think I'll have to go back tomorrow. This is the last of my clean clothes."

"Mmm, me, too. I think we're all in the same boat. Don't you think we've rounded up all the strays by now?" Shivering, Tish glanced down at her front and began to button her shirt. Then she wiggled about and unzipped her bedroll.

"Yeah, probably." Jeff was doing the same thing and as he maneuvered to free the end of his bedroll, he bumped hips with her.

"Sorry," he murmured.

"It's okay," she muttered.

Trying to keep his mind where it belonged, Jeff managed to stretch out in his bedroll, pull up his extra blanket and flip the covers over himself. Seeing that Tish was settled in, he reached toward the lamp.

"Don't turn it out just yet, okay?" she asked.

"Oh. Sure."

His sleeping bag had a built-in pillow that could hardly be called one, so he raised one arm and cradled his head on it. Looking over at her, he saw that Tish was staring up at the very low ceiling. "Hope you're not claustrophobic."

"Fortunately not."

"I don't imagine you did a lot of camping out when you were a kid, eh?" She'd cut him off the last time he'd mentioned her early years. Jeff wondered if he could get her to open up here in this nonthreatening environment.

"None at all. Sleeping on the nasty old ground in a smelly tent with all manner of bugs and vermin is not for well-bred young ladies." Her voice had a trace of repressed anger.

"That sounds like a direct quote. From your mother?"

"My *step*mother, or whatever. And my father was paranoid that I'd be kidnapped and held for ransom since it was common knowledge that he had a lot of money."

Jeff could scarcely make out her features in the dim light. "That much money, eh?"

"Yes. Filthy rich, as the saying goes. Plenty of cold cash and a heart carved out of ice to go with it."

Whoa! Jeff wondered if she knew how bitter she

sounded. Not as angry as she'd been the other day at the mention of her father. But rather sorrowful and regretful.

"A cold fish. Well, a lot of successful men get to the top by kicking and clawing their way up the ladder, often using ruthless methods to gain control. Many of their business associates dislike and fear them, I hear."

"Not my father. He wasn't ruthless in business. He was heartless and utterly without remorse with his own family."

That's when they heard a huge crash and a loud scream, the sounds coming from close by outside their tent.

Chapter 4

"I'm going out to see what happened," Jeff said as he grabbed his boots and began pulling them on.

"I'll go with you," Tish said, sitting up.

"No, stay here." He searched through the pile of wet things, looking for his denim jacket. "No use both of us getting soaked again." Finding the jacket finally, he opened the tent flap and crawled out.

The rain came down in buckets as he shrugged into his jacket. He hadn't bothered with jeans since pulling on the soaked pair would be no easy feat in the cramped tent and he didn't want to get his other dry pair wet. Scrunching up his shoulders, Jeff made his way toward the far side where a small lantern lent enough light for him to see that the stakes had come loose and the tent had fallen in on the occupants.

"It's too muddy here," Pete said as Jeff joined the others in trying to raise the tent. "Stakes won't stay in the ground."

"We need to move it over there," Derek answered, pointing to a higher ridge where the ground was rocky but solid.

The four men put their backs into it and lifted the tent stakes and all, leaving Tanya scrambling out of her bedroll, looking wet and annoyed. A short distance from her, John sat on his sleeping bag pulling on his boots and muttering under his breath. The rain pelted everywhere and quick, jagged spurts of lightning lit up the night sky while thunder rumbled in the distance. Carrying his end, Jeff followed as they maneuvered the tent up the small incline.

"I'll stake my end in first," Jim called out.

Justin came hurrying over with the mallet and pounded the stake in while Jim held it fast. Justin hurried around to where the others held their stakes and made short order of firmly pounding each one in.

"Okay, guys, thanks," Pete said, then shouted above the rain's noise. "John, Tanya, you're all set over here."

Wrapped in her bedroll, her booted feet sticking out and carrying her other clothes, Tanya stomped up to the tent. "Are you guys sure this will hold? I'm not fond of these middle-of-the-night surprises."

"Think of it as an adventure," John said, trailing behind her.

"I hope you brought your hair dryer, Tanya," Jeff teased her.

She made a face at him and ducked inside the tent.

"She's cranky when she's wet," John said, chuckling. "Thanks, guys."

"Hey, John," Pete said, grabbing his arm, "keep the wrestling in there to a minimum and the tent will hold."

"Yeah, yeah." And he disappeared inside, closing the flap after himself.

"Well, that was fun," Derek muttered, slogging through

puddles toward his own tent as Jim, Pete and Justin trailed after him.

Jeff made his way back to the far tent and just for his own peace of mind, whacked each of the stakes with the mallet to make sure they were holding steady. Satisfied, he opened the tent flap and ducked inside. "One of the tents collapsed, but we fixed it."

"You're soaked again," Tish said, going up on her knees and grabbing his towel. "Here, let me help you."

Quite willing at this point to accept her help, Jeff yanked off his boots and shrugged out of his jacket. With his back to her, he let Tish dry his hair, then his damp shoulders and back. He felt her small but strong hands move over his cool flesh, warming wherever she touched, and his pulse began to escalate.

"Turn around," she directed.

Sitting Indian style, he swiveled about and found that she was quite close. He could have easily finished up himself, but he was enjoying her ministrations way too much to stop her now. Carefully, she patted dry his face, then shifted her attention to his chest, dabbing at the hair there. Her touch was arousing him despite his best effort at control.

In the dim light of the small lantern, he saw her eyes drift lower. She went to work on his legs next, her gaze returning to his briefs, once more wet.

Tish stopped, sitting back on her haunches, averting her gaze. "I'll give you my towel. It's not too wet, and you can finish up, okay?" Slowly, color moved into her face as she became aware of his discomfort. "I—I think you might have to slip those off since they're sopping wet." She seemed unable to keep from staring at the gray cotton briefs that had become all too tight.

Time seemed to stand still as Jeff waited to see what Tish would do. Her eyes moved up his body and locked with his dark green gaze. There was a war going on inside her, he could tell, but he couldn't help her with this one. She'd have to make the first move and he could see by her expressive face which way she yearned to go.

The moments ticked by and finally she came to a decision. "For your sake," she began, her voice low and husky, "I should walk away from you. You'd be so much better off. But I can't seem to do that. I want you too much. I want you more than I've ever wanted a man in my life."

He hadn't known he'd been holding his breath, but he let out a relieved sigh at last. Raising his hand to her silken cheek, he stroked her soft skin. "I won't hurt you, Tish. Not ever."

"But I might hurt you," she whispered.

"I'll take my chances." His hand moved to cup the back of her neck and drew her closer. His lips touched hers, gently at first, then more passionately. Jeff's other arm went around her as he deepened the kiss. Her response was instantaneous and avid, her mouth opening to admit his tongue, to allow him to explore while their hearts beat furiously in unison.

Outside the rain beat against the walls of the tent and poured into the nearby mountain stream. A craggy bolt of lightning flashed, clearly visible through the tent walls, followed by a thunder clap that reverberated along the ground beneath them. The elements of nature, fierce, wild and wonderful, impossible to control. Like his need for this woman, Jeff thought as he arranged their sleeping bags as a mattress and spread the blankets for cover warmth.

Easing her down on her side, Jeff joined her and smelled the rain on her hair, inhaling her special scent that was sweeter than anything he'd ever known. In the dim lamplight, her large luminous eyes watched him, hazy with an arousal he himself struggled to control. Slowly, he thought.

He wanted to go slowly and prayed he could hold off, for she was so beautiful.

"I tried to stay away from you," Tish whispered, her voice tremulous. "I honestly did, but I kept being drawn back. It's like you're in my blood and I've got to have you."

He stroked her rain-washed hair back off her face, smiling down at her. "From the first moment I saw you come riding in on Belladonna, looking for all the world like the lady of the manor, those gorgeous eyes examining me from head to toe, I knew I'd never be able to let you go."

A small frown appeared to mar her lovely features. "You don't know me. There are things—"

"Shh," he said, a finger to her lips. "Not tonight. Whatever they are, they can wait. We'll take care of them together. Tonight we don't think, we just feel." His hand glided along her shoulder down her rib cage and came to rest on her hip. "And you feel so good."

Her small hand moved to tangle in the hair of his chest. "This is what excited me tonight, when I saw you with your shirt off. My hands itched to touch you. You're so strong, so beautiful."

His smile came easily. "You're the one who's beautiful and tonight, you're mine."

"I don't take this lightly, Jeff. I don't do this easily. I'm following my heart here, and I don't seem to have a choice where you're concerned, but I can't say I'm not afraid."

He could see she meant what she said and wished he could find the words to take away her fears. "Life's a crapshoot, Tish. There are no guarantees. I wish I had a better answer, but I don't. Just tell me what you want."

Her eyes burned into his, fiery in the dim light, filled with resolve. "You," she said, her voice husky. "I want only you."

If only she knew how completely she already had him,

Jeff thought. Aroused beyond belief, Jeff took her mouth as his big hands molded her small body to his.

Fingers made clumsy by passion, he unbuttoned her shirt, never taking his mouth from hers. Wiggling and squirming, he managed to slip the shirt off her shoulders as his lips skimmed her cheeks, her chin, her lovely throat and back to settle on her mouth. The breathless kiss went on and on until his need had him shifting restlessly.

Sitting up, he tugged at the hem of her T-shirt. Tish sat up, too, allowing him to tug off the shirt and toss it aside while his eyes feasted on her beautiful breasts. As she watched him, he filled his hands with her, gently caressing until her eyes closed and her head dropped back. When he put his mouth to her, she moaned out loud, her body arching.

Jeff shifted her onto her back and sent his mouth on a journey, tasting everywhere. Her skin was firm and smooth as he reveled in the feel and scent of her. He felt her hands in his hair, urging him to explore where he would, and he didn't disappoint her.

He gazed at her face and saw that she appeared to be floating, absorbing the sensations, straining to get closer as he feasted on her willing flesh. This was what he'd been dreaming of, to touch her everywhere, to kiss her secret places, to make her want him as much as he wanted her. Her arms circled his neck and he shifted his mouth to the satin column of her throat before returning to the wonder of her lips.

His hand traveled lower to tug off her silk panties as her hips lifted to accommodate him. Returning to kiss her, to distract her, his fingers skimmed along the length of her lovely legs then moved inside and found her ready. Unable to resist, he sent her soaring and swallowed her astonished response. He felt the waves pummel as they tore through her. With what little breath she had left, she whispered his name.

He let her return slowly, all the while placing soft kisses along her heated flesh. Then, to his surprise, she reached over and her fingers closed around him. Jeff pulled in a shocked breath as her exploring hand brought him perilously close to explosion. It was time to take the control back.

Shifting, Jeff eased off his briefs and positioned himself above her, slipping inside as smoothly as if they'd been lovers for years. Recovering quickly, she rose to meet him thrust for thrust, her eyes hazy but open and on his. It occurred to Jeff as he moved within her that the conqueror was being conquered as well.

They found the rhythm instinctively, moving together as one. He felt her arms go around him as if needing to hold him ever closer moments before they tumbled over the edge together.

His weight must be crushing her, Jeff thought as he braced himself to roll over. But Tish's arms tightened around him, holding him close. "Don't go."

"I'm too heavy on you," he insisted, though he really didn't want to move.

"No, you're not."

Jeff drew in a deep breath. "How do you feel?"

"Stunned. Astonished. Marvelous." There was a smile in her voice, in her eyes.

"Not sorry, then, eh?"

"Sorry? How could I be sorry when no one's ever made me feel the way you do?"

He couldn't think how to answer that, but he felt what little tension remained drain from him. It had seemed that she'd talked herself into making love with him, given in because her desire had left her no choice. And he'd been afraid that afterward, she'd have regrets. Thank goodness she didn't.

"You remind me of my grandfather," Tish said, snuggling into him, rubbing her cheek against his five-o'clock shadow.

"Your grandfather?" Jeff asked. "Well, that's flattering. I guess."

She smiled and went on to explain. "My Grandma Alice told me that the closest she ever got to heaven was when she was making love with my grandfather. They were married sixty-seven years. So, yes, you remind me of him."

"Now, I'm sure I'm flattered." He shifted so he could look into her eyes. "Do you think we could last together for sixty-seven years?"

He felt a subtle withdrawal, physically and emotionally, as if the question bothered her. She took her time answering. "I don't know, Jeff," she finally answered, sounding sorry she'd ever introduced the subject. "These days people don't seem able to stick together for long."

"There are still plenty of people who stay together through thick and thin. If their bond is strong enough, they can handle anything that comes their way."

Instead of answering that, she stretched to kiss him, as if her actions would change the subject. He didn't mind, his body already wanting more. He took his time exploring her mouth unhurriedly and her body with his hands, watching her reaction to his touch. Leisurely, he investigated every curve and hollow, searching out all her sensitive spots as her breathing went shallow. He was throbbing within her now and she was no longer able to lie still. The journey was just as sweet, just as fulfilling.

When he all but collapsed on her, Jeff decided they both needed a little rest. Rolling over, taking her with him, he stretched out on his back and settled her head just over his heart. He pulled up the blankets and covered them both.

As he closed his eyes, he heard her sigh contentedly. Drifting off to sleep, Jeff couldn't ever remember feeling better.

The ride back to Red Rock Ranch the next day was slow. Lucky for everyone, the rain had stopped but it was quite cool. The three cowhands had left at daybreak with Tanya and John following after breakfast. At Jeff's insistence, Tish and he had lingered behind, letting their horses mosey along, in no hurry to return. He was aware of the speculative looks they'd gotten that morning, but he'd ignored them all. After all, they were two consenting adults and their relationship was no one's business.

Except for a stretch where the path was quite narrow and could accommodate only one horse at a time, they rode side by side on the open range, talking about this and that, nothing important. By the time they stopped for lunch around one, Jeff was more than ready to hold her close in his arms.

He spread out the blanket he'd had in his bedroll while Tish scrounged in her saddlebag for some fruit, cheese, crackers and cans of soda they'd chilled overnight in the mountain stream. But before she could put together their small meal, Jeff pulled her into a fierce hug and eased her onto the blanket beneath them. Jeff was eager for her, hungry, and she was just as anxious, returning his kiss with all the ardor he could have asked for.

They were alone on the mountainside since the others were far ahead of them, yet when Jeff's fingers began unbuttoning her blouse, she stopped him. "Please, let's wait. I don't feel right out in the open like this in broad daylight."

Jeff frowned, feeling the frustrations of a new lover suddenly refused. "I want to see you in the daylight. I don't want us to hide under darkness. Are you ashamed of our relationship?''

''No!'' She was quick to reply. ''Please, Jeff. There'll be other times. I've already given you more than I thought was in me, far more than I'd planned.''

Chagrined, he backed off, kissing her lightly, then sitting up. ''All right, I'll cool down. But it won't be easy.'' He noticed some purple and white wildflowers growing in the rocky soil and went over to pick a few. Returning, he handed them to Tish, a sort of peace offering for pushing too hard.

With a smile, she thanked him then spread out their lunch, slicing pears and apples along with chunks of cheddar cheese. Nibbling on a piece of pear, she again looked thoughtful. ''I can't imagine why you'd want to take on someone like me who's lugging around all this baggage.''

Jeff cupped her face, making her look at him. She was so lovely even with her dark eyes so solemn. He'd said he'd take things slowly, let her come around in her own time, but he couldn't help saying the words. ''I've got all this love stored up inside me, Tish, just waiting for the right person to share it with. You're that person.''

''Don't!'' Tish sat up taller, moving away from his touch. ''Don't mention love to me. I've had too many people in my life do things in the name of love, terrible things. I don't understand love. The very word frightens me.''

Seeing how agitated she'd become, he tried to calm her. ''Shh, it's okay. I'll teach you.''

She didn't answer, just finished her pear and stared off into the distance, closing up.

Jeff felt shut out, felt there was something more in her past that she hadn't shared with him, something that had made her afraid to love. ''What is it, Tish? Tell me what you're afraid of.''

She shook her head. ''I wouldn't know where to begin.''

His lunch forgotten, Jeff moved closer, putting his arm around her. "The same way you told me about Eric— slowly, in your own words."

She kept staring at the clouds gently moving in a dreary sky, one hand tracing the seam of her jeans. She was quiet so long that Jeff wondered whether she'd speak at all. Finally, she did, her voice low, strained.

"My father's name is Charles Buckner. You may not have heard of him, but on the East Coast, many people know him as a wealthy financier, a shrewd but fair businessman, a generous philanthropist. As his only daughter, I was doted on. Growing up, he denied me nothing and spoiled me rotten. As I moved into my teens, I always thought his love and affection for me was why my mother was so cool and indifferent. I thought she was jealous of Dad's feelings for me. Little did I know." Pausing, she drew in a breath as if to steady herself. Her hand settled on Jeff's resting at her waist, her fingers lacing with his.

He noticed that her hand was cool, and decided the weather had nothing to do with that. Her emotions had her churning, the memories he was forcing from her tying her in knots. Still, he didn't back down because he honestly felt whatever was troubling her needed to be said, to be out in the open before they could truly share an intimate relationship. Evidently whatever it was still had the power to freeze her up some twenty years later.

"I'd graduated from college that spring and finally gotten Eric out of my life. I was twenty-two with the world at my feet, or so I thought. I'd planned on going into public relations at one of Dad's companies, to start at the bottom and learn the business from the ground up. I remember my folks had gone away for the weekend and I was all alone in the house, probably for the first time ever.

"It's a huge house in upstate New York, and I wasn't really alone because there was Wanda, the housekeeper who'd been around as long as I could remember. She lived in, but there was also a cleaning woman who came twice a week and a cook who came for dinner parties and a whole gardening crew. To this day, I can't remember what I was searching for when I went up into the attic the afternoon they were due home. Anyhow I was rummaging through this old trunk and I found a box containing some of my baby pictures that I'd never seen. Naturally, I was interested, so I looked at them, then searched for more. That's when I ran across several documents that changed my life.''

Jeff wondered if she was aware that she was squeezing his hand as if holding on for dear life. He didn't make a sound or a move, but let her pause long enough to find the strength to go on.

''I couldn't figure it out at first. The top page was a legal document stating that a woman named Angela Rosetti was relinquishing all rights to an infant girl named Grace for the sum of twenty-five thousand dollars. It was signed by Angela and my father and witnessed by our family lawyer and someone else whose name I didn't recognize. It wasn't until I noticed that the document was dated one day after I was born that I really paid attention.''

Tish drew in a shaky breath. ''The second page was a legal document stating that the same child named Grace was legally adopted by my father and my mother, Eleanor Buckner, dated the same day, and that the child's name was changed to Tish Buckner. At this point, I assumed that Angela Rosetti had been an unwed mother and that my father and mother had adopted her baby girl, me. The money exchanged bothered me, but it was the third page that ravaged my world.

''It was a letter from Angela Rosetti to Dad, handwritten in ink, with several blotches as if tears had fallen on the paper. In it, she begged him to take good care of their daughter. *Their* daughter, not *her* daughter as I'd begun to think. She went on to say she was sorry that she wasn't good enough for him, that she'd believed him when he'd told her he loved her and only her, that he'd leave his wife and marry her. She went on to say she'd honor her promise to never try to see the baby, even though he hadn't honored his promise to her, because she wanted what was best for the child's future. She ended by saying she would always love him. The final document was a birth certificate for a baby girl, Grace, stating the mother to be Angela Rosetti and the father to be Charles Buckner.''

Jeff shifted slightly and saw a lone tear trail down her cheek. He caught it on his finger and held her tighter.

Once begun, Tish seemed to need to say it all. ''I sat there a long time, trying to figure things out. When I heard my parents returning, I carried all four papers downstairs and confronted them. My father became furious, first with my mother for not burning those papers years ago and then me for snooping, as he called it. When I told him the box they were in had my name on it, he calmed down, but not much.

''Charles Buckner is known as the persuader in business circles. The best negotiator on the East Coast, one magazine article had labeled him. So he went to work trying to win me over. He breezed over the fact that he'd been on a business trip early in his marriage and run into a woman named Angela Rosetti, small and pretty with long dark hair. He'd had an affair with her, the only time he'd been unfaithful in his marriage, he swore. Some months later, Angela Rosetti contacted him and told him she was pregnant.''

Tish swiped at another tear, speaking over her shoulder to Jeff. ''I'll bet you never thought I'd have such a sordid tale in my background.''

''Honey, you don't know what sordid is.''

''I think I do. You see, my father confessed then, right in front of the woman I'd always thought of as my mother, the woman who all my life had been cool and indifferent to me, that he'd learned Eleanor couldn't have children so when Angela called with the news that she was pregnant, he decided they'd adopt her child. Simple as that, he'd said, smiling. But his wife's eyes were cold as winter, with just cause, I felt.

"I interrupted him and told him I'd read Angela's letter and she didn't seem happy about the adoption, that she'd loved him and had believed he'd leave his wife and marry her as he'd promised. As easily as he'd swat a pesky fly away, he dismissed her words as the raving of a poor, pitiful woman, saying she'd come from the wrong side of the tracks, a second-rate background, blue-collar parents, not our kind. Then he added the words that have haunted me. Don't you see? he asked me with a straight face. I did it for you, so you'd have a better life than you could have had with her. I did it because I love you."

Jeff honestly didn't know what to say. He turned her so she faced him, clutching both her hands, but her eyes were downcast, and he waited for the rest.

"I couldn't leave it alone. What about a mother's love for her child? I literally screamed at him. What about your wife? How could you bring your illegitimate child into this marriage, causing her to resent me all my life? And his wife, who was not really my mother, didn't bother to deny my accusation. But his only answer was that he did it in the name of love. By then I was hurt, angry, furious really. I railed at him that he evidently thought my real mother was good enough for a fling but not good enough to marry the great Charles Buckner. He stormed out then, telling me he didn't want to discuss this anymore. His wife started crying and went to her room."

"How did you manage to coexist with them after the truth was finally out?" Jeff wanted to know.

"I didn't. You know, thinking back, I'd wondered most

of my life how odd it was that Eleanor was tall, blond and fair, and my father was over six feet with sandy-brown hair. And here I am not very tall with this dark brown—almost black—hair and an olive complexion. However, I thought I was a throwback to some European relative.

"And I was, only they were Angela Rosetti's relatives who came from Italy. As I mentioned, I couldn't let things be. I hated my father for lying to me and for what he'd done to Angela, bullying her into selling her child, probably blackmailing her somewhere along the line so she'd never contact him again. And I wasn't too fond of Eleanor who'd blamed an innocent child and made her pay for her husband's infidelity. So I went searching for Angela Rosetti."

"Good for you," Jeff said, proud of her.

"Unfortunately, I was too late. I traced her family to Philadelphia and went there only to find she'd died three years before. She'd never married and had used the money from my father to care for her sick mother. Her married sister, Dolores, knew all about Charles, knew that Angela loved him, yet they welcomed me with open arms. She told me that Angela didn't want to accept the money, but their mother was so ill and she didn't have insurance. They're such nice people. I still keep in touch with them."

"What about Charles and Eleanor?" he asked.

"I never spoke to my father again after that day. I moved out, lock, stock and barrel. I heard that Eleanor died about five years later and Charles is still alive, probably still scheming. All in the name of love, of course."

So now he knew why the very word upset her. "You're right. People make a lot of mistakes and blame it on love."

"Yes, they do. Dad said he was trying to protect me. From what? I asked him. From a life of poverty with low class, uneducated people, he'd answered. Nice viewpoint, eh? Growing up, I'd never realized what a snob he was.

But love isn't only about protection. Love without truth is a travesty."

"Like Eric claiming to love you when the truth was he was using you."

Head bent, she nodded. "Yes, exactly."

"Tish, when I said I had a lot of love stored up, that was the truth. I couldn't love my selfish, drunken parents and I had no real friends, shuffled through the foster care system and living on the streets. East was my first friend and I came to love him as the father I never had. Not only because he took me in, taught me, nourished me, but because he earned my respect, my trust. He's honest and always tells me the truth. So, I agree with you."

Slowly, she raised her head. "I'm glad."

"But I also don't want you to be afraid of love. Eric's so-called love was self-serving and so was your father's. But mine isn't. You'll see that in time. You'll trust me because I have no ulterior motives, just these solid, overwhelming feelings for you. And if you're going to say it's lust not love, please don't. I admit to lusting after you—" he smiled "—but it's far more than that. And it's real."

The eyes that met his were still troubled. "I want to believe you, to trust you. But I need time."

Jeff smiled. "I know and I'll try not to rush you. I can be patient when the prize is worth the wait. And you definitely are." He eased her into his arms, kissed the top of her head and just held her as they sat silently enjoying the view. He knew it had taken a lot out of her, revealing so much.

Holding the wildflowers he'd given her, she inhaled the sweet fragrance. "I think flowers are nature's greatest invention. They're like children—all they ask is that you tend them and love them. That must be why my adopted mother never could grow a flower of any kind in her garden. She tried and tried, but she was so filled with resentment that she couldn't have babies of her own yet had to raise her husband's child that her garden was barren.''

Silently, he held her, hoping his presence would ease her troubled memories. Later, Jeff couldn't have said how long they stayed like that, listening to each other's heart beating, just being quiet together. He only knew that that had been a turning point in their relationship. It hadn't been easy getting her to trust him enough to open up, but he felt that now that she had, in time she'd learn to love him.

Leaning back in his airline seat, Jeff smiled, remembering how things had been when they'd finally arrived back at the ranch. Even though John and Tanya had shared a tent that rainy night, they received no sidelong looks, no knowing glances. But the agents had quickly singled out Jeff and Tish and labeled them a romantic twosome.

He had to admit they probably gave themselves away. Although they spent the next week doing work on the ranch with the horses and cattle much as they had the previous week, there was a decided difference in their demeanor. The looks they'd shared, even across a crowded room, had been heated and simmering. The moment Jeff entered a room, his eyes automatically searched for Tish, and she seemed to do the same. If she'd been chatting with others in a group, she soon made some excuse and headed toward Jeff. As often as not, the two of them would then slip away to be alone.

Of course, people noticed. Like during the goldfish incident.

Naturally, there was no room for pets in the lodge with agents coming and going. But one day in town, Jeff decided to surprise Tish so he bought two goldfish with all the equipment—bowl, rocks, food, a decorative ceramic arch. He hurried back, planning to set it all up in her room while she was out, with the aid of Naomi Star who had keys to all the rooms.

Unfortunately, as Jeff rushed to the elevator, the plastic bag filled with water and fish broke open. There they were, Naomi and Jeff, on the lobby floor, trying to capture the flopping fish before they died without water. The commotion brought several people running. Next thing he knew, there were five or six people scurrying after fish, getting more water, mopping the floor.

And that's when Tish walked in.

His surprise sort of fizzled, but by the time he set everything up on her dresser, with the whole entourage watching, of course, she was shaking her head and smiling. It was hard to miss the loving looks passing between them so, despite Tish's wish for secrecy, everyone knew.

When they'd all left and Jeff and Tish were alone in her room with the fish, he took her in his arms and kissed her long and deliciously. Easing back, Tish gazed up at him. "You're too much, Jeff Kirby. I never know what you're going to do next."

"That's what keeps life interesting," he said.

Still, she stared at him, as if trying to see into his mind. "You're completely opposite of what I thought I wanted in my life. You're funny when I felt I needed solid and serious. You're adventurous when in my personal life, I need calm. But—but you make me smile, laugh, feel good." She inched closer. "And when you kiss me, oh, Lord! Bells and whistles and horns."

Jeff just grinned and kissed her again.

That incident and others had him feeling fairly confident that Tish was learning to care more and more for him every day. And still she hadn't said those three little words he'd been longing to hear. He was wondering if she ever would when something happened that brought them both up short.

The day had started out like any other. Tish had been

working with the newborn calves and Jeff had been helping Tex, one of the more experienced hands, break in a horse. By late afternoon, both Tish and Jeff were tired and looking forward to some private time together. So they'd gone to their rooms, showered and put on fresh clothes, then ridden out to a favorite spot they'd discovered alongside a brook in the shadow of the mountains. It was twilight, that lovely time when the day was almost ready to drift away and the night not quite prepared to put in an appearance.

Plum and crimson and amber put paintbrush streaks across a clear blue sky as they rode out of sight of the Red Rock Ranch. They spread their blanket under an old cottonwood tree and scarcely had it hit the ground before he scooped her in his arms, hungry but not for food.

"Oh, you feel so good," he murmured into her hair, hugging her close. "The thought of this is what kept me going all day."

"Mmm, me, too," Tish whispered into his ear. "Kiss me, Jeff. I can't wait any longer."

And he had, many times while he made love with her as the golden sun slowly sank out of sight. Afterward, they'd eaten their picnic dinner that Jeff had talked Elsa into packing for them. They'd talked and nibbled on cold chicken and potato salad between kisses, drawing out their time together. Finally, most reluctantly, they'd packed up their picnic things, climbed on their mounts and ridden back to the ranch.

The rotating red light atop the ambulance was the first unusual thing Jeff spotted as they came within sight of the ranch buildings. It was parked in front of the lodge used by the tourists and alongside it was a police car and a group of people milling about.

"Must have been an accident," Tish ventured as they slowed the horses near the barn. Terry, one of the groomers, came out to take Belladonna's reins. "What happened?" she asked the young man.

"One of the guests had a heart attack," Terry said as Jeff swung down off Domino. "He died instantly."

"Do you know his name?" Tish asked.

"Afraid not." The young man led both horses into the barn.

Jeff took hold of Tish's elbow as they hurried over to the building. They were just putting the gurney into the ambulance, a sheet draped over the victim's body including the face. Then the ambulance attendant closed the double doors.

Tish recognized Doreen Novak standing by the lodge door, her face red from weeping. "Oh, no," she whispered to Jeff. "It must be Henry Novak."

Jeff knew that Tish had spent some time with the Novaks after learning they were from the same town in upstate New York where she'd grown up. She'd even given them a lengthy tour of the area. The couple, in their sixties, had just retired and seemed in good health.

Leaving Jeff, Tish hurried over to the distraught woman. "Doreen, I just heard. Henry?"

"Yes," the widow said, fighting a fresh rush of tears. "We'd just finished dinner," she continued, her hands worrying a crumpled tissue, "when Henry said he thought he had indigestion. The food here is so good we always eat too much. He asked me for an antacid and I'd just opened my purse to get it for him when he grabbed his chest and fell to the floor. His face was so red and a sort of gurgling sound came from his throat, then he went limp. Oh, God, I screamed and people came running. Someone gave him CPR, but it was too late."

Tish held her hand tightly. "I'm so sorry, Doreen."

"He didn't get to enjoy but a month of his retirement."

She turned her tear-streaked face to Tish. "Just like that, he was gone. Oh, Tish, I never even got to say goodbye."

"I'm sure he knew you were there at his side," Tish told the distressed woman, her arm slipping around her frail shoulders.

"I wish I'd have told him I loved him this morning. You know, it was our habit to say the words to each other every morning and night, but he'd gotten up early to go for a walk and I slept in. I—I feel so terrible. I didn't get a chance to tell him I love him."

Tish patted her hand. "You've been married how long? You told me forty-six years, I believe. I'm sure Henry knew you loved him deeply."

"I suppose you're right. But I wanted to tell him again. Why oh why didn't I get up with him this morning?" She cried softly into the new tissue Tish gave her.

Amos Turner, the manager of the tourist lodge at Red Rock, came over, his round, ruddy face the picture of sympathy. "Doreen, they're taking Henry to the hospital. Would you like me to go with you to help you fill out the paperwork?"

Looking shaky and confused, Doreen looked at him. "Yes, Amos, that would be so good of you." She turned grief-stricken eyes to the ambulance now silently gliding down the driveway. Amos guided her over to his big Lincoln and helped her inside before driving off in the same direction as the ambulance.

The police had finished questioning witnesses and seemed satisfied so they, too, drove off.

Tish strolled back to where Jeff was quietly talking with Slim. When she reached his side, he slipped his arm around her.

"Are you okay?"

Tish nodded. "I need to go inside."

"Sure." With a nod to Slim, Jeff took her arm and

walked with her to the main building. She was strangely
silent, pale, her expression troubled as if she were thinking
about something deeply. He knew that she'd been friendly
with the Novaks though they hadn't been close friends. Yet
Henry's death seemed to have affected her.

As the doors silently slid open, Tish took Jeff's hand.
"Will you come with me to my room, please?"

"Whatever you want."

Once they were inside her room, which was very much
like Jeff's, she turned to him. "Doreen told me something
tonight, that she hadn't told Henry that she loved him this
morning and now, suddenly, he's gone."

Where was she going with this? Jeff wondered. "I'm
sure he knew she loved him. They've been married forever
and—"

"Yes, of course. But her point was that even though we
know someone cares for us, it's important to tell them regularly and often." She draped her arms over his shoulders
and looked into his dark-green eyes. "I've been selfish,
Jeff. I've heard you tell me that you love me and the words
thrilled me, made me glad inside. But I've never told you
because…because of all that went before, I suppose. And
you're right. All that happened in the past has nothing to
do with us, not really."

He smiled down at her, deep affection in his eyes. "I'm
glad you finally see that."

"I love you, Jeff. I love you with all my heart." Rising
on tiptoes, she reached to kiss him.

At last she'd said the words he'd been longing to hear,
and she sounded as if she meant them. His arms around her
tightened and he accepted her kiss as he accepted her words
of love, with pleasure, with joy.

At last when the kiss finally ended, he looked into her
fabulous brown eyes now filled with love, love for him.
"Thank you for that. I kind of thought you felt that way,

but I couldn't be sure without the words. Do you see what I mean?''

''Yes, I do. Doreen said that, even after forty-six years of marriage, every morning and night they said those three little words to each other. I found that so heartwarming. I think she can take comfort in the fact that although Henry won't be with her anymore, he died knowing he was loved. That wasn't the way of things in my family.''

''Nor in mine. But I'll bet East and Alicia say those words to one another every day. I can tell from the way they treat each other.''

''Yes, that's it. You can't say *I love you,* then treat someone poorly.'' She drew in a deep breath. ''I've been meaning to tell you for a while, but the time was never right. Now, it is.''

''Then say it again,'' Jeff requested, holding her closer.

''I love you, Jeff Kirby,'' she answered, her gaze on his lips.

''And I love you, Tish Buckner,'' he said, taking her mouth in a kiss that was like a promise.

Chapter 5

Jeff carried his leather bag down the broad concourse at Kennedy Airport, his strides lengthy and impatient as he glanced out the windows at a rainy morning. He wasn't hungry, wasn't even sleepy.

Anxious was what he was. Anxious for some answers as to how Tish was doing, what her most recent prognosis was.

Outside the terminal, Jeff pulled up the collar of his leather jacket against the rain and walked to the taxi curb, quickly hailing a cab.

Tossing his bag inside, he climbed into the back seat and tugged the door closed. "How long to get to Metropolitan General Hospital?" he asked the heavyset, balding driver.

The man shrugged. "This time of morning, rain and all, fastest would be to take the Van Wyck Parkway to the Grand Central, then the Long Island Expressway to the

Midtown Tunnel. An hour and fifteen, maybe an hour if we're lucky.''

Jeff held out a twenty. "This is yours above the fare if you make it in under an hour.''

Wordlessly, the driver nodded, put his meter into play and whipped into the next lane.

Gloomy weather, Jeff thought, trying to relax, slightly wired from all the caffeine. Gloomy suited his mood perfectly. He'd been to New York City before and hadn't cared for the crazy way the cabbies drove, but today, it was just what he needed. He watched the driver weave in and out of lanes as he headed for the ramp to the Van Wyck.

Traffic was heavy, even at this early hour. Commuters, he supposed. The rain dripped and tunneled down the window and kept the wipers busy on the windshield as he stared unseeingly at the passing scenery. In his mind, there was but one thought, one prayer, like a mantra: *Let her recover. Please, let her recover.*

Some fifty minutes later, the driver pulled to a screeching halt in the circular drive of the large Manhattan hospital. Jeff paid the meter fare and handed him the twenty before climbing out. Hurrying inside, he stopped at the information desk on the first floor.

"Tish Buckner,'' he said to the cheerfully smiling volunteer.

She typed the name into her computer, then waited as the information came on screen. "She's on the fifth floor, in surgical ICU. Only family members allowed to visit.'' The middle-aged woman peered over her glasses. "Are you related?''

"Yes,'' Jeff answered. "Thank you.'' He rushed off toward the bank of elevators. He heard the woman call after him, but he didn't stop. He'd find out all he needed to know upstairs.

Trying his strained patience, the elevator was slow in

arriving and when it did, an attendant and a patient lying on a gurney took up all the space. He punched the button again. The next car arrived filled to near capacity, mostly with hospital personnel in green scrubs so familiar to Jeff. He shoved in, quickly turning to face the front, ignoring the annoyed glances of the other passengers who had to step back.

He was in no mood for the amenities this morning, not until he was apprised of Tish's condition.

Getting off on the fifth floor, he looked around and spotted the nearest nurses' station. He approached a harried nurse who was on the phone, scribbling something on a chart while another phone rang incessantly. Since no one else was around, Jeff waited impatiently. She disconnected, then took the other call. When she finally hung up, he stepped closer. "Tish Buckner. Can you tell me where she is?"

The nurse finished the notation she was writing, then looked up. She undoubtedly saw a tall man with tired, worried eyes who needed a shave and about twelve hours of sleep, but he managed to give her a smile nonetheless. She responded as most women did and smiled back. "Down that corridor, turn left and take it to the end. That'll be ICU."

"Thanks." Jeff followed her directions and came to a pair of windowless double doors. Next to them was a desk where another volunteer sat reading the paper. "Tish Buckner," he said to her.

She set aside the paper and checked her chart. "She's in ICU after surgery yesterday. Are you a relative?"

"Yes. May I see her please?"

"What's your name?"

"Jeff Kirby."

The woman checked her chart. "You're not listed here as next of kin."

"I'm her husband," Jeff replied. "Listed or not, I need to see her. Who's her doctor?"

Again, the woman looked on the chart. "Dr. Edmund O'Neill."

"Fine. Page him, please. He's talked with my father, East Kirby, in California and arrangements were to have been made."

"I don't see a notation anywhere here, Mr. Kirby." She picked up the phone. "I'll page Dr. O'Neill."

Frustrated, anxious, annoyed, Jeff set down his bag and slipped off his leather jacket, placing it on the bag. It was warm in here, as it was in most hospitals. They had to follow rules, he knew only too well. However, knowing Tish was on the other side of those swinging doors and he couldn't go to her was raising his blood pressure.

He began to pace the small waiting area as he heard the page for Dr. O'Neill over the PA. The familiar hospital scents drifted to him, medicinal along with cleansing solutions and that indefinable almost tangible smell of fear, especially in the ICU area. Distant bells pinged, phones rang, pages were repeated in well-modulated tones and nurses in rubber-soled shoes rushed by. It was his world, the one he'd chosen, yet he desperately hated being on the other side as the relative of a gravely ill patient instead of part of the medical team.

A television bracketed to a shelf on the wall had CNN on, the volume low. There were three plastic chairs and an upholstered green couch in the waiting room. A woman softly crying in the far corner was the only other occupant. Jeff walked back and forth, feeling like a caged lion.

By his watch, it was a full twenty minutes before a man wearing a long white hospital coat over a white shirt and dress pants came hurrying toward him. In his late forties, Jeff estimated, he had thinning black hair and wore glasses over dark-brown intelligent eyes. He held out his hand as he approached.

"You're Dr. Kirby?" he asked.

"Yes, sir," Jeff answered, shaking his strong, firm hand. "Third-year resident. How is she?"

Edmund O'Neill shoved his glasses more firmly into place on his nose. "A lot better than when they brought her in yesterday. She's suffered a severe concussion and broken clavicle, for starters. We had to remove her spleen and minute bomb fragments. She had a collapsed lung but it's functioning fairly well now and we doubt there's permanent damage there. The trauma to the head is our main concern, the one that's put her into the coma." He studied Jeff's reaction for a moment. "I'm being very frank with you only because you're a doctor, and because East told me you could handle the truth."

"I appreciate your candor, Doctor. What's her prognosis?"

"Guardedly optimistic. She's quite healthy and was in excellent physical condition before the accident, so that's in her favor. I operated and stabilized the floating clavicle by putting in two permanent screws. She's holding her own, but we really can't tell yet at this stage. Time will let us know more. If she comes out of the coma in the next twenty-four to forty-eight hours, it will mean the swelling in the brain has gone down and she'll have an excellent chance of a total recovery. If not, well, we'll have to reevaluate."

Jeff swallowed hard. He'd thought he'd been prepared but, although the news wasn't hopeless, it wasn't as good as he'd hoped, either. "Can I go in to her?"

"Yes, and I'm sorry I didn't get around to putting your name on the approved visitor list. As usual, it's a little crazy around here. I had no idea she was married until East Kirby called me personally and told me about you. Normally, we don't allow visitors to stay with ICU patients around the clock, as I'm sure you know. Because of your credentials, I'm making an exception. He's a very persuasive man, your father.''

''Yes, he is. And thank you.'' Jeff couldn't help wondering just what his father had told O'Neill to get unlimited visitation for him.

Walking over with Jeff to the volunteer, Dr. O'Neill gave her his new instructions. ''Dr. Kirby has my approval to stay with his wife as long as he wants.'' He turned back to Jeff. ''I suggest you get some rest after you see her. She's not awake and probably won't be for hours yet.'' He gave him a tired smile. ''You look like you could use some sleep.''

''Thanks, but what I need is to be with Tish.'' He glanced at his bag and jacket. ''Can I leave this here for now?'' he asked, well aware that visitors weren't permitted to take things into ICU as a safeguard against patient infection. ''I came here straight from the airport.''

''Absolutely,'' the doctor said.

''Thanks, I'll pick them up later.'' He shook hands with O'Neill again, feeling grateful for East's call and for the close-knit community of medical personnel. Pulling in a deep breath, he stepped through the double doors.

A shoulder-high circular desk in the center dominated the large room. Along the perimeter were the private ICU cubicles, each with sliding glass doors closing them off from the main area where several nurses went about their duties. The nurse behind the desk whose name tag read Thelma looked up from a monitor as Jeff walked over.

''Tish Buckner,'' he said. ''I'm her husband.''

''Yes, Dr. Kirby,'' she answered with a smile. ''I just got the word from Dr. O'Neill.'' Rising, she led him toward the third cubicle. ''I'm assigned to your wife,'' she added.

''How's she doing this morning?'' he asked, knowing

this nurse was the one monitoring all of Tish's vital signs, administering the medications the doctor ordered, and would be aware of the slightest changes in her condition. The machines hooked up to the patient relayed any small change to the central nurses' station.

"Holding her own, Doctor," she answered in that maddening way some medical personnel had of saying something while revealing nothing.

Jeff grit his teeth as they stopped in front of cubicle 3. "I'd like to see her chart, if I may."

She thought that over for the briefest of moments. "Certainly, as long as her doctor authorizes it." She gave him a polite smile. "If you need anything, please press her call button and I'll check with Dr. O'Neill."

She had to follow protocol or she'd be in trouble, Jeff knew, but felt annoyance at the delay nonetheless.

Steeling himself, he slid open the glass door. Despite all the patients he'd seen hooked up to machines during his years in training, gazing at the woman he loved with tubes running in and out of her was a shock. She had an IV line in one arm, the bag of solution dangling overhead, and a hep-lock in the other in case they needed to take a blood sample. A catheter tube ran from under the crisp white sheet to a pouch on the far side of the bed and a blood pressure monitor was wrapped on one arm, automatically recording a reading at regulated intervals. The clear tubing of an oxygen canula ran under her nose. The machines blinked and winked and bleeped occasionally, the various colors chasing each other on electronic graphs, oddly frightening even to the experienced.

It's so different when you're emotionally involved with the patient, Jeff thought.

He stepped close to the bed and saw that Tish was very pale in sharp contrast to her usual healthy tan, and she looked so small, so helpless. The figure 8 bandages crisscrossed her sternum, keeping the area immobile so the fractured clavicle could heal. There were bruises and scrapes on her arms and hands and even a few on her lovely face. Her dark hair was tucked close around her head and her long dark lashes rested on her cheeks.

Choking back his emotions, Jeff pulled the lone chair over closer to the bed with trembling hands. Still, he stood, taking one of her small hands in his, gently caressing the bruised flesh. "I'm here, honey. Tish, you're not alone. You've got to fight. We—we've got a lot of living to do yet. Don't give up. I'm here."

Slowly, he lowered himself to the chair. Exhausted, physically and emotionally, he bent his head to lay it on the side of her bed. He hadn't been a praying man, though he'd become one during his ordeal of being buried alive. This was just as desperate a plea, if not more so.

Please, God, let her live, he silently prayed. *Please.*

Jeff awoke with a start, shocked to find he'd fallen asleep in that cramped position. His eyes flew to Tish but he saw that she hadn't moved a muscle. He got up and stretched to get the kinks out as Thelma came in to take her patient's temperature and pulse.

Glancing at him as he rolled his head around, Thelma apparently felt a measure of sympathy. "If you'd like to get something to eat, you can, you know. I'm right here and I'm not going anywhere." When he looked at her, she gave him a small smile.

The attractive thirty-something nurse was a natural blond, wore only a touch of pale-pink lipstick and her blue eyes were kind.

He scrubbed a hand over his unshaven face. "I must look like something the cat dragged in, up all night on the red-eye," he explained.

After marking down Tish's temperature, Thelma looked

up. Her eyes seemed appreciative rather than critical of the way he looked, but she probably thought he could use a shower. "Since you're a colleague, Dr. O'Neill told me to tell you that if you wanted to clean up in the doctor's lounge, it's located on the third floor. He also said you could see your wife's chart." She handed it to him.

"Thanks." After she left, Jeff sat down and perused Tish's chart, but he didn't learn anything he didn't already know.

Leaning close to her bed, he stroked the backs of his fingers along Tish's cheek. "You're going to make it, babe. I just know you are. You have to. I can't live without you."

He sat like that for a few hours, touching her gently, stroking her tenderly, talking softly to her. Finally, knowing he'd feel a lot better if he took a shower and put some food in his stomach, and realizing he had to take care of himself for Tish's sake, he left the ICU and told Thelma he'd be back in about an hour.

He was back in short order having shaved and grabbed a quick shower in the doctor's lounge. Edmund O'Neill had been there having a cup of coffee before his next surgery. He'd shown Jeff where to stash his bag until later in an empty locker at the far end. He'd chatted briefly with Jeff about the hospital in California where he was a resident and about his medevac specialty. The casual acceptance had improved Jeff's outlook.

Dressed in clean clothes, a blue shirt and khaki slacks, he felt a lot better. He'd taken the time to go down to the cafeteria where he'd gulped down two glasses of orange juice, a bagel and coffee before returning to the ICU.

Tish hadn't moved, nor had anything changed.

Sitting down alongside her bed, Jeff chided himself. What had he expected, that he'd return to find her sitting up in bed, laughing and joking with the nurses? She was alive. He had to focus on that. And the fact that she was strong and healthy. She would make it. She had to.

He took her hand in his, turning it over, seeing the strength there in her slender fingers, yet the vulnerability of the small bones. Since meeting Tish Buckner, he'd imagined a lot of scenarios, but this hadn't been one of them, with her in a coma and him by her bedside, waiting, hoping, praying.

Jeff yawned, realizing he was tired yet not really sleepy. He gazed at her features, her lovely face now marred by a cut on her forehead and a bruise on her chin. How he loved to just look at her. During some of their nights together, he'd sometimes awakened and just lay there looking at her in the dim night light as she slept. He fervently wished they were back there in those wonderful days when they'd been together and she'd been well, happy, laughing.

Swallowing hard and blinking back tears, Jeff knew his emotions were very close to the surface due to his concern for Tish and his lack of rest. Yet he didn't want to rest, wanted instead to be right here, alert and available, when she woke up.

His medical training had included the study of head traumas, of the coma condition, and the best advice for relatives had been to stay by the patient, talk to them, touch them, let them know you're there and waiting for their return. People who'd awakened from comas had mentioned hearing voices, some even remembering actual conversations that had gone on around them while they'd been under.

So, because he thought it might hasten her recovery, and because he wanted Tish to know he was there, he began talking to her as he sat holding her hand. Talking softly, lovingly.

"I guess I never told you much about my early years. I always found reasons to change the subject because, well, it wasn't pleasant, remembering. But also because I'd been so used to not opening up about my past. I'm sorry I shut you out, babe. I didn't mean to. Looks like we have plenty of time now.''

After confiding about his painful childhood for several minutes, Jeff got up, feeling restless. He walked over and straightened covers that didn't need attention, pausing to stroke her face again. "Oh, God, Tish, I wish you'd open those big, beautiful eyes and look at me, just once, babe. You can go back to sleep then, but I wish I had a sign that you were trying hard to come back to us.''

But she just lay there, not moving.

Leaning back, Jeff sighed, wondering if the rain had stopped. There were no windows in ICU. After dozing for a while, he gazed out the glass sliding doors and saw that it was shift change time for the nurses. Had he been here that long? He stretched again and his aching muscles reminded him that he had been sitting for a long time.

The door slid open and the new nurse came in, introducing herself as Doris. She was older with gray hair and glasses, but she was quietly efficient, checking Tish's vital signs, marking on her chart.

"I understand Dr. O'Neill's orders are that you're permitted to remain with our patient here as long as you like, Dr. Kirby,'' she said. "However, if you want to check into a hotel and get some rest or leave for a meal, please know that I'm here and I'll be monitoring your wife every moment.''

He smiled at her. "Thank you. I think I will leave to make a couple of calls and to grab a sandwich, but then I'll be back. I'm not checking into a hotel, though. I'm staying with her until she comes out of the coma.''

He saw the carefully veiled expression on the nurse's face that told him she was used to family members having hope. "That's fine. We can't bring a cot into this small space, though, and you look like you could use some rest.''

"I'll be fine. I can sleep anywhere. That chair's quite comfortable." Hadn't he spent years on the run, sleeping on the hard ground, on wooden benches? There'd be plenty of time for a soft bed after he knew Tish was out of danger.

"Well, all right, then. If you need anything, I'll be at the desk." As silently as she'd entered, she left.

Jeff walked over to his wife and gazed at her for a long while, holding her hand in his. "I'm going out to call East, which I should have done earlier, and to grab a bite to eat. Then I'll be back, sweetheart. And I'll give you chapter two of the fascinating saga that is my life so far." He leaned down to kiss her pale cheek.

As he straightened, he felt her hand move, the fingers grab his. "Tish!" he called out. "You moved! You're coming back to us. Thank God. Oh, honey, it's Jeff. Come back to me, please."

Reaching for the call button, Jeff pushed it hard, then turned back to her. "Tish, do it again, sweetheart. Squeeze my hand."

There was mist, at first filmy, then heavier. She struggled through it, trying to see, to look around. Why couldn't she see? Her eyes fluttered, but it was no use. Her lids were too heavy.

Tish heard a voice as if from a distance, calling to her. A man's voice. She strained to make out the words, to recognize the voice. There was gentleness in the sound and she seemed to recall the same man talking to her in a soothing way.

Then suddenly he said something very close to her ear, his words begging her to return to him. Where was she that she had to return? Where had she gone and why was he just out of reach?

The mist swirled with an ebb and flow of its own, confusing her. She tried desperately to move, to reach out, but she could only grasp someone's hand. She wanted to ask questions, but she couldn't move her lips. Why couldn't she speak? Why couldn't she remember where she was and how she'd gotten here?

Now it became quieter and she could hear his voice more clearly. It was Jeff! Oh, how badly she wanted Jeff to be with her but, try as she would, she couldn't communicate. Tish felt tears forming, tears of frustration. Jeff was talking to her again, telling her to hold on, that he'd called for help. Who was coming to help her? She was locked in this terrible nightmare, unable to reach Jeff. He sounded so worried. I'm here, darling, she wanted to yell out, but no sound came from her parched throat.

She could feel him next to her, squeezing her fingers, kissing her hair. Her Jeff, her husband, the man she'd almost lost and found again in Australia. It was his voice she'd been hearing speaking softly to her hour after hour. It didn't matter that she couldn't always make out what he was saying. The fact that he was here with her was the only thing that mattered. She wanted to tell him how very much she loved him, had always loved him, even when her own pain had kept her from telling him so. She wanted to feel his arms around her because when he held her, she knew nothing could harm her.

But something had harmed her or she wouldn't be here like this, unable to reach out to the only man she'd ever loved. Something terrible must have happened. If only she could remember. But the mists were closing in again and Jeff's voice was getting fainter. No! Tish wanted to cry out, to bring him back. Don't go away, please.

And then there was only darkness again.

Doris came hurrying in, a frown on her face. "What is it, Dr. Kirby?"

"She moved. Just now, she squeezed my hand." He gave the nurse a quick smile. "She's coming out of it."

Doris moved to the bed as Jeff stepped back, checked the machines, paying particular attention to the blood pressure monitor. She checked Tish's eyes, then took her stethoscope from around her neck and bent to listen to her patient's chest for several long minutes. Finally, she turned to him.

"It was just a muscle spasm, Dr. Kirby. They happen occasionally and—"

"No, damn it! I tell you she squeezed my hand when I bent down and kissed her cheek. I felt it." Feeling frustrated, he rubbed Tish's hand and gently squeezed her fingers. "Do it again, sweetheart. Show her."

But there was no response.

"I understand how you feel and I believe her hand did move. But it was involuntary. She didn't *make* her fingers move, they just did." Her eyes sympathetic, she touched his arm. "I'm sorry."

Jeff let out a huge sigh. "Yeah, me, too." He turned and left Tish's room and the ICU area. He needed some air, some food. Some hope.

Down the hallway, he found a bank of phones and dug out his credit card. Quickly he dialed in the numbers and a minute later, East's deep voice answered.

"Dad?" Jeff swallowed around a clogged throat. "I'm here in the hospital. I'm sorry I didn't call sooner."

"That's all right," East answered, reading between the lines, hearing the fatigue and despair in his son's voice. "How is she?"

"Holding her own is all they say, whatever that means. A minute ago, I was holding her hand and she—she squeezed my fingers. Dad, it was so real. I know it happened and yet, the nurse says it was involuntary, a muscle spasm."

East heard the hopelessness and knew he had to encourage his son not to give up. "You've probably studied that particular phenomenon already, but you want to believe she squeezed your hand on purpose. I don't blame you, but false hope is hard to live with. Real hope isn't." East cleared his throat. "You know, when you were kidnapped and I didn't know where you were or who had you at first or where they'd taken you, I felt like I imagine you're feeling now. Defeated. Despondent. Filled with despair.

"One night, in Alicia's arms, I broke down. And you know what she told me? That if I gave up hope, my son would be as good as dead. Hope was all we had to go on, forcing us to keep searching, to look for more clues, to pray and to believe that eventually we would find you. And we did. You have to believe, son. Tish will come back to us, but you have to believe it. Because although she can't speak or open her eyes, when you're there and talking to her, she knows. She hears and she can tell if you've given up on her or if you believe she's fighting to return. Don't ask me how, but I believe she knows. You have to be strong, for her, for yourself."

Again, Jeff swallowed as a rush of emotion had the backs of his eyes stinging with tears wanting to fall. He blinked them back and nodded. "Yeah, you're right. Thanks, Dad. I—I needed to hear your voice. It always helps."

"Do you want me to go there, Jeff? I can catch the next plane...."

"No, but thanks for the offer. You belong there with Alicia. How's the baby doing?"

"They're both doing well. Alicia sends her love."

Feeling too choked up to talk any more, Jeff nodded. "Thanks. I'll call again later." He hung up, bowing his head and swiping at his eyes with his hand. The hand that had felt Tish move.

She would recover, he repeated silently. She would be

back with him, loving him, wanting to make their marriage work. She would be well and strong. He would see to it if he had to sit beside her for the next entire week. People awoke from comas all the time, hardly the worse for having been away. This was her body's way of healing itself. The fact that it took a terrible toll on the people who loved her didn't matter. If they believed, they'd be able to handle it.

Because, Jeff thought, stepping away from the phone and drying his eyes, as he'd once told Tish, she was worth the wait.

Chapter 6

Later, Jeff ran into Dr. O'Neill, who was rushing through the double doors of the ICU, his white coattails flying. "Doctor," Jeff said, stopping, "is there any change in Tish's condition?"

"No, I'm afraid not, Doctor." He rubbed a spot just above his right eye. "As I'm sure you're aware, these things take time. The nurse told me she had a neurological reaction. A muscle spasm. Strictly involuntary, of course. There is eye movement there, a good sign. Are you talking to her?"

"Yes. I was hoping she might respond to my voice or my words but, so far, nothing."

A couple of nurses turned into the ICU corridor, causing the two doctors to step to the side. "Keep talking to her. Medical studies show that coma victims do hear, do listen. That's why, in discussing her condition or prognosis, I always step out of the room. I don't want what I say to nurses or a relative to influence the patient's recovery."

"Right. Thanks, Doctor." He hadn't learned much, but at least there'd been no bad news.

Dr. O'Neill patted Jeff's shoulder. "Hang in there. I'll see you later." And off he went.

Jeff walked through the doors into the overly warm, muted atmosphere of the ICU. He nodded to Doris who was carrying a stack of clean sheets toward a cubicle.

"I've just changed her sheets and given her a back rub," she told him, pausing. "We don't want her to get bed sores."

"If there's any of that I can do for you, I'd be glad to help out," he offered.

"I'll remember that," she said, giving him a smile before going on her way.

Jeff let himself into Tish's cubicle and it seemed as if he'd never left. She looked the same, although he thought perhaps her hair had been combed and rearranged. Walking up to the bed, he smiled down at his wife, trying desperately to let his love and concern come through in his voice as he touched her lovely hair.

"Remember how you used to love to have me brush your hair, Tish? You'd sit on the bed after your shower and I'd brush and brush for fifteen, twenty minutes, until your hair was totally dry. And you'd purr like a kitten." He chuckled so she could hear. "Remember that scrawny cat that used to come around our apartment looking for food? You never could turn away from an animal in need. You started feeding him and next thing I knew, he'd moved in with us. This so-called *free* cat had to be checked out by a vet, get shots, be neutered." He laughed again. "But you loved him and I loved you for it."

Gently, he brushed her hair back off her forehead, then let the backs of his fingers trail down her soft cheek. "They tell me that cut won't leave a scar, so don't worry about it. The incision on your collarbone will, but we can think of it as a badge of honor. You survived, babe, and that's the main thing.''

Sighing tiredly, he eased his weary body into the chair, wishing he could go for a run which would undoubtedly help his cramped muscles. But he was too tired. Trouble was, he couldn't turn off his mind.

Leaning forward, he decided to talk some more to Tish. Something might penetrate her coma and besides, it kept him from thinking too hard, from worrying too much.

Jeff caressed Tish's hand with his thumb, leaning close to the bed, speaking softly. ''I don't know if you know about East's past—or how I came into his life. At one time, he'd been one of SPEAR's top field men. Then one night, on a high-speed chase through the narrow, twisting roads of Beverly Hills Canyon, he accidentally killed a kid on a bicycle who darted in front of his car. He was cleared of any wrongdoing, but East couldn't accept that and blamed himself. He'd always held himself to standards even higher than the agency demanded, and by his own standards, he was guilty and needed to be punished. Sometimes, we're our own worst enemy, you know.''

Pulling in a deep breath, Jeff went on. ''East didn't trust himself in the field anymore, haunted by the boy's death, so he voluntarily withdrew. They didn't want him to leave, but he was adamant. He spent three months at Condor Mountain, alone, unapproachable, shunning all company and conversation by day, hiking the mountains at night. On one of those nights, he ran across me.

''I was penniless, cold, hungry and just about as low as a guy can get, someone with no foreseeable future. A fourteen-year-old runaway with no family. And East took me by the hand and led me up the mountain to the Monarch Hotel. He cleaned me up, fed me, put me to bed on clean sheets and let me sleep twenty hours. Then he talked with me.''

Jeff gazed at Tish's face as he wound down. "He told me I could be anything I wanted to be if I studied and worked hard enough. He said he'd help me every way he could. Or, he added, I could go back to living on the streets. Naturally suspicious, I asked him why he was doing this for me, this kid he didn't even know. That's when he told me about the boy on the bicycle. Maybe if I help you, he told me, I'll be able to sleep better. I was like his penance, you know. He had only one rule, that I never lie to him. And I never have."

Leaning back, Jeff rubbed the back of his neck. "So East took over the running of Condor Mountain Resort as a civilian employee and he enrolled me in school. I'd missed a lot and it took me a while to catch up, but it seems I love to learn so I did well. Eventually, East put me through college and we had long talks about what I wanted to do with my life. After a while, I knew I wanted to be a doctor, so he said he'd take care of med school and all my training. And he introduced me to SPEAR. Slowly, I began to realize that I wanted to be a part of the team.

"But the greatest thing East did was to give me unconditional love. I wonder how many kids really have that even from their real parents. He taught me by example, the finest way to learn because it always stays with you. He was tough when I needed discipline and there for me when I went through some difficult times. He changed me from a scared but mouthy kid with a chip on my shoulder a mile wide to someone I could be proud of. Basically, he taught me the value of truth and honor, of love and forgiveness. He taught me to be a man and I'll love him forever for that alone. When he finally adopted me, it was the happiest day of my life up to that point. He's a wonderful, kind, caring man. If I turn out half as good, I'll be happy. The thing is, East gives me credit for healing him, for allowing him to forgive himself for his part in the accident where the boy died. But actually, he healed me.'' He smiled at her. ''A mutual admiration society, eh?''

Jeff glanced at his watch, saw that it was nearly nine in the evening. ''Honey, I'm going to stretch out on this chair and grab some shut-eye before I keel over here. You keep on resting, keep on fighting because I love you, unconditionally and every other way, and I want you back with me.''

Repositioning the chair near her bed but far enough away so that the nurse could come in and do her thing, Jeff also found a small stool and set it in place. With a huge yawn, he sat down and stretched out his long legs, propping his feet on the stool, and laying his head on the extra pillow he'd taken from the closet. Though he'd thought to rest his body only since his worried mind would make sleep impossible, he was unconscious within minutes.

Shifting his cramped body in his sleep, Jeff's feet slipped off the stool and he awakened with a jolt. Disoriented for a moment, he gazed around the dim room, then remembered that he was in Tish's ICU cubicle. The machine lights were still winking and blinking and Tish still hadn't moved.

Rising, he stretched his sore muscles and looked through the glass doors. One nurse was on the phone and two others were in the far cubicle across the way. He'd learned that each nurse was assigned two ICU patients, but that they helped one another out in an emergency. This seemed to be one of those critical times, Jeff decided as a man in street clothes with a stethoscope hanging around his neck, presumably a doctor, rushed in through the double doors and hurried over to the far cubicle.

Checking his watch, Jeff saw that it was a little after five in the morning. Apparently the patient in question was having some sort of difficulty and his doctor had been summoned. Curious, he slid open Tish's glass door to see if he could figure out what was going on.

A man in green scrubs that Jeff hadn't noticed before was working on the male patient, administering oxygen from what Jeff could see. Wandering to the circular desk, he glanced over and saw that Thelma was back on duty and Doris was gone.

"What's happening?" he asked quietly. Everyone in ICU spoke in soft tones so he'd fallen in line.

"The patient in cubicle 1 is in distress." Aware that Jeff was a doctor, apparently Thelma felt free to speak more openly than she would to a lay person. "He has all sorts of things wrong with him. Prostate cancer too far gone for surgery, emphysema and the pneumonia that put him in here. Such a shame. He's only fifty-two."

"That's a lot to fight off," Jeff commented.

As he stood watching, he saw the doctor step back from the patient, remove the stethoscope he'd been using and glance up at the clock. Bad news, Jeff thought. Usually that meant the doctor was pronouncing a patient dead, noting the time.

Which was exactly what had happened as the stern-faced doctor came out, followed by the man in scrubs, probably the physician on call. In whispered conference, they stood at the far side of the circular desk.

As Jeff turned to go back to Tish, he heard the double doors hiss open and two distraught women came rushing through. The taller one spotted the doctor and rushed over to him.

"My father, how is he, Dr. Burns?" she asked. "I got this call and—"

Taking her arm, Dr. Burns talked to her in low tones as he led her to her father's cubicle while the other woman followed. The taller woman bowed her head, apparently weeping softly, but the smaller one let out a wail that could have been heard outside ICU.

Jeff closed the sliding doors and moved to Tish's bed to allow the family some privacy. She hadn't moved despite the woman's shriek. He sat down, feeling depressed.

It took a special kind of person to work in ICU. Only the seriously ill were brought there. Although he'd been in medicine for quite a while now, a patient dying always got to him. No matter how advanced medical science was, at times nothing more could be done.

His green eyes settled on Tish lying there. If he mentally removed all the medical equipment, she might look as if she were asleep. And she was, but unnaturally so.

He leaned forward, trying to will her awake. "It's time, honey. Time to wake up, to talk to me. I'm so lonely here without you, Tish. I need you to be here with me.

"I'll bet you're trying to come back. I'll bet you're scared and feeling all alone, too. You're not alone, you know. I'm here and East sends his love and so does Ally. They had their baby, a little girl. Named her Annie. Mother and baby doing fine. Maybe one day, you and I will have—" No, he thought, halting his flow of words. Best not to go there. Best not to talk about anything that might agitate her.

"I know how you feel, you know. Exactly how you feel. You wonder where everyone is, how come you're all alone, why someone isn't rescuing you. Is that about it, honey? Yeah, I'll bet that's how it is with you because that's how I felt when those SOBs buried me alive."

Dropping back in the chair, Jeff pressed his fingers to his closed eyes. He didn't want to think about that horrific time several months ago, back to that hellhole those monsters had left him in to die.

Shaking off his dark train of thought, Jeff leaned down and placed a soft kiss on her hand. "Oh, honey, I wish I wasn't talking alone here. I wish you could answer. I just want you back with me. Maybe soon, eh?''

He lay his head on the edge of the bed and stayed like that for a long while.

Chapter 7

Thelma quietly stepped into her ICU patient's cubicle to check Tish Buckner's vital signs. She smiled when she saw that Dr. Kirby was resting with his head on the edge of his wife's bed, his hand curled around hers. Except for a couple of quick meals, he hadn't left her side, sitting there night and day, since he'd first arrived. Such devotion was wonderful to see in this day and age, Thelma thought as she walked around to the other side of the sickbed to check the blood pressure cuff.

When she'd finished charting her readings, Thelma paused a moment to study the young man sleeping so soundly. Even though he needed a shave, he was certainly handsome, tall and well muscled. They were married yet had different last names, she'd noticed. A modern marriage, she supposed. Still, only a devoted husband would hang around a comatose spouse around the clock.

As she continued staring at him, he smiled in his sleep. Probably dreaming of happier times, Thelma decided, and left the cubicle as soundlessly as she'd entered.

Jeff *was* back in happier times, but he wasn't dreaming. He was remembering their time together at the Red Rock Ranch in Arizon…

They'd ridden their mounts to their favorite spot, a large overhanging cottonwood tree alongside the cool mountain stream. It was late afternoon and Jeff and Tish were several miles from the Red Rock Ranch, off the beaten track, safe from prying eyes since no one used the somewhat overgrown trail leading to this little corner of paradise, as Jeff had begun to call it. Here they could be alone, could talk to one another without being overheard, could touch and look their fill of one another. Could even make love, the area was that private.

They'd taken to riding out nearly every evening, knowing that soon this idyllic time would be over and they'd both go their separate ways. On this day, Jeff had been busy for hours helping Slim with his accounting books and he hadn't seen Tish until they'd set out. Which was the reason he didn't know why she seemed so lost in thought, almost melancholy.

He waited until they'd spread out the large plaid blanket and set down the picnic basket Elsa by now was used to packing for them. Lying down on his side, Jeff patted the space next to him. "Come here, please. I want so badly to hold you."

Tish had wandered over to the stream's edge, but walked back and sat down, a frown on her face, her eyes on her hands twisting a tissue.

"What is it? Is something wrong?" Jeff asked, getting worried.

"I was talking to Reggie earlier today," she began.

The big, boastful jerk was always hanging around her, Jeff knew, even though everyone else was aware that he and Tish were a couple now. "And what did our learned friend have to say?" When she didn't answer and seemed to be searching for the right words, he sat up. "Did he say something to upset you?"

"In a way." She glanced off to the horizon, then finally swung her gaze to his face. "You see, Jeff, I'm—I'm—"

Now he was getting nervous. "What? Just tell me."

"I'm thirty-six years old," she finally blurted out, her brow wrinkled. "And Reggie told me you're only twenty-four!"

Jeff just stared at her. "Is that it?" He watched her slowly nod. "That's what's got you so upset?" He couldn't help it. He laughed out loud, relief flooding through him as he pulled her into his arms. "You had me really worried there for a minute."

Tish eased back from him. "You should be worried. I can't get involved with you, Jeff. Don't you see? I'm twelve years older than you."

He was still smiling, still euphoric that her news was so minor. "So what? I don't see the problem."

Her face was unsmiling, her brow creased with concern. "You don't understand. People will say that I'm robbing the cradle. I've got an established position in SPEAR and you're just starting out."

"Oh, come on. I'm not *that* young. I've finished college and medical school, my internship, am now working on my residency. Besides, what do you care what people think? My dad's thirty-five, and married to a woman exactly my age, and things couldn't be more perfect between them."

Her eyes were downcast. "Yes, if the man's older it sometimes works. But when the woman's older…"

"It also works." Jeff placed two fingers beneath her chin and tugged, making it impossible for her not to meet his serious gaze. "Listen, I've been looking for you all my life, Tish Buckner, and I'm not letting you go."

Her eyes on his darkened and she was quiet for some time, as if struggling with a difficult decision. "Don't, then.

Don't let me go, not ever. I know it's not the best thing, for either of us, to want you the way I do. The timing's lousy. But I can't help myself when it comes to you, and that's never happened to me before. I'm usually in control of myself, but with you, I lose control the moment you touch me.''

Jeff rose to his knees and brought her with him and they knelt that way, mere centimeters apart as he framed her lovely face with his big hands. "Go ahead, lose control." Slowly, ever so slowly, he bent his head and grazed her lips with his, back and forth. Gently, he kissed her and she returned the slight pressure.

He felt her small hands curl into the material of his shirt at his back as she drew him nearer, then gloried in the feeling of just holding her close. "You feel so good," he whispered.

"Mmm, so do you. How is it that no one else can make me feel so much?"

"No one else better try." His tongue traced the outline of her lips, then he kissed the corners of her mouth before trailing up her satin cheeks to kiss her eyes closed. She was swaying now and he kept them both steady as he returned to her waiting mouth and kissed her long and deeply. Jeff felt the passion she seemed to struggle to hide flare up instantly between them.

He urged her closer, swallowing the small sound she made deep in her throat as his arms wound around her. The sun was sinking slowly behind the mountain, but he paid no attention. The stream alongside them ran swiftly over smooth rocks as it journeyed downhill, but Jeff didn't hear the lapping water. His concentration was fully on Tish as he continued to assault her senses, nibbling at her lips, his hands beginning to explore, his tongue beginning to invade her mouth.

Emotions warred within him, the unreasonable fear that

he would lose her before he'd won her, pleasure and impatience and need. His need for her. Only her.

He knew she was steeped in sensation as her mouth answered his, as her eyes closed to hold in the feeling, as the soft sounds she made urged him on. Jeff's fingers fumbled with the buttons of her blouse, finally shoving the folds of the cotton cloth apart so his hands could cup her swollen breasts.

Never breaking the kiss, he felt her hands unbuttoning his shirt and pushing it off his shoulders. When they were both naked to the waist, he pulled her to him, the soft pillows of her breasts rubbing against his solid chest. The erotic friction had his pulse pounding and his blood rushing like the racing stream nearby.

Easing back from her, he waited until her eyes opened and he saw the hazy mists clear, then he thrust his hands into her hair, massaging her scalp with his blunt fingers. He heard her soft moan as she swayed in his arms and moved restlessly under his touch. He looked deeply into her eyes. "Tell me what you want me to do."

She hesitated only a moment. "This," she said huskily as she pressed her mouth to his for a long, soul-shattering kiss. "And this." She threaded her fingers along his broad chest, her fingers buried in the soft hair there, causing Jeff's heart to stumble, then race.

"You're wearing too many clothes," Jeff whispered.

"Why don't you do something about that?" she challenged.

With a slow smile, Jeff lay her down on the blanket and made quick work of yanking off her boots, then her jeans and underthings. As always, he paused, struck anew at the beauty of her female form. The setting sun sent rays of gold and crimson and streaks of orange onto them, dappled by the leaves of the cottonwood as they fluttered in a light breeze.

Tish seemed to hold her breath, no longer self-conscious under his lengthy study of her, her eyes challenging him to take her to the next plateau. But apparently she ran out of patience for she tugged him down and burrowed her breasts into him. A groan Jeff couldn't prevent escaped from him as he nuzzled her neck. "Oh, yes, and this, too," she whispered.

Finally, Jeff lifted his head to trail hot kisses along her throat and lower, closing his lips over the peak of one breast. He could feel her heart thundering beneath his mouth. Leaning back, he covered both breasts with his hands, finding her small and firm, her skin soft as satin. He inhaled the sweet feminine fragrance of her and the urge to rush all but overwhelmed him. Consciously, he slowed his hands, his mouth.

He wanted to take her up slowly, to make her half mad with need, crying out for him, opening to him. She deserved slow loving and an easy touch. Gently he came back to her lips and feasted there, drinking from her.

When her hips arched in unconscious invitation, he took his mouth along her throat and traveled slowly downward, tasting the heady flavor of her breasts and brushing his face along the tender skin of her flat stomach. He caught her throaty moan as she closed her eyes on a sensual sigh.

Her hair was spread on the plaid blanket in a wild tangle exactly as he imagined it in his restive dreams. Her eyes were misty with passion and her full mouth was swollen from his kisses. As he looked at her, she moved fitfully and reached a trembling hand to the waistband of his jeans. When he didn't help her out, she tugged open the top snap and slipped her hand inside, her fingers closing around him.

Jeff jolted at her touch, afraid it would all be over if he didn't take control. Easing back, he shed the rest of his clothes and came back to run his hands along her strong, slender thighs. Gently caressing up and down, he kept his eyes on hers, aware that she'd wanted to take control. But not this time. Quickly, before she could react, he replaced his hands with his mouth.

Stunned as the first waves ripped through her, a look of dazed pleasure registered on her face. Breathless, her hands clutched at his arms as she shook with the power of it. Before she was fully recovered, he drove her up again, watching her climb, watching a sensual flush infuse her face.

This was what he'd been after, Jeff knew, to give her this mindless loss of self where no disturbing thoughts could intrude, where past problems were only wisps of smoke and where age differences mattered not at all. There was only here and now, this peaceful afternoon, this blanket that held two magic lovers. His thoughts centered totally on pleasing and being pleased, on letting go of the world for at least a little while.

And in so doing, finding each other, finding love.

Coming back to earth, Tish looked up at him and saw a smile play around his clever mouth. "Pleased with yourself, are you?"

"I am. Do you want to stop or do you want more?"

"I want more." She opened her arms. "Come here."

More than ready, Jeff poised himself above her. "Don't close your eyes." He wanted her to watch as he joined with her. And when he finally did, she arched to meet him, her body straining to get closer, closer. He found the rhythm and saw she was perfectly attuned to him, keeping up, moving with him.

He drove himself into her with a fierceness he'd never experienced before. He watched her eyes try to stay focused on his, until they finally drifted shut as a stunning peak shoved her over the edge. Unable to hold back another moment, he let himself follow.

* * *

Jeff awoke from a dream, a good dream, and reluctantly opened his eyes. After his sweet recollection of their lovemaking at the Red Rock, he'd finally drifted to sleep. He was in Tish's hospital cubicle, his head on the edge of her bed, his neck hurting from the awkward position. Leaning back, he rose to rub the back of his neck and saw that Tish hadn't moved. He let out a frustrated sigh.

He picked up the small bottled water he'd brought in and drank deeply. His watch told him he hadn't been asleep all that long, yet his body felt as if he'd been in that contorted position awhile. Wishful thinking, hoping the hours would rush by so now it would be time for her to wake up. So he could talk with her. So they could get on with their lives.

Feeling out of sorts, angry at the circumstances and the traitor whose selfish, diabolic agenda had caused the woman Jeff loved to be so badly injured, he strolled back to her bedside and tried not to let his feelings transmit themselves to her. He stood staring down at her frail body, her lovely features. "If wishes were horses, honey," he whispered, "you and I would be riding off into the sunset right now." Wearily, he left her cubicle.

Thelma was at the circular desk working on charts. "I'm going out for a while, Thelma. I've got to make a few calls, get something to eat. Let me give you my cell phone number in case she awakens, okay?"

"Certainly, Doctor." Efficient as always, she wrote it down, then gave him a small smile. "It'll do you good to get some air."

Nodding, Jeff left, anxious to leave the hospital atmosphere with its unrelenting routine and muted PA announcements and antiseptic smells. It was different when it was his work atmosphere. So very different.

Striding down the hallway, he reached the bank of phones and called East, updating him. "I wish I could tell you some good news, but unfortunately there's been no change.'' Glancing out the window, he saw that the sun was lowering in the sky. Another day nearly gone and no improvement. To say that he wasn't discouraged would be a lie, and he knew his voice conveyed his feelings all too well.

"I'm sorry, Jeff. Does the doctor tell you anything?"

"I wish. He says to hang in there." Jeff ran a hand through his hair. "You know, I've heard of people remaining in comas for weeks, months, even years. Dad, that can't happen. Not to Tish."

"It won't, son. She'll be back with us as soon as the brain swelling goes down." East had kept in touch with the doctors as well. "It's difficult, I know, but keep the faith."

"Right." He needed a change of subject, something more cheerful, more hopeful. "Are Ally and Annie home yet?"

"Yes, and they're both well and happy. The baby's got red hair, Jeff." There was a smile in East's voice. "When Tish wakes up, why don't the two of you plan to come here to Condor for a while. Rest up."

"It's a thought, and thanks." Although he didn't know how Tish would react to being around a baby just now. "I'll have to play this by ear, Dad. When we parted in Australia, we hadn't really reconciled fully, just agreed to talk again after her New York assignment."

"Maybe being in this terrible accident has given Tish another perspective, Jeff. Life-altering things usually do, remember?"

"Yes, I remember, every day. We'll see if she feels the same."

"I might see you soon. They've asked me to go to New York as part of the bombing investigation. I'm not sure how much help I can be, but especially since you're there, I'd like to go."

A familiar face, someone to talk with, someone who cared to be with him. Jeff closed his eyes, hoping he didn't sound as pathetically grateful as he felt. "I'd like that," he said gruffly.

East picked up on it, as usual. "Okay, then. I'll be in touch. Call if there's a change."

"You bet." Jeff hung up and wandered to the windows. Springtime in New York. The trees were in bud, the weather balmy, the rain over. If he couldn't run, maybe a walk would do him good, some fresh air.

He headed for the elevators.

It was twilight when Jeff returned to the hospital and he felt all pumped up. He'd taken a long walk which felt good, using muscles too long confined to a chair. He'd run across a small Italian restaurant and he'd stopped in, thinking the menu had to offer choices far better than hospital food.

It had. He'd finally found his appetite again. Maybe the exercise of his walk had helped. Feeling more than human when he'd left, his spirits lifted and he rushed back to the hospital. Breezing past Doris who was at the desk since the shift change, he hurried into Tish's cubicle, his heart full of hope.

And she hadn't changed an iota, hadn't moved a muscle.

Deflated, he sagged into the chair and just stared at her for a long time. This kind of waiting would try the patience of any man, Jeff decided. He could handle deadlines, if only he knew something would be over on a certain date at a particular time. It was the not knowing that ground away at a person. The fear that even if she awoke, would she not be her old self? Would the bomb fragments or the surgery have injured her so extensively internally that she might come to, but be a shadow of her former self?

It didn't bear consideration. Drawing in a deep breath, Jeff sat up taller and brought his thoughts under control.

Upbeat, he told himself. He had to be upbeat, to talk to her about things that would warm her heart, make her *want* to return, urge her to fight to be with him again.

So he scooted the chair closer to the bed and picked up her small hand, turning it over in his, studying the smooth skin that he'd kissed so many times before. Hands that had touched his body everywhere and touched his heart. He bent to press his lips to her fragile fingers, then cleared his throat as he pushed back his negative thoughts and fears.

"Hi, sweetheart," he began. "I was gone for a little while. Talked with East. Ally's home from the hospital with Annie, their little girl. All of them send their love and prayers to you. They want us to visit them after you get of here. And you *will* get out of here, babe. Soon.

"I walked for a while. It's in the seventies out there, spring in New York. I saw a policeman on horseback and several others getting ready for the big Easter parade along Fifth coming up soon. Remember the night we watched that Fred Astaire movie in our apartment and sang along with Judy Garland? Neither of us can carry a tune, but we had fun anyhow." He squeezed her hand lightly. "I want so badly to do everyday normal things like that again with you, Tish. Movies, walks, sleeping curled up in each other's arms." He sighed, trying not to sink into a depressing tone.

"I'm stuffed to the gills. I stopped on my walk at this little hole-in-the-wall Italian restaurant. The waiter's name was Tony—what else? He had the requisite black mustache, curly hair and big white apron. There were these murals on the wall, scenes of Venice with the gondolas. Not very good drawings, but they added to the atmosphere. And, naturally, there was the Italian recordings in the background, thankfully not too long. Mario Lanza, I think. You'd know. I remember how you always recognize who's singing on the radio and I rarely do. You have a much better ear for voices than I do.

"Anyhow, I had spaghetti bolognese and the sauce was scrumptious. I asked for mushrooms because you know how I love mushrooms, and Tony brought me half a pound, I think. The bread was to die for, crusty on the outside, soft inside. And, I confess, I had some red wine, Chianti. Not wonderful, but it couldn't have been too bad 'cause I had two glasses. God, Tish, I wish you'd have been with me. You know how I hate to eat alone. You always scolded me because I missed meals when I was on duty at the hospital, but mostly it was because I'd rather go hungry than eat alone.

"But I had to tonight because I haven't been eating much and I want to stay strong so that when you wake up, I can pick you up and take you out of here. I always loved picking you up and holding you. You fit in my arms perfectly, like no other. Because there'll never be another woman for me, Tish. You're stuck with me forever."

Jeff searched his mind, trying to come up with light-hearted things to talk about. "I know you'll come out of this, babe, because you're tough. At first glance, people think you're small and fragile, but inside, you've got a core of iron. One tough cookie. Remember that time on the ranch when that cowhand Mac and I were about to go at it and you rescued me?" Jeff laughed. "The big bully caved in to you like I'm sure he's never done with anyone else." I remember that day so well....

On a bright, sunshiny morning at the Red Rock Ranch, Jeff sat down to breakfast alongside Slim in the main dining room. He was in a good mood. Excellent, matter of fact. Things were great between him and Tish, he felt rested and had gained some of his weight back and felt he was truly over his ordeal of being buried alive.

"Good morning," he said with a smile. Glancing around, he saw that only a few other people were still lingering over that second cup of coffee. He'd slept in this morning and it had evidently improved his mood. "Looks like another great day out there."

"Yeah, guess so," Slim said, leaning back in his chair and studying Jeff.

Jeff buttered his toast, then felt the manager's eyes on him so he looked up. "Something the matter?"

"You know, I don't usually pay attention to rumors, but this one maybe we both should think about. Word is that Mac's still real mad at you for humiliating him like that at the branding last week. They say he's gunnin' for you."

Jeff busied himself cutting a piece of sausage. "That so? What do you mean, gunnin' for me?"

"Like maybe he wants to teach you a lesson." Slim wasn't smiling, was in fact wearing a worried frown.

Damn but he didn't need this right now, Jeff thought. Still, he knew Slim wouldn't have brought it up unless he meant for Jeff to take it seriously. "What do you suggest I do to diffuse the situation?"

Slim shrugged. "Don't rightly know. Maybe an apology, for starters."

Jeff's fork clanked on the plate as he dropped it and swung toward Slim. "Apologize for keeping a big bully from going after a smaller, brand-new kid who was shaking in his shoes? Talk about humiliation, you should have heard Mac, the way he talked to Teddy, criticizing, dressing him down in front of everyone."

"I didn't say Mac didn't deserve what he got. But you asked me how you could get back on his good side."

Jeff picked up his fork. "Mac doesn't have a good side. He's mean as...well, as a wild bull. Frankly, he shouldn't be in charge of anything or anyone."

That put Slim on the defensive. "Mac's got his good points, though he hasn't shown any to you. He works hard."

"So does everyone else without running roughshod over a newcomer trying to learn." He put a bite of eggs and sausage in his mouth, but tasted only his growing anger.

He ate in silence for several minutes while Slim sipped his coffee. Finally, having lost his appetite along with his sunny mood, Jeff wiped his mouth and tossed the napkin on the table. "All right, what *else* do you want me to do?"

Slim shook his head. "I'm not telling you what to do. It's up to you. I'm only warning you that you have a mean pit bull mad as hell at you and if you don't do something, you'd best watch your back at all times."

Jeff drew in a calming breath and thought about what East would want him to do. After a moment, he scooted back his chair. "Okay, I'll go apologize. But damned if I feel he's due one."

Looking up at him, Slim nodded. "Son, we all have to do things now and again that stick in our craw."

"If you tell me I'll be a better man for it, I'm liable to punch you, too." Picking up his hat, Jeff marched off and out the back door, not even stopping to compliment Elsa on his breakfast this morning.

He found Mac in the far side of the cow barn where he'd finished castrating a couple of two-year-old males. The steers were bawling their heads off, but Mac seemed oblivious as he stood at the tin sink cleaning his long knife.

Probably not the best time to approach the SOB, Jeff thought, but he wanted to get this over with. "Mac," he began, stopping a short distance from the burly cowhand.

Mac slowly turned, his eyes hard and angry-looking, as always. Leaving the water running, he straightened to his full five-seven height and glared at Jeff without saying a word. His black Stetson shaded his face from the overhead lights, but Jeff could see his mouth was a thin line.

Jeff shifted his feet, then settled on a nonthreatening stance as he took off his hat. "Listen, about last week, I'm sorry I got carried away.'' He held out his right hand. ''No hard feelings, I hope.''

Mac's eyes narrowed as he moved his hand back and forth on the blade of the long, curved knife. ''No hard feelings?'' he snarled. ''Hell, yes, I have hard feelings. You were way out of line, boy.''

Another one who called him *boy*. He was getting damn sick and tired of it, but he decided to ignore the insult and give it one more shot. ''Listen, I don't want there to be bad blood between us. I've apologized and I hope we can go on from here.''

''Oh, you do, do you?'' Mac's pudgy face gleamed in the bright lights as he took a step toward Jeff. ''Listen, boy, I don't like you, not one little bit. You and me, we're never going to be friends. Understand, boy?''

Jeff had had enough. ''Just so you know, I don't want to be your friend. And I'm not your *boy,* you hear?''

Mac's expression turned ugly as he started toward Jeff.

''Oh, there you are,'' came a soft voice from behind Mac. Tish had walked in through the open back door. ''I've been looking all over for you, Mac.'' She totally ignored Jeff as Mac, confusion and surprise on his features, half turned toward her. ''I was wondering if you could help me?''

Just as surprised as Mac, Jeff just stared at her.

''What do you need?'' Mac finally asked her.

She stepped closer to him, smiling. ''There's this calf in the next barn in the end stall. You might know him, spotted, kind of small for his age. Anyhow, no matter what I do, he won't take the bottle.''

Exasperated, yet taken in by a beautiful woman seeking his advice, something that didn't happen hardly ever to Mac, he relaxed a bit. ''There must be some hands over there can help you.'' He tossed a glaring look at Jeff. ''I'm a little busy here.''

"Somebody named Lefty told me you were the real expert, that you could get any calf to drink. He says you've saved a few who were fighting being weaned." She smiled at him again. "Could you show me how? I'd be really grateful."

Obviously torn between vengeance and flattery, he chose Tish. Tossing the knife into the sink and turning off the water, he gave her what passed for a smile. "Okay, lead the way."

She gave him a dazzling smile. "Thank you so much." She started toward the door, then when she was sure Mac was following her, she glanced back. "Oh, and Jeff, you could come, too. Maybe you could learn something." And she glided off to the barn next door with the two men trailing after her.

Jeff smiled to himself. He already had learned something. Wasn't there a saying that you could catch more flies with honey than vinegar? Damned if he had the patience or the makeup to play that game with bullies like Mac. Still, he had to admit, it worked.

In minutes, she had the two men in the hay-strewn stall, Jeff holding down the recalcitrant calf while Mac was down on one knee holding the bottle just so, explaining his award-winning procedure to Tish who looked for all the world as if she were hanging on his every word. When the bottle was empty, the calf full and the session over, she thanked Mac profusely.

Rising, Jeff could have sworn the man blushed as he smiled and told her it was nothing. He left the barn whistling.

Jeff got to his feet while Tish waited, making sure Mac was truly out of the barn, then she turned to him, a mischievous smile on her full mouth. "More than one way to skin a cat, Jeff Kirby," she said, moving up close to him.

Slipping his arms around her, he smiled down into her

eyes. "I suppose that big mouth Slim told you where I was and why."

"Could be," she answered coyly.

"What makes you think he won't come after me anyhow since he refused to accept my apology?"

"You mean your very sincere, heartfelt apology?"

He raised his brows. "You were eavesdropping?"

"I heard every word. You're not real good at backing down, are you?"

"No, but neither is he. And he's the bully."

"Mmm-hmm. He didn't look like much of a bully kneeling in here feeding that little old calf."

Jeff drew in an exasperated breath. "Women can get men to do all kinds of things they wouldn't do for another man."

"I think you're right."

Jeff glanced around and noticed that they were all alone in the big barn except for a few calves in their stalls. He took her hand and led her down the walkway to the wooden ladder leading up to the hayloft. "Ever see the view from up there? You can see for miles."

"Is that so? Well, I wouldn't want to miss that." She started up the ladder.

Jeff followed, enjoying the view already as her denim-clad bottom teased him every step of the way. They scampered up and walked over to where a high window looked out on the ranch, the outbuildings, pastureland, the lazy stream ambling along, all the way to the majestic mountains in the distance. As Tish stood looking out, Jeff slid his hands along her arms urging her to lean against him. They enjoyed the view for several minutes, until Jeff thought of something else he'd rather do.

Slowly, he turned her within his arms so he could look into her fathomless brown eyes. "Have you ever made love in a hayloft?'' he asked, his blood beginning to heat at the mere thought.

Tish scrunched up her face. ''Let me think. Let's see, once when I was…no, that was alongside a stream. Maybe that night…no, that was in a tent during a rainstorm. A hayloft? No, I don't think I have.'' She gazed up at him, her heart in her eyes. ''What'd you have in mind, Dr. Kirby?''

''Just this,'' he said and bent to kiss her.

In moments, they were two people totally engrossed in each other. Jeff hadn't known he could feel so much pleasure as he impatiently undressed Tish, stripping layers from her with trembling hands. The freshly pressed yellow blouse was tossed unceremoniously aside, followed by slim jeans and leather boots that hit the hay-covered wooden floor with loud thuds. Two silken swatches of what passed for underwear went flying as well, for in his haste he'd almost ripped them from her.

How was this possible, that no matter how often he made love to her, he was hungry for her again? And Tish was no less eager as her fingers flew on his buttons while he shoved off his jeans.

Need for her pounded through Jeff as he knelt with her on the thick hay, lacing his fingers through hers. Her skin was fragrant, delicate, the texture of fine satin. He sent his mouth on a journey of discovery, always brand-new, always thrilling as her breath trembled from her. Hands still locked, he followed her down and watched her eyes widen as he filled her completely. She arched to take him deeper.

Now he could feel her needs vibrate through her, drawing him in, as slick, damp skin slid over warm, moist skin. Her fingers curled around his as she changed from passive to frenzied. He held off the moment, watching her go up and up, until she became greedy and finally desperate. She moaned her demands and begged for release as he held her in check, increasing their pleasure by delaying the inevitable.

From below there came the bawling of a forlorn calf and the slamming of a door, then horse's hooves as a rider left the area, but they neither saw nor heard. Fingers twined, hearts pounding in sync, Jeff thrust deeply, then withdrew until she raised her hips to urge him back, then he thrust again. His eyes on hers, he emptied his mind of everything but this woman who filled his thoughts more thoroughly than anyone he'd ever known.

There in the ranch's hayloft that he'd coaxed her up to visit because he couldn't wait for their usual evening rendezvous, he took her with a raging hunger he was very much afraid would never let him be. As he swallowed her cry of completion, Jeff wondered how he'd ever again manage to be without her....

Chapter 8

Now, staring down at Tish lying so very still on her hospital bed, Jeff was still wondering the same thing, how he could ever manage to live without her.

Remembering their days and nights at Red Rock Ranch last year, Jeff thought that their time together had had almost a surreal quality to it. No question that it had been real, that it all had happened, yet in many ways, the time period was almost dreamlike.

Which was why it had had to end, sooner or later, he supposed.

Looking at Tish's lovely, unlined face, so serene in her deep sleep in the ICU, he wondered if there'd ever be another time like that for them. When they could—

Suddenly, a blipping noise began chiming from one of Tish's machines. His heart thudding, he quickly checked them out and realized it was the one monitoring her breathing.

Rushing out, he almost ran into Doris who'd already had

the warning at her desk monitor. "Something's wrong," Jeff told her.

"Yes, I know." She hurried to check the instruments, then the patient whose breathing was now troubled. Tish's chest was heaving and she appeared to be straining.

"Do you want to call Dr. O'Neill?" Jeff asked, his concern building.

Another nurse stepped into the cubicle and quickly assessed the situation. "I'll call the attending, Doris," she said.

"Yes, please do." Doris had her stethoscope on Tish's chest, listening. The patient was obviously in distress, her face breaking out in a sweat.

"Is there anything I can do?" Jeff asked, hating feeling so helpless.

Doris spared him a quick glance. "Would you please step outside, Dr. Kirby? We'll handle this." She'd no sooner finished her request than a tall, dark-haired man wearing a white jacket walked in. Doris stepped back, giving him room. "Dr. Monroe, this is the patient's husband, Dr. Kirby."

Monroe was in his fifties, Jeff guessed, slightly overweight and wearing an expensive toupee. He moved right to Tish without another glance at Jeff. "Yes, please step outside until we're finished." He leaned down to the patient, listening with his stethoscope.

Jeff didn't want to leave. After all, it wasn't as if he were the ordinary lay person. He was medically trained and—

Doris touched his arm. "Please, sir. The waiting room is right through the double doors. I'll come get you as soon as the crisis is over."

He struggled with his need to be with Tish and his desire to be cooperative with the medical staff, much as he'd want any patient's relatives to be if he were in charge. Most reluctantly, he backed out of the cubicle and walked through the double doors.

Two other people were in the small ICU waiting room, but Jeff didn't spare them a glance. Concern wrinkled his brow as he began to pace, running through possibilities in his mind. Something related to her surgery? Her heart unable to handle the strain? A bomb fragment they hadn't located previously now loose and floating, causing internal problems? Another lung collapse? A sudden blood pressure drop due to…due to what? He hadn't been talking to her about anything upsetting, so she couldn't have heard bad news.

His mouth a grim line, Jeff marched back and forth. The damn television was on, the volume much too loud. What was wrong with people that they had to have entertainment every waking hour? This was a hospital, for God's sake!

Aware that his thoughts were bordering on unreasonable, still he felt he had every right to be upset. But not to lash out, which was why he kept quiet as the two young people on the couch went into a giggling fit over the TV show.

How could life be normal, even funny, when Tish was struggling to live?

Afterward, Jeff couldn't have said how long he paced the ICU waiting room like the proverbial caged lion. He knew it was close to half an hour though it seemed much longer before they let him back in. By that time, he was frazzled, worried beyond belief and highly annoyed, but, to his credit, he tried not to let them see.

Dr. Monroe met him at the circular desk as he finished writing on Tish's chart. "You were told earlier that your wife had a collapsed lung along with her other injuries, right?" he asked Jeff.

"Yes, I believe so. Is that what caused her distress?"

"Yes. We've removed the canula and put on an oxygen mask for now. She'll be closely monitored and most likely it can be taken off in a couple of hours. I just want to make certain her oxygen level stays within range." He removed his rimless glasses and put them in his shirt pocket. "Everything else is normal, Doctor."

Normal? Nothing was normal, Jeff thought. How could he call Tish's condition normal? "Any sign she might be coming out of the coma soon?"

The doctor's round face broke into a sad smile. "I wish I could say yes, but we simply don't know. There's no activity to indicate an imminent change. You must know how these things go, Doctor. She could wake up an hour from now, or next week. Or not until Christmas. We have no way at this time to judge."

Well, that was helpful. He didn't know why, but Jeff didn't like this doctor. Still, he had no right to be ugly to him, to rail and lash out as he wanted to do. "Thank you, Doctor." He turned and entered Tish's cubicle.

She lay there looking much the same, except for the oxygen mask enclosing her mouth and nose. Her face seemed a bit flushed, probably from her efforts to breathe. Her chest was moving gently with each breath, no longer heaving or struggling.

Jeff took her hand in his. "You gave us a scare there, babe. But they say you're all right now."

"Yes, she is," Doris said from behind Jeff. "I'm sorry you were worried, but these things happen occasionally, as I'm sure you're aware."

Jeff hadn't heard her come in, moving as she did on those silent nurse's shoes. He didn't turn to look at her. "You don't think we should notify Dr. O'Neill?" He was, after all, Tish's doctor.

"I've put a note in his box, though it's no longer an emergency. When he gets it, he'll come by. He's due later on rounds anyway." She paused, as if uncertain whether or not to speak. "Dr. Monroe is an excellent doctor," she told Jeff, trying to sound reassuring, perhaps sensing Jeff's attitude toward the attending physician.

"I'm sure he is," Jeff said, his eyes on Tish, his thumb caressing her hand.

"Well, if you need anything, let me know." As soundlessly as she'd entered, Doris left, closing the cubicle door.

Wearily, Jeff moved the chair close beside the bed again and dropped into it. "Don't do this again, babe. I can't handle any more frights." Leaning back, he scrubbed his face with an impatient hand. He was really losing it, giving warnings to a comatose patient.

When, oh, when, was all this going to be over?

Releasing a deep sigh, he dropped his head back and closed his eyes. He felt about as low as the day he'd proposed to Tish. How ludicrous that asking someone to marry you should turn into such a sad event.

He remembered all too well. It was on an evening two nights before they were both scheduled to leave Red Rock Ranch. Jeff was going back to his apartment in Los Angeles, his R and R over, to resume his hospital duties. Tish was supposed to return to her home to await her next SPEAR assignment.

But Jeff had other plans, plans he intended to share with her that evening as they rendezvoused on their blanket at their favorite spot. With his eyes closed, he could picture the scene perfectly....

It was later than usual, just past eight in the evening, already dark but the moon was high in the sky, almost directly overhead with no clouds visible. A perfect night for love, Jeff thought as he spread the blanket and sat down to wait.

Tish had been tied up with the last riding lesson for the young tourist boy, Luke, the one she'd been teaching during the family's stay at the Red Rock Ranch. He was going home tomorrow so she'd promised him extra time. Jeff had finished his chores and gone on ahead. As he stared up at the faraway stars, he rehearsed in his head what he planned to say to her. Several times, he edited his words until he heard Belladonna approaching.

Rising, he went to meet her as Tish slipped off the mare. He leaned over to kiss her, then tied up her horse several trees over from where Domino stood pawing the ground, as restless as Jeff himself was.

"Are you hungry?" Jeff asked as they both settled on the blanket and he opened the lid of their basket. "I had Elsa pack light because it's kind of late for a big meal. Just cheese, crackers, fruit and—" with a flourish, he pulled out a bottle of chilled champagne "—and this." He removed two fluted glasses as well.

Tish's eyes took on a suspicious light. "Are we celebrating something?"

"That depends on you." Jeff worked on uncorking the champagne and all the while, Tish was quiet. He wondered if she'd guessed what was coming or if she'd not given the possibility of their future together another thought after their last discussion. She'd confessed to being in love with him, but not anything beyond that.

The cork popped and he lost only a small drizzle, then poured champagne into the two glasses she held. Setting the bottle back in the basket, Jeff took a glass and raised it. "To us," he said.

"To us," she repeated, though her words were slow and hesitant. They each sipped in silence.

He'd never been one to beat around the bush, so Jeff decided to come to the point. Taking her free hand in his, he gazed into her eyes. "Tish, you know that I love you."

A frown appeared on her face quickly, then disappeared as she took her hand back, as if fearful of what was coming. "Jeff, we've known each other less than two weeks."

"I don't think time's a factor. Some couples go together for years and finally discover they're in love. Others, it takes a month, maybe a week. Sometimes only a moment. That's how it was for me." Refusing to let her withdraw, he took her hand again. "I fell in love with you that first day when I saw you on Belladonna."

He waited, but she said nothing, finding their two joined hands fascinating as she stared at them. Jeff felt a nervous flutter. In all the speeches he'd rehearsed, her unresponsiveness had never been a part of any of them. "Say something, anything."

"I don't know what you want me to say, Jeff."

"Best scenario? I want you to say you love me, too."

"I've told you that, but—"

"And that you want to marry me."

She glanced up, looking as if she were truly caught off guard. "You're asking me to marry you?"

"Yes. Don't tell me this comes as a total shock. We've been together constantly since that first evening. We've made love over and over. From the way you responded, I thought you felt the same as I do." When she said nothing, he had to go on. "Surely you didn't think we were having just an affair. Do I seem a cavalier sort of person to you, someone who'd make love to a woman, then kiss her good-bye and move on?"

She looked away at the faraway mountains. "No, you don't. Nor am I the type for casual affairs."

"Then, what's the problem?"

Tish let out a ragged sigh. "I care for you, Jeff, of course. But marriage? It's not just the age thing, though that's a bigger obstacle to me than you. It's that we're in totally different places in our lives and our careers. You're just starting out, with two more years in residency to go, then finally you'll be more active in SPEAR full-time. I'm in my prime now, constantly assigned into the thick of things. And I like it that way. I'm good at my work, proud of what I do.''

''It never occurred to me to ask you to give up SPEAR.''

She looked up then, seemingly anxious to make him understand. ''We wouldn't have much time together, you stuck in L.A. for several years yet, me traveling around the world most of the time.''

''People in committed relationship, married people, find time to be together. All right, so we'd be separated some, but that would only make the time we had together all the better.'' She didn't look convinced.

''There's another factor here. Jeff, I know firsthand how dangerous life as an agent is and, as a medevac, you'll also be in every trouble spot, working under fire, putting your life at risk to save others. What if…if we have children? And I want to have children. Naturally, that would mean I'd quit SPEAR. But could I bear to stay home with children whose father might never live to see them grow up?''

Jeff struggled with a growing frustration. ''Look, Tish, we're getting way ahead of ourselves here. East and Ally are married and—''

''And she's retired from the field and he runs Condor, a safe assignment.''

He knew she had a valid point. ''All right, bad example. But lots of men have dangerous jobs. Firemen, policemen, servicemen. And a civilian can be on his way home, step off a curb and get run over by a bus. There are no guarantees of a long, perfect life for any of us, Tish.''

''Maybe not, but we don't need to shorten the odds.''

He dropped her hand, growing angry despite his best intentions. ''So then, you plan never to marry, to have children, even though you just said you wanted them, because their father works in a risky environment? Are you waiting to meet some nice safe boring guy, someone you can be sure will be around to see your children grow up? All the while, loving me?''

Almost roughly, he took hold of her shoulders. "Admit it. You care about me. You love me. Don't you?''

He could see the moisture gather in her eyes. "Yes, I do love you. But…''

He dropped his hands. "If you *really* love someone, there are no *buts*. You work through the problems. You compromise. You take a chance, on that person, on a life together.'' He speared her with his hot, angry gaze. "Or are you too afraid?''

Jeff watched her struggle not to cry, blinking back tears begging to fall, her lower lip held tightly between her teeth so it wouldn't quiver. Finally, she got up. "Yes,'' she said softly, "I am afraid.'' Hurriedly, as if she might change her mind if she lingered, Tish ran over to Belladonna, untied her and jumped into the saddle.

In minutes, as Jeff sat watching, Tish was out of sight.

He wanted to hit something really hard. He wanted to take back his words, rephrase them, try again.

Rising, he slowly gathered up their picnic things and walked over to Domino. Climbing on, he decided he'd let Tish be tonight. He wouldn't try to see her or talk to her. He'd let her sleep on it and by tomorrow, perhaps after thinking things over, she'd be in a better frame of mind.

Starting back, Jeff decided that was the right thing to do.

Only in the morning when he went down to breakfast, he learned that Tish had left Red Rock Ranch at 6:00 a.m.

Her departure had rocked him to his very soul. He'd tried not to react when Slim told him the news, but he was sure the older man could read his expression and know how disappointed he was.

Slim's strong, weathered hand squeezed Jeff's shoulder, conveying without words that he understood. They were in the dining room, standing off to the side where the ranch manager had led Jeff after spotting him as he entered.

Jeff swallowed around a suddenly dry throat. "Did she say why she was leaving so early?" he asked, the need to know stronger than his desire for privacy.

Slim shook his head. "Not a word to me. Naomi Star caught me when I came in for breakfast. She said Tish showed up at the front desk with her two bags, signed herself out and climbed into a cab she'd apparently arranged to pick her up."

Thrusting his hands into the back pockets of his jeans, Jeff struggled for control as he rocked on his booted feet. "I don't suppose she left a note for me with Naomi." It was more a statement than a question.

"'Fraid not. When Naomi asked her when she'd be returning, Tish just shook her head and hurried outside." Slim studied the young man's face, debating how much to say. "Did you two have a quarrel? Naomi said Tish looked like she'd been crying."

Damn! Jeff ground his teeth, fluctuating between hurt and anger. "A quarrel? Not exactly. I asked her to marry me."

Slim's eyes turned sympathetic. "I take it she turned you down."

Jeff's laugh had a bitter edge. "She admitted she loved me, then left me high and dry."

Wearily, Slim nodded. "Women! I'll never understand them."

Jeff sighed. "You've got that right."

"Maybe if you go after her, get her to talk…"

"No!" Jeff let the anger race through him and it felt good. "I'm not crawling back to her, begging her for another chance. If she doesn't want me, then fine. If she changes her mind, she'll have to come to me." With that, he turned on his heel and left the dining room, his shoulders square, his stride angry.

Stretching out his long legs, Jeff snapped out of his reverie and gazed at his wife in her hospital bed. "You sure put me through a miserable couple of weeks that time, Tish. Not as miserable as right now, of course. But this is different. This time, I'm worried and, I have to admit, more than a little scared. But back then, I was angry and deep down inside, hurt.

"You have no idea how rejection like that can sting. I told you I loved you and you said you loved me, too. Then you rode off and left me. I knew you had issues about love, about marriage, about men who claimed to love you, like your father and later, Eric, the man you thought loved you. And I know a couple of weeks isn't a long time, but our feelings were real."

Jeff ran a hand through his hair, remembering his frustration. "Maybe you didn't believe that I cared so deeply. Maybe you were afraid to trust your own feelings. Or perhaps you were simply afraid of marriage, of commitment. Lots of people are, only a lot of times it's men who are afraid."

He leaned forward and again took her hand. "Even though I was angry, I couldn't forget you. Lord knows I tried. I left Red Rock the same day you did, only later in the afternoon, catching a plane to L.A. Back a day early and they could scarcely believe that anyone would cut short a vacation."

Caressing her hand, Jeff found himself remembering the reunion that followed, and a small smile broke through. "I hadn't heard from you in several weeks and I'd pretty much convinced myself it was over. I hated going to sleep because you were all I dreamed of, so I worked double shifts, tiring my body so I could fall into bed and not be haunted by dreams of you. It didn't work very well. Which was why I was so shocked when you showed up that day last autumn at my L.A apartment, out of the blue...."

Los Angeles, early October

Climbing the stairs to his third-floor apartment, Jeff felt as if there were heavy weights in each of his shoes. He was bone tired, all his energy depleted. He couldn't remember the last time he'd had a really good meal, away from the hospital—like a steak and all the trimmings served at a table—instead of a bagel caught on the run or a cup of soup he drank standing up. Although he was hungry, he was too tired to fix a meal. Maybe after he slept awhile. He wasn't due back at the hospital for twelve blessed hours.

Reaching the third floor, wondering how he'd driven home as worn-out as he was, he fumbled with his keys, searching for the right one. As he turned down the hallway, he glanced up, then stopped dead in his tracks.

Sitting on the carpeted hall floor in front of his apartment door was Tish wearing a navy shirt over khaki slacks and navy running shoes.

As he stood staring at her, Jeff wondered if he was hallucinating in his dissipated state. How had she found his address? Through SPEAR operatives, of course. His knees feeling weak from fatigue and the climb, he braced one hand on the hallway wall as he gazed at her.

Damn, but she looked good. She slowly stood, silently facing him, the expression on her beautiful face hard to read. She'd let her hair grow, the ends just barely touching her shoulders. Her eyes were watchful and her whole demeanor was hesitant.

Jeff finally found his voice. "Tish," he said. All the anger he'd carefully nursed along, all the hurt he'd hated to acknowledge, left him as his eyes caressed her from afar. "You're looking great," he added, slowly walking closer.

But when he reached her side, even as tired as he was, he could see the dark smudges of fatigue beneath her eyes, the trembling of her lower lip. Jeff frowned, but refrained from reaching out. "What is it? What's wrong?"

Tish averted her gaze. "Could we go inside? I—I'd like to talk with you."

"Sure, sure." He found the right key and opened the door, standing aside so she could enter. Following, he saw the small apartment as if through her eyes, and almost cringed. It was a rental, plain and simple, adequate for the few hours he spent in it.

The furnishings came with the place, a long and comfortable sofa that had seen better days, an easy chair and ottoman that didn't match, two wood tables and a lamp. Books he'd been studying last night were stacked on the floor, a pair of old moccasins next to them. A jacket was draped over the arm of the chair and two empty pop cans were on the table next to a half-eaten candy bar. To the left through the arch was the kitchen, small but serviceable. To the right was his bedroom and bath.

Jeff felt he ought to explain. "This is temporary, naturally, until I finish my residency." He scooped up a pile of newspapers from the floor next to the couch and set the stack on the ottoman. "I'm here so seldom that I—"

"Jeff," Tish interrupted, "you needn't defend where you live."

The apartment had one good feature, a fairly large picture window that, although it looked out onto the parking lot, made the place seem light and airy. He watched her walk over to it and stand gazing out. He wished he knew what she was thinking.

Scrubbing a hand over his face, acutely aware he needed a shower and shave, he moved over to join her. "Would you like something to drink?'' It was the first week of October and already cooler. "I could make some coffee.'' Maybe the caffeine would help him stay awake, to focus more easily on her unexpected visit.

"No, thanks. You needn't bother." She didn't take her eyes off the scene outside the window. "I've been wondering where you live, trying to picture you here."

That sounded good, he thought. At least she'd been thinking about him. "So now you know." He decided to get down to it. He took a step closer to her. "Why'd you come, Tish?"

Finally, her eyes swung toward him. "I needed to tell you. I've taken a leave of absence from the field."

That surprised him. He'd told himself during one of his sleepless nights that of course she couldn't marry him, that she was already married to SPEAR. "I know how much you love working. You must have a good reason."

Her brown eyes were steady on his, but he saw a muscle twitch beneath one and he again wondered why her skin looked so bruised, as if she'd had a lot of sleepless nights.

"I do have a good reason. I'm pregnant. Two and a half months."

Jeff couldn't help himself. He just stared for several long moments, then his face split into a huge grin. "That's wonderful." In his exuberance, he picked her up and swung her around in his strong arms, then bent his head to kiss her.

She held back at first, stiff and unyielding. But then, just when he was beginning to regret he'd touched her, she made a low groaning sound in her throat and her arms snaked around him, urging him closer. Her mouth moved over his, making him recall the wonder of her kisses.

Home. Jeff felt as if he'd come home. She tasted even better than he'd been remembering and she smelled so clean and sweet. He gathered her closer and the kiss went on and on, both of them caught up in the power of it. One thing they'd had from their very first meeting was an electric excitement between them that threatened to ignite with the merest glance.

Finally Jeff released her and met her eyes, which were already a shade hazy. He'd hoped to see joy or signs of pleasure on her face, but instead she looked melancholy. Hadn't she told him once that she wanted children? Surely she hadn't changed her mind. Naturally, he'd rather she'd have come to him because she wanted him desperately, not because an unexpected pregnancy meant she needed a father for her child. But after all these weeks without her, he wasn't about to make an issue out of it.

"Aren't you happy about the baby, Tish?" he asked softly.

She drew in a deep breath and wandered over to his couch, sitting down. "Yes, I am, although truth be known, I'd rather have waited a few more years. I've always wanted a child, one I could raise with all the motherly love I didn't have growing up." She paused, waiting until he sat down beside her.

"I knew I would have to make a decision soon about having a child before I reached the age where it might be dangerous to go through a first pregnancy. I also knew that I'd have to give up working in the field then, and I wasn't ready for that quite yet." For the first time, she looked up and smiled. "The best laid plans of mice and men, eh? I guess the decision's been made for me."

He slipped an arm around her, needing to feel close again. "I'm glad, Tish. Really glad."

She frowned, as if there were more she had to say. "Jeff, wait a minute. I want you to know that I'm not here because I expect something from you. I'm not telling you about the baby to force you to marry me. It's just that I feel you have a right to know."

It was Jeff's turn to frown. "Force me to marry you? Are you kidding? I asked you back in Arizona to marry me and you ran off."

She nodded, looking chagrined. "I know. I didn't mean to hurt you, it's just that I needed time. Everything happened so fast. Then when I found out about the baby, I took some time to think things over. I came to the realization that my life as a field agent is definitely over." She looked deep into his green eyes. "I want this baby, Jeff. *Your* baby."

"And the baby's father? Do you want him, too?"

"Yes, very much. I love you, Jeff. I'm sorry if I've given you a hard time, but this was a life-altering decision. And I wasn't sure you'd want a baby just now, when you're still a resident and all."

Now he gathered her close, heartened by those three little words she'd finally uttered. "Of course I want the baby. Honey, I've come through so much in life—surviving alcoholic parents, living on the streets, being buried alive and left for dead—that I believe we can handle most anything that comes our way. Together. And I can't imagine anything more wonderful than coming home to you and our baby. Nothing could be more perfect."

"But what about money? I won't be bringing any in and I'm not sure how much residents make, but I've heard it's not a lot. I've got some saved, but not much. And I won't go to my father."

He smiled and kissed the top of her head. "Not to worry. East set up a trust fund for me the day he adopted me ten years ago. I can dip into that if need be. He'll be thrilled about our marriage because he's the only one who knows how much I've missed you. And he'll be happy for us about the baby, too. Ally's expecting, you know." He hugged her tightly, thinking he'd walked into the middle of a wonderful dream, hoping he'd never wake up. "I can hardly wait to tell him."

Tish pulled back, frowning again. "Could we sort of keep our marriage private for now?" Noticing his face, the surprise-bordering-on-hurt look, she put her hand on his chest. "Just for a little while, Jeff. I...we're so different, you and I. What if it doesn't work out for the long haul? I mean, it's okay if we talk about the baby because we can hardly keep that a secret for long. But not the marriage, not for a while. Let's just get married quietly, please." Her eyes on his were pleading.

Slowly, Jeff dropped his arms, disappointment etched on his tired features. "I thought every woman dreamed of a big wedding with all the frills?"

"Perhaps, but sometimes you have to adjust your dreams."

Wasn't that the truth? "You think we'll fail so you want to save face in case we do?"

She grabbed hold of his hand, trying to make him see. "Do you remember an agent from California, Brenda Wicks? She and Brian Temple had a similar story as ours a couple of years back. They'd worked together in SPEAR, she became pregnant and they got married. Big church wedding, everyone invited. Well, they separated two months after the baby was born. She'd made such a big fuss, then all she felt was humiliation. She moved to the East Coast and dropped out of sight. I don't know where Brian is."

She certainly knew how to take the shine off good news, Jeff couldn't help thinking. He let the silence between them build, then finally decided there was only one way to handle this. He would prove to her that no matter how many other such stories she had or how many marriages went bust, they would make it.

Placing both hands on her shoulders, he leaned to her.

"I'll go along with this, but not for long. I love you and I want you to be my wife. I want the whole damn world to know it. We're not going to fail. You got that, Mrs. Kirby-to-be?"

She gave him a shaky smile. "Yes, Mr. Kirby. I mean Dr. Kirby."

"Good. Now I need to take a shower and to shave before I drag my fiancée into bed where I've been dreaming of her for far too long. Do you think you could find something to eat in my meager kitchen while I clean up?"

Her smile was broader this time. "I think so."

"Terrific." He kissed her lightly, then stood. "I'll be ready in ten minutes."

"Ten? That's mighty fast work."

"I've waited all these weeks to get you back under the sheets. I'm not going to waste another minute." Walking backward, he grinned. "You know, we never did get under sheets. We were always in tents or on that blanket under the stars."

"I don't mind if it's the ground or the floor or your bed. As long as I'm with you." Obviously feeling better, Tish started for the kitchen. She was almost there when she was tackled from behind and wound up being carried in the opposite direction. With a yelp, she clung to him. "What are you doing?"

"I decided to forgo the food." In the bathroom, he let her slide down his body suggestively. "Want to scrub my back?"

"Mmm, and other interesting parts," Tish said as she pressed her mouth to his.

Chapter 9

Dr. Edmund O'Neill came out of Tish's ICU cubicle and found Jeff waiting for him at the nurses' circular desk. He'd lost a patient an hour ago, a sweet woman his mother's age who'd gone into a diabetic coma and never awakened, so he wasn't in the best of moods. Some patients got to you more than others.

Like Tish Buckner. So lovely and so lost in her silent world. Edmund looked at Tish's husband, Jeff, a young doctor in training, and his chest tightened. The man looked tired, worried, anxious for just one small word of hope he could cling to. Edmund wished he could offer him just that.

Pushing his glasses higher on his nose, the doctor handed Tish's chart to the nurse and turned toward Jeff. "Let's go over here," he suggested, leading the worried husband to a small alcove near the double doors.

His glance took in Jeff's appearance, rumpled clothes, needing a shave, his dark-green eyes troubled. "She's holding her own, Doctor," Edmund began. "I know you're hoping for something more positive and I wish I could give it to you. But as a medical man, I'm sure you know that your wife's injuries were serious. A severe concussion alone can put a patient into a coma for some time while the swelling recedes and the brain heals itself.''

Jeff thrust his hands into his pants pockets, nodding. ''Yes, I know. You'll have to forgive my impatience. I want so badly for her to wake up. I feel so helpless.''

''Actually, I think you're contributing to her recovery. I'm a firm believer that coma patients are struggling to come back, drifting deeper, then floating near the surface again. And a familiar voice urging them back, hearing that someone cares and is right by her side so she's not alone, I know that helps a great deal. I've seen miraculous things happen more than once. You may feel powerless, but you're helping her even if it doesn't seem that way.''

''I certainly hope so. You know, this has given me real insight as to how a patient's relatives feel.''

Edmund nodded. ''I went through something similar a while back when my father was hospitalized with terminal cancer. For days I sat by his side, wishing I could do something and feeling as helpless as I know you do. I think that experience made me a better doctor, and this will make you more compassionate, as well.''

But Jeff's thoughts were still on Tish. ''Her lungs, are they fully functional on their own now after that scare we had?''

''Yes. I've removed the oxygen cup. She's breathing on her own without distress. I've also ordered a reduction of her pain medication. Up till now, I knew she needed it. But it was also keeping her deep in the coma. So now we'll see if she'll slowly come to.''

Jeff frowned. ''But does that mean she'll be experiencing pain without that medication?''

''Some, perhaps. Not like she would have before. Pain,

as I'm sure you know, is sometimes necessary and even helpful. It tells us where and what we need to treat. We can't tell that if she's constantly heavily sedated."

"I hate to have her suffer any more."

"It will feel more uncomfortable for her than painful. And once she awakens and can talk to us, she can tell us about her pain and we can evaluate further. Don't worry. We won't let her lie there suffering."

Jeff knew that and knew they were doing all they could. It's just that he couldn't help worrying. Yet he liked and respected this doctor. He held out his hand. "Thanks for answering all my questions, Doctor."

"Anytime. They'll page me if there's a change." He patted Jeff's shoulder. "Get some rest. You look like you could use it and she's not going anywhere."

Dr. O'Neill hadn't really told him anything, yet Jeff felt better as he watched the slight man leave ICU. He strolled over to where Doris was placing various medications into small paper cups on a tray.

"I'm going to grab a shower, Doris. I'll be back shortly."

"Take your time, Doctor. I'm here for her."

He smiled wearily. "I know you are and thanks."

Jeff looked in on Tish, but of course she hadn't moved since he'd stepped out for Dr. O'Neill's exam. Shoving open the double doors, he yawned expansively. It was odd, the way he felt. He was tired, yet had trouble sleeping. Maybe because he was afraid to dream.

In the doctor's lounge, he opened the locker O'Neill had told him to use and pulled out his leather bag. Rummaging for clean clothes, his hand found his cell phone. He hadn't taken it into the ICU because cell phones would interfere with the various medical machinery there. Now, he checked his messages and found three. He ignored the first two as inconsequential, but he needed to call back the third party.

Sitting down on a red fake leather two-seater, Jeff pushed in the code for East. His dad answered on the second ring.

"Hey, Dad, it's me. You called?"

Standing at the kitchen counter in his suite at the Condor Mountain Resort in California, East tried to gauge his son's mood by his voice. "Yes. How are things progressing?"

Briefly, he updated East on Tish's condition. "So now we're waiting to see if lessening her pain medication will bring her back."

East sat down on the tall stool at his island counter. "I see."

"How's the baby and how's Ally doing?"

"All Annie wants to do is eat. She was nearly nine pounds at birth, can you believe it? Ally's fine, nursing her every two or three hours. I worry she can't rest, but she feels strongly that mother's milk is best."

"I'm sure she's right."

East heard the weariness, the underlying fear of losing someone you love that was next to impossible to cover up. "How are you holding up, son?"

Jeff closed his eyes as he leaned back. "Hanging in there, as they say. What else can I do?"

East read between the lines. "I don't suppose you've slept any? You could go check into a hotel, you know, and catch up on your rest. They'd call you if there's a change."

Jeff took his time answering. "Would you if Ally were in that room hooked up to machines, not knowing if she'd ever awaken?"

East had known before he'd suggested the hotel what his son's reaction would be. "Point taken. Listen, I called because I'm catching the red-eye to Kennedy tonight. As I said earlier, they want me to visit the bomb site, though I don't know how much help I'll be. Years ago, I was involved in something similar so I guess the powers that be think I'll spot something they missed."

"I'm glad you're coming. I'd like to see that scene myself, but I can't leave here just now."

"I'll check it out for you. Before I go there, I intend to stop at the hospital right after I land." And see for himself how Jeff was faring, insist they go get something to eat, maybe spell him at Tish's bedside so his son could get several hours of uninterrupted sleep.

"All right, then. I'll see you sometime tomorrow morning. Sorry I can't meet you at the airport."

"Don't worry about that."

"Dad?" Jeff waited for his father's response. "I'm glad you're coming." And he hung up before he embarrassed himself.

Leaning forward, his elbows braced on his knees, he hung his head, trying to regain his composure. Nobody would blame him, he supposed, if he broke down. Even strong men wept when someone they loved was threatened in some way. Jeff liked to think of himself as strong, but he wasn't sure how much longer he could keep up the facade. East, he knew, would see through it in a moment.

Scrubbing a hand along his unshaven jaw, he knew he should get up, take a shower, shave, put on clean clothes. And he would, in just a minute.

Leaning back, stretching out his legs, he closed his eyes, needing a few minutes before he could call up enough energy to get cleaned up. He was agitated to think about the future.

Instead, he thought back to a happier time—the week he and Tish ran off together to Las Vegas and got married....

Las Vegas, early October

It hadn't been easy, getting time off from the hospital after his emergency R and R while he recovered from his kidnapping ordeal. The medical administration would be only so understanding before they'd toss you out of the program. He'd come too far to let that happen. Yet he didn't want to lose Tish nor to delay the wedding because of her pregnancy.

A real dilemma. East had taught him that honesty was the best policy so he'd gone to his supervisor and basically outlined the situation, leaving out some of the more personal aspects. Dr. Wilson was a decent guy and a fair man. But he wasn't too tolerant of slackers. However, he knew that Jeff worked his butt off, taking double shifts to help out others, a team player. He'd given Jeff from 8:00 a.m. on Tuesday morning, after working all night, until midnight Wednesday when he'd have to report for another eight-hour shift. That was all the time he could spare.

Tish thought that was pretty ghastly. Jeff just felt grateful he had at least that much time.

Neither of them had ever been to Las Vegas. They couldn't take the time to drive, so they'd flown, not telling a soul. As tired as he was after ten hours on the job, Jeff knew he'd never be able to make the long drive anyway.

To say that their first impression of Vegas was like visual overload was definitely accurate.

They'd stepped off the plane at noon on Tuesday, each carrying one overnight bag. Although it was October, it was quite warm, more so than in L.A. They'd taken a cab to their hotel, the Venetian, and on the way, gawked at the sights like every other tourist. Huge skyscraper hotels fought for attention along The Strip, each with neon lights flashing in every imaginable color. On one corner was New York, New York, the hotel that featured a working roller coaster at the very top, the screams of passengers carrying all the way down to the sidewalk which was crawling with people. So many people, all presumably going somewhere.

In front of the MGM Grand was a huge gold lion silently guarding the entrance and the walkway to Caesar's Palace had magnificent Roman statues along each side leading to the mammoth pillars surrounding the front entrance.

"I've never seen anything like this," Tish said as the cab swung into the circular drive of the Venetian, which was fashioned after Venice, of course.

"Look over here," Jeff said, pointing to the gondola making its way along the canal that circled the property. A young couple snuggled together while the gondolier guided the boat and serenaded them, barely able to be heard above the street noise.

"It's utterly amazing," Tish decided, stepping out of the cab as Jeff held the door open for her.

Still gaping wide-eyed, they strolled through the gold-and-ivory splendor of the lobby to the check-in desk. Pocketing their coded card key, Jeff refused the bellman's offer of assistance, preferring to carry their two small bags himself. They headed for the bank of elevators, passing through a huge expanse of gambling machines.

Awestruck, Tish just stared. "I never imagined there'd be so many people sitting around gambling so early in the day."

"Almost every slot machine is being used and look over there at the Twenty-One tables. Every seat taken."

Just then, a nearby player hit a jackpot and the slot machine's lights flashed on and off while bells and whistles rang out louder than ever. The players in the vicinity crowded around the man who'd put in the winning coin, trying to see how much he'd won. Suddenly a man in a black suit pushed through the crowd and shook the stunned player's hand before inserting a key and turning off the ringing bells.

Fascinated, Jeff and Tish stood watching as an attractive, scantily clad woman with a camera came rushing over and asked the man to stand next to the machine while she snapped a couple of pictures. Jeff and Tish pressed closer, curious like everyone else.

The man in the black suit was telling the winner to follow him to the payoff window. Beaming a smile, the stunned tourist marched after him. As the crowd began to disperse, Jeff finally caught a glimpse of the amount. "Wow, look at this. He won just over ten thousand dollars."

"I wonder how much he's poured into these machines before this big win," Tish commented.

"You're a cynic," Jeff told her as they resumed their search for the elevators.

"You're probably right. I think the fun is in trying to beat the house, if you can afford it."

They spotted a sign that read Elevators and stopped at a huge arch where a tall, barrel-chested man was seated at a desk with a name plate that identified him as Max, part of the security staff.

"May I see your key, please?" he asked.

Jeff dug it out of his pocket and showed him.

"Thank you. Take the elevators to the left, please."

Impressed, Jeff took Tish's hand. "Nice to know they have good security. No one without a key can get past Big Max."

They rode the elevator up to the fourteenth floor where the doors silently slid open and they stepped out. After they located their room, Jeff inserted the card key and swung open the door.

Tish walked in as Jeff flipped on the lights and set down their bags. "Now this is something," she said, looking around.

"All the rooms are suites in the Venetian," Jeff explained. He opened the door to the bath, which was decorated in gold and white and was almost larger than his whole apartment.

Tish checked out the big king-size bed, then she walked down two steps to a sitting room with a couch, two chairs, a huge television set and windows along one whole wall. She pulled back the drapes and sheers. ''Look at this view!'' Las Vegas was spread out below with all its glitzy splendor and in the distance were magnificent mountains jutting up into a cloudless sky.

Jeff came up behind her, sliding his hands along her bare arms as he leaned her against his body. ''Not bad, eh?''

''I think I could get used to this,'' she whispered.

He turned her in his arms and kissed her long and deeply. ''And could you get used to that, every day, every night?'' He still wasn't comfortable with her insistence on secrecy, but he'd agreed, feeling certain she'd change her mind in time.

''Oh, yeah,'' she whispered and reached on tiptoes to kiss him again.

Ever since they'd agreed to get married two days ago in his apartment, Tish had been very loving, and much less skittish and hesitant, Jeff thought. It was as if once the decision had been made, she was content. He prayed her mood would last, that he could make her happy.

Stepping back, Jeff looked around and spotted a telephone book on a large desk alongside the phone and a fax machine. Did people really come here to work? he wondered.

''I'm going to look up the address for the Chapel of the Bells. According to one of the doctors who got married there, it's a very nice wedding chapel.''

''Okay.'' Tish wandered off to examine the bathroom.

In minutes, Jeff had the address and phone number jotted on the notepad he'd found on the desk. He dialed the chapel, hoping they weren't booked solid. Unfortunately, they were, but they recommended another wedding chapel nearby, the Chapel of Dreams. By the time Tish returned, exclaiming over the gold faucets and mirrors everywhere, he had their appointment confirmed.

"How does four this afternoon in the Chapel of Dreams sound to you?" he asked.

"As good as any, I guess." Suddenly serious, she walked over to where Jeff was seated in one of the chairs and sat down on his lap. "Are you sure, absolutely sure, you want to go through with this, Jeff? I seriously doubt that fatherhood was on your mind when we made love back in Arizona. I can handle this on my own if you—"

He cut off the flow of words by kissing her soundly, then framing her lovely face. "The operative word here is *we,* Tish. We made love and as a result, we made a baby. You didn't do it alone and I would've been furious if you hadn't told me. I want to be this baby's father, not because it's the right thing to do, but because I already love him or her. It's part of us, a miracle. I've delivered babies, Tish, and every time, I'm blown away."

"You're not just saying what you think I want to hear?"

"Absolutely not. What can I say to convince you?"

A mischievous smile started at the corners of her mouth, then traveled to her eyes as she glanced over his shoulder at the big bed just waiting for them. "Don't tell me. Show me."

Smiling, Jeff tugged her up two steps and, falling back onto the mattress, he pulled her atop him.

They made love for over an hour, slowly, perfectly, then they called down for room service and ordered a gargantuan late lunch. However, they discovered they weren't all that hungry after all and, after nibbling around the edges, they dived back into the luxurious king-size bed and made love again.

Finally aware of the clock ticking away, they showered and dressed carefully, for this was their wedding day. At

Tish's insistence, Jeff wore a charcoal-gray suit with white shirt and striped burgundy tie, a somewhat sedate outfit she'd bought for him yesterday while he'd been at the hospital. Pausing, he gazed again at the platinum wedding band with small diamonds all around that he'd purchased just yesterday, then tucked the velvet box in his inside pocket.

As he inspected the knot of his tie, remembering again why he hated to wear the darn things, Jeff heard the bathroom door open and turned from the mirror.

She was wearing a pale-peach dress that had a filmy layer of material over silk, and matching shoes. Her dark hair curled at her chin and her beautiful brown eyes were shiny and bright. She was stunning, Jeff thought, every man's dream.

He walked toward her, afraid to touch, to spoil the perfection. But Tish felt no such reluctance as she looked him over, brushing imaginary lint from his broad shoulders then reaching up to stroke his face. "Perfect," she said then kissed him lightly.

"Lady, you light up the room. You're absolutely gorgeous."

"Mmm, I bet you say that to all the women you marry."

"No, there's only you. Always you, Tish."

The eyes that gazed into his were serious. "For me, too, Jeff. From that first moment, it's only been you."

He reached for a package on the table and held it out to her. "This came while you were showering."

Tish recognized the lobby florist's box, opened it to reveal a perfect white orchid. "It's so beautiful, Jeff."

"It's for the wrist, but we can pin it on your dress if you'd rather."

"No, like this." She slipped her hand through the elastic band, then held out her arm. "Lovely."

"Almost as lovely as you." He stepped closer and kissed her hair, breathing in her special scent. "One more thing."

He reached in his pocket and pulled out a small black jeweler's box, holding it out to her.

"You've already given me so much," she protested, but her curiosity got the better of her and she opened the box. Two small diamond earrings winked as they caught the light. "Oh, they're lovely."

"I wanted you to have something special to remember the day."

She smiled up at him. "As if I wouldn't remember this day." She noticed a hint of sadness on his face. "Are you sorry that East and Ally aren't here?" she asked with a worried frown.

Yes, he was, but he hoped he could be forgiven one small lie. "All I need is you." He checked his watch. "We'd better go."

Jeff had stashed away some money, an old habit from his street days, and had dipped into that fund to try to make their impromptu wedding as special as possible under the circumstances. He'd hired a white limo and it was waiting at the circular entry of the Venetian when they stepped out. As Tish settled in, Jeff popped the cork on the champagne he'd also ordered, and poured some into the two flutes.

Handing her one, he smiled. "To us," he said. "The three of us."

Tish's smile was a bit nervous, but she touched her glass to his and echoed his toast before taking a small sip.

"I don't believe your doctor would want you to have alcoholic beverages, but a sip or two won't hurt." He took the glass from her. "But that's all." He set his own glass down and leaned back, slipping an arm around her, drawing her near.

He noticed that her hands were trembling. "Nervous?"

"A little," she admitted. "You?"

Jeff held out his hand, fingers splayed. "Steady as a rock."

"Good. One of us should be."

He'd grown serious again. "I want you to know that you can always count on me, Tish. I'll always be there for you and I'll always tell you the truth." Because of her past experiences with her father and Eric, he wanted her to know that he was different.

"I know, Jeff." She snuggled into him as they rode the rest of the way in silence.

Afterward, they could laugh about it, and did. Actually, they almost had a fit of giggles as soon as they stepped into the foyer of the Chapel of Dreams to the sound of an overhead bell tinkling, and looked around.

Red, apparently, was the color du jour, Jeff decided since it was everywhere from the flocked fleur-de-lis wallpaper to the crimson chandelier and the scarlet carpeting. Two ruby-red brocade chairs placed at an angle by the wide window draped in vermilion damask were the only furniture in the room. A carved wooden door on the far wall was closed, but the muted sound of voices on the other side could be heard.

This might have been a mistake, Jeff thought as he turned to Tish. "I know this isn't exactly what you've dreamed of for your wedding."

She took his arm, shaking her head. "Listen, I'm fine with it. Don't worry."

He relaxed fractionally as he checked his watch. "We're right on time. I wonder where—"

Just then the wooden door swung open and a plump blond woman wearing a full-length wedding dress, her train trailing behind her, stomped into the waiting area. Whipping off her veil, she swiped at tears streaming down her chubby cheeks. "I'm not marrying you, Norman," she wailed. "Not now, not ever."

As Tish and Jeff stepped back out of the way, the groom, resplendent in a pale-blue tuxedo with frilly shirt, came charging after her. "Denise, wait a minute. I did *not* hesitate. I had something in my throat is all."

Swirling her skirts around angrily, Denise glared at the man she'd obviously planned to marry. "Don't lie to me, Norman. When the minister asked, do you take this woman for better or worse and all the rest, you hesitated. For a full minute. Were you thinking about Zelda, Norman?"

"No, honey, I swear to you." The man, sweating profusely, tried to take her hand, but she shook him off. "Zelda and I are through, over, finished. It's you I love, honest."

Flames shot out of Denise's blue eyes. "Then why'd you hesitate? Why didn't you jump right in and say I do, huh? Answer me that, Norman."

Running a hand through his thick black hair, Norman shuffled his feet nervously. "I told you, I had a lump in my throat, honey. I had to swallow, then I answered real fast. Nerves probably. You know what they say, guys are always nervous on their wedding day."

"Brides are supposed to be nervous on their wedding day, not grooms." She narrowed her eyes, studying his face. "No, you're lying. I can always tell 'cause your nose kind of twitches when you lie. Like when you told me you were bowling with the guys and lost track of the time and you were late for our rehearsal dinner. Remember that? You were with her, weren't you?"

"No, I swear, on my mother's grave."

Denise looked shocked, then furious. "Your mother's not dead, Norman."

"Oh, yeah. I meant my father's grave." He swiped at his damp forehead. "You got me so rattled I can't think.

Please, honey, let's go back in and let the minister finish. Everyone's waiting at the restaurant for our reception, I got the plane tickets for our honeymoon and—''

The door opened and a short, dark-haired woman wearing a colorful kaftan in a wild print stepped into the room, a frown on her face. As Jeff and Tish watched in fascination, she walked over to the frazzled couple. "Denise, Norman, I have to have an answer. We have other appointments." With a wave, she indicated Jeff and Tish. "Are you coming back in so we can continue? Surely this is a minor misunderstanding."

Denise, who was a good head taller than the newcomer, squared her pudgy shoulders and shifted her irate gaze to the woman. "Minor? You think it's minor when the man I'm about to marry is thinking of his former girlfriend as he's about to take his vows?"

"Now, honey," Norman began, his voice soft compared to her screeching, "please believe me. I think only of you. I want only you." He dared to take her elbow. "Let's go back in and—"

"Get your hands off me! Go find Zelda. I'm through with you." That said, she turned in a swirl of gauzy skirts and satin train and marched through the front door, slamming it behind her.

Looking stunned, Norman just stared after her.

The petite woman sent Jeff and Tish an apologetic smile, then touched Norman's arm. "I'm sorry things didn't work out. However, I'm afraid we'll still have to charge you since we fulfilled our part of the agreement."

A look of weary acceptance on his face, Norman reached into his pocket and pulled out a folded check. "Here." Eyes downcast, he left the building.

The woman rearranged the folds of her kaftan and turned again to Tish and Jeff. "We apologize. These things hap-

pen, though rarely. We'll be ready for you in a moment."
She quickly disappeared and closed the door.

"Well, that was interesting," Jeff said.

Tish looked puzzled. "Can you imagine, she wouldn't
go through with it because he hesitated? I feel like going
after him to let him know he's better off without a woman
who'd break off a wedding for something so minor."

Jeff shrugged. "Maybe there've been other incidents. It
didn't seem to me that they were exactly star-crossed lovers."

"No, you're right." Looking up at him, she laughed.
"Quite the way to start off our wedding, eh?" And she
giggled.

Joining in, Jeff took her hand. "Years from now, we'll
look back on this and—"

"—and be glad we didn't have some ordinary wedding
where everything was perfect, right?"

"Right." Pulling her to him, Jeff kissed her.

"Ahem." The woman in the kaftan was back, having
entered on little cat feet for neither had heard her.

"You must be our four o'clock," she said sweetly, smiling as if nothing out of the ordinary had taken place. "I'm
Evelyn. Please, follow me."

As she floated through the doorway, filmy skirts flying,
Jeff leaned down to whisper in Tish's ear. "I love you. Just
wanted you to know."

"And I love you," she said, taking his arm. "This is
fun, Jeff, something to tell our grandchildren. We can always have a traditional wedding later, but this, well, it's a
once-in-a-lifetime experience. Let's enjoy it."

He kissed the top of her head, enormously pleased she
was being such a good sport. He'd had a feeling that most
of the Las Vegas wedding chapels were a little quirky.
From what they'd seen so far, they apparently attracted
quirky couples as well.

They followed Evelyn.

The main room was equally flashy with two rows of benches covered in red velvet on each side with an aisle between, then three stairs leading up to an area carpeted in white and surrounded by heavy cardinal-red drapes fringed with tassels. Waiting at the top was a tall man dressed in white from top to bottom, his tuxedo circa 1950 or earlier.

Jeff tried to keep a straight face as Evelyn arranged the two of them on the bottom step, then took her place alongside Tish. A short balding man wearing white pants and a Hawaiian shirt in a print that matched Evelyn's dress stepped out from behind the folds of the drapes and walked over to stand next to Jeff. Holding Tish's hand tightly in his, Jeff knew if he looked at her, he'd lose control and burst into laughter.

The man in white, whose thinning black hair was carefully combed over his narrow head, a white prayer book tightly gripped in one hand, finally spoke. "We welcome you, Tish Buckner and Jeffrey Kirby, to the Chapel of Dreams where you will be united in holy matrimony. I'm Reverend Alexander Kaminski and your witnesses are Evelyn and Tom Doran. Have you other guests coming or shall we begin?"

"No other guests, Reverend," Jeff answered.

"Very well," he said in his slightly nasal tone as he held the prayer book in a death grip and closed his eyes.

Suddenly, the wedding march blared forth from hidden speakers, jolting Jeff and Tish who both looked around, startled. Jeff dared to look at her, his eyes dancing. This would be one to remember all right, he thought.

They waited out the song which seemed interminable, the abrupt silence following it also a shock to the senses. Finally, Reverend Kaminski opened his eyes and his book and raised one hand, beckoning them to come forward.

Jeff and Tish slowly walked up the steps until they were standing in front of the preacher.

"Dearly beloved," he began.

No dearly beloveds here, Jeff thought as the man droned on. He felt a pang of regret at the absence of East and Ally as well as some of their friends. This would be legally binding, but one day, they'd have a real wedding with everyone they cared about as witnesses. And a big joyful reception.

They responded as instructed and spoke their vows. Then it was time for Jeff to bring out the ring. He noticed that despite the untraditional surroundings, Tish's eyes were misty as she gazed into his while he placed the platinum band on the third finger of her left hand. He laced her fingers through his as they both turned back toward Reverend Kaminski who finished the ceremony in short order. Probably had a four-thirty booked, Jeff thought. Or perhaps a four-fifteen. Weddings were a big business in Vegas.

"I now pronounce you man and wife," the Reverend said. "You may kiss your bride."

Turning to his wife, Jeff gathered her close and smiled into her eyes before capturing her mouth in a long, thorough kiss filled with promise. As he let her go, he felt a tapping on his shoulder, looked up and saw the Reverend thrusting out his hand.

"Congratulations," he said, shaking first Jeff's hand, then Tish's. "Please pay Evelyn on the way out." With that, he turned and walked toward the drapes, disappearing within its folds.

So much for ambiance and good wishes, Jeff thought, shaking hands with the two silent witnesses. They followed Evelyn out to the foyer where Jeff handed her a check he'd already made out. "I believe this is the amount you mentioned."

She glanced at the check and nodded. "Yes, thank you."

She handed him the signed marriage license. "Good luck." A quick smile and she hurried off.

Jeff sighed deeply, then checked his watch. "Thirteen minutes. Must be a record."

But Tish wasn't upset. "Hey, get 'em in, get 'em married and get 'em out. That's their motto."

"You're right," he said, slipping his arm about her. "You should have heard Evelyn on the phone. Will you be wanting a cake? That will be *X* number of dollars. Flowers? Music? The long or short ceremony? A limo? A photographer? A reception? Yeah, we can do that, for a price." He shook his head. "Kind of impersonal, when you think about it."

Tish hugged his arm as they stepped out into the waning late afternoon sun. "Not to worry, sweetie. Who needs pomp and circumstance? We're just as married as those who spend thousands on a big wedding and reception."

But Jeff felt as if he'd somehow cheated her. "I know, but I wanted more for you."

She stopped as they reached the waiting limo. "Don't, Jeff. Don't let the way it was done spoil the happiness we should be celebrating right now."

She was right, of course, so he nodded and finally found a smile. "When did you get so wise?"

"When I fell in love with you."

"Mmm, was that ever the right answer." He kissed her, right there on the curb, then helped her into the limo. "We've got this thing rented for two more hours. Want me to tell the driver to drive us around a while or do you want to go back to the suite?"

"Let's go for a drive," Tish answered. "And maybe I could have just one more tiny sip of champagne, Doctor?"

"All right, but just one tiny sip." He slid the window open and instructed the driver, then closed the two of them off in their intimate little world. One sip of champagne and then they leaned back, stretched out their legs and, arms around one another, lazily gazed at the passing scenery.

It was nine o'clock by the time they got back to their hotel. After their limo ride, they decided they were hungry so they wandered through the Venetian's lobby, stopping at each of the restaurants to check them out and peruse the menus posted by the entrance. Finally Jeff told Tish to decide and she said the baby felt like Chinese. So they stopped in the oriental restaurant and each ordered something different so they could sample a variety of dishes.

They ate with chopsticks, neither very adept, but it was fun trying. Then, their hunger appeased, they strolled hand in hand through the noisy, crowded casino. After watching for a while, Jeff urged Tish to try and got her a couple of rolls of silver dollars. To his amusement, she took her time choosing just the right machine, one where Elvis sang a song each time a large or small jackpot was scored. She sat down on the stool while Jeff stood behind her, watching.

To Tish's utter amazement and delight, she hit a jackpot for three hundred dollars after only twenty minutes. Smiling, she watched the hotel employee count the money and hand it to her.

"You're on a roll now, babe. Pick out a new machine."

But Tish shook her head, hiding a yawn behind her hand. "No, I'm going to take my money and fold. Otherwise, I'll just give it all back to them."

"Or double it," Jeff added, ever the optimist.

She took hold of his hand and tugged him toward the elevators. "This mother-to-be is tired."

Of course, that did it since Jeff didn't want her to overdo and jeopardize the baby. He struggled with a yawn as well as he inserted the card key in their door, suddenly aware that he'd worked all last night and had been up all day.

He'd been so revved up arranging the wedding and all, that the excitement had kept him going.

"What do you say we undress and snuggle down?" Tish suggested, already stepping out of her shoes.

"I'm all for that." Jeff shed his jacket, then wandered over to check out the movies offered by the hotel. But the rustle of silk behind him caught his attention. He turned and saw Tish take a floor-length pale-blue gown from her leather bag. The movies forgotten, he moved to her and took her in his arms.

"Why don't you put that on so I can take it off you?" he whispered in her ear, kissing her silken throat. After all, it was their wedding night.

"It's such a lovely gown. Don't you think I should leave it on?" she asked as a shiver skittered up her spine under his knowing touch.

"For a while, maybe."

"I think I'll take a relaxing bubble bath," Tish said.

Jeff let her go, watching her take the gown into the bathroom and close the door. Perhaps Tish was suddenly shy with the thought that this was their wedding night. They'd made love in Arizona under the stars and on a blanket by the stream many times. And a couple of times in his small apartment.

But this was different. This was their wedding night and they were in a lovely hotel in a luxury suite. Although the wedding itself had been offbeat, he was certain that Tish like most women would always remember her wedding night.

He would make it special, for both of them.

Chapter 10

Sometime later, Tish stepped out of the bathroom in a steamy cloud of her favorite scent. Just past the doorway, she stopped, her eyes going wide with wonder.

It was amazing what you could accomplish in a luxury hotel with a little time, a credit card and a concierge with a romantic soul, Jeff thought, smiling at her expression. He let her absorb the changes he'd arranged so quickly and discreetly.

There were candles, nearly a dozen, ranging from tall and slender to chunky and fragrant, on the nightstands, the tables, even the television. The pungent aroma of vanilla wafted through the warm room. Music from the stereo in the sitting area drifted to the upper level, something low and bluesy. The drapes had been opened wide, leaving only the sheers that allowed a full moon to add to the candlelight's magic.

Her eyes shining, Tish turned to Jeff. He'd removed his jacket and tie as well as his shoes. He stood in his stocking feet watching her. "You've been busy," she said, smiling up at him.

She was heart-stoppingly beautiful, he thought, the pale blue of her gown a lovely contrast to her golden skin. Her hair glistened in the candlelight. The silky material clung to her lush curves and ended at her bare feet, her toenails painted a bright pink. She was feminine perfection, Jeff decided, and she was his.

"Just setting the scene," he answered, moving her into the circle of his arms, holding her lightly. Prolonging the pleasure, he let her need build slowly as his fingertips caressed her smooth back.

"It seems as if you've done this a time or two," she whispered as her skin began to tingle beneath his clever hands.

He aligned their bodies more perfectly, more intimately, and watched her eyes go smoky. "Not like this." He drew in a breath and her scent wrapped around him. "Your cologne. I don't know what it's called, but I can't get it off my mind. Like you."

"A chemist friend makes it up for me. He's very talented."

There was that quick flare of jealousy that he was unable to prevent before he tapped it down. "And he is…"

"Out of my life."

He gazed deeply into her eyes. "And all other men you've ever known?" he asked, wanting to know, needing the words.

"What other men? There are no other men in my life. I like to concentrate on one thing at a time. And since meeting you, there's been no one else. Is that what you wanted to hear?"

He drew her closer, where she could feel his rising need. "It is what I wanted to hear. What do you want to hear?"

His hands had moved inside the gown, touching the flesh

of her back, gliding down her rib cage. He felt her breathing go shallow. "You're doing just fine without my coaching."

"I understand that women have fantasies, too, not just men."

"A few. I'd rather hear the truth, how you really see me, not what you think I want to hear or what you believe I fantasize about."

"The truth?" Jeff nuzzled her neck with his mouth and felt her shiver. "Okay, the truth according to Jeffrey Kirby." He drew back as if to check her over. "You're lovely, a very feminine woman, yet you're strong inside. You have the most incredible eyes, so expressive…"

"They're too close together." She was swaying now, moving with him.

"Your hair is…"

"Like I said before, an ordinary, boring brown."

He pulled back and gave her an exaggerated frown. "Hey! You wanted the truth as I see it, didn't you? Don't interrupt and don't contradict." He bent to nibble her ear.

She laughed at his playful reprimand, obviously enjoying this. When his tongue outlined her lips, skimming the surface from corner to corner, then back again, the journey very slow, very seductive, all laughter left her. She didn't move, didn't seem able to as her face registered the shock of sensation ricocheting through her. Her lips trembled where his tongue glided and her hands curled around his forearms.

Jeff noticed her flushed face, saw the stunned passion in her eyes, always new, always glorious. A slow climb up the mountain was always more exhilarating than a frantic rush. He wanted to coax her along until she was edgy and eager. He thought about her beauty, the sweetness of it, the wonder. And he thought about how short, how precious life was—and how fortunate a man he was to have Tish Buckner Kirby here in his arms, his to love all night long, all life long.

Tish touched a shaky hand to his chest as she caught her breath.

"Tell me what you feel," Jeff said, curious.

She took her time finding the right words. "You make me feel more alive than I've felt in...in so long I can't put a time frame on it. I see mysterious green eyes with just a hint of danger in them, or are they just shadowy in the moonlight? Either way, I find that oddly exciting. That you can make me tremble so readily, want so desperately, still surprises me, even though it's been like that from the day I met you."

Suddenly, he pulled her into position and heard her quick gasp. "May I have this dance?" he asked. Both of them shoeless, he led her down the two steps to the carpeted sitting room, the low thrum of a love song whispering from the stereo. His thighs in his suit pants were rubbing against hers wrapped in satin, the gentle friction of their movements causing his blood to heat.

The sexy sigh of a saxophone had her melting in his arms, swaying with him to the dark rhythm, her head on his shoulder. Needing to be closer, Jeff stopped to yank his shirt off over his head, several buttons popping as he tossed it aside. Then he pressed her close to his chest. The soft satin of her gown allowed her breasts to yield against him, and he felt his head spin at the contact. He saw Tish close her eyes and felt the candlelight flicker and warm their skin as he moved slowly around the small room. Drugged in pleasure, he drew out the moment.

"You dance very well," he whispered into her ear. He slid his hands along her spine, then settled at her waist as his lips sampled her neck. She didn't answer, just made a low sound in her throat and reached up to thrust her hands into his hair.

Deeply aroused, Jeff welcomed the move when Tish's mouth sought his, when her tongue slipped between his parted lips. She made a muffled sound as his hands bunched into the satin material at her waist, gathering it up higher and higher. In moments, he had most of it clustered up to where he could cup her soft flesh in both hands and press her intimately against the hard evidence of his desire.

His touch was unhurried, a lazy seduction that held her prisoner nonetheless. He felt her press closer to the mouth that caressed her own, enjoying the magic of her body against his. Her hands ran along his bare shoulders and caressed the muscles of his arms, exploring his strength. Dreamily, she let him lead her.

Moonlight turned her skin creamy. He found her impossibly soft, unbearably sweet-tasting as his mouth moved to kiss the tender spot behind her ear. He felt her knees begin to buckle as she shuddered briefly.

Stepping back, Jeff bent to pick her up and carried her up the stairs. Carefully he laid her down on the king-size bed that had been turned down for them. Tish stared up at him as his dark-green eyes devoured her. Seemingly uncomfortable under such close scrutiny, she reached a hand to his belt buckle.

''Can I help you with this?''

He needed a little more time. ''In a moment.'' He trailed his fingertips along the underside of her satin-covered breasts and saw the peaks harden at his touch. Needing to be flesh to flesh with her, he whipped the gown from her in one quick movement and set it aside, then lowered himself to her. He cupped both breasts in hands that weren't quite steady, then met her eyes watching him in the gentle light of the candles. ''Do you know how many nights I've lain awake thinking of you, wanting you like this? Just you and me locked away in a quiet room somewhere, knowing that you're mine for all time?''

"No, tell me," she whispered, her voice husky.

His fingers molded her swelling flesh. "Forever, I think." His head dipped down, his tongue gliding over her breasts until she gasped out loud at sensations he knew were pulling at her.

Expertly, Jeff moved down her, trailing kisses over her still-flat stomach. Then he paused, his big hand caressing her belly, suddenly filled with wonder. Inside there was his child, *their* child, who would be born of their love. A tiny little life already growing. The miracle of it overwhelmed him as he raised dazed eyes to hers, unable to put what he felt into words.

Tish placed her hand atop his. "I know," she whispered softly.

He moved up to kiss her, putting his heart in it, surprised and pleased that she knew exactly how he felt. He lingered, then slowly began demanding a response from her that she was finally helpless to withhold. In moments, he took her from dreamy to desperate, his mouth devouring, his fingers seeking. She could no longer lie still beneath him, her fitful body arching as he ran his hands up the inside of her thighs.

Restless needs within Jeff fought for dominance. The need to make her wild, to make her want as much as he did, to make her his in more than a shared name consumed him. Desire was a thunderous sound in his ears, the feel of her skin teasing his senses. He slipped his fingers inside her and felt her arch as she dug her nails into his shoulders.

A rush of heat and she crested quickly, then fought for breath only to find he was driving her up again. Suddenly, a stunned release had her moaning his name. Finally, looking dazed, her eyes opened to find him watching her.

"You're mine, Tish. Say it," he said, his voice ragged.

"There's never been a question," she answered breathlessly. "I'm yours, Jeff."

Quickly, he removed the rest of his clothes, then came

back to her. As she fought to slow her breathing, he kissed her eyes closed. She was glowing, yet reaching for him again, but he evaded her hands as his mouth moved hungrily to her breasts once more. Restlessly, she shifted beneath him, her hands clutching his shoulders as he wandered lower.

She whispered his name and he felt the sound rocket through him. Her hands on him were no longer timid, no longer patient as they sought to give, to touch, to learn him more thoroughly as he was learning her. Her desire fueled him further, taking him to the swift edge of reason as he returned to crush her mouth with his.

Overwhelmed by her responsiveness, he softened the kiss, shifting to tenderness. He'd known from the start that there was passion in her, kept carefully in check, but he hadn't dreamed how much. Nor had he thought how deeply it would touch him. She had allowed him to see her vulnerability and he would do no less. Drawing back from her slightly, he let her restive hands find him, then guide him inside her.

He wanted to watch her climb, watch her soar, his own completion suspended by the joy of her response. Her eyes were open and on his, her skin damp with passion, her mouth a breath away from his. There was an aching pleasure on her face as she reached for the stars. And then he gave them to her....

The door to the doctor's lounge in Metropolitan General Hospital opened and two young men in scrubs walked in, talking in low, serious tones. They glanced at Jeff, then moved to the far corner where they continued their conversation.

Reluctantly, Jeff stood and stretched, hating to let his thoughts of happier times—of their wedding night—drift away. If only the wonder of that night could have stayed with them. But if there was one thing he'd learned a long time ago it was that nothing stays the same.

Grabbing his leather bag, Jeff went into the shower room to clean up. It was empty this early in the morning and he was grateful. He wasn't very good company right now. He set the bag on the floor and took out his shaving kit. Examining his face in the mirror, Jeff frowned.

The man staring back at him looked exhausted, albeit with good reason. It was hard to remember how many hours ago he'd been in a bed where he could stretch out his long legs and sleep until he woke up. Plugging in his razor, he knew it might be quite some time before that would happen again.

Pausing, he drew a hand over his shadowed cheeks and chin. Maybe he should grow a beard. A beard might disguise that suddenly gaunt look he had since this whole ordeal began. But it wouldn't erase the dark smudges beneath his eyes or remove the worry from his expression.

He flipped on the razor and began shaving.

When he finished, he quickly undressed and turned on the water in the farthest of two stalls. He started out with the temperature as hot as he could stand, letting the soothing spray ease his cramped muscles. Next he lathered up and vigorously rubbed his skin with the soapy washcloth. Ducking his head under, he shampooed his hair. Finally he rinsed off and gradually turned the water to cool, then cold. Awake for sure now, he stepped out and grabbed a towel off the rack.

A few minutes later, he was dressed in black slacks and a black cotton shirt. Quickly, he brushed his teeth, combed his hair, packed his things in his bag and zipped it closed. Just as he was leaving, a doctor shuffled in, dark circles under his eyes, his scrubs splattered with blood. Jeff nodded to him and left the shower room.

The lounge was once more empty and he debated about

pouring himself a cup of coffee from the ever present pot on the corner table. On closer examination, he decided the contents looked like sludge. East should be arriving soon. He'd take him down to the cafeteria and they'd have breakfast. Not that he was especially hungry, Jeff thought as he walked out into the hall. But he knew he had to keep up his strength.

He headed back to ICU to check on Tish and to wait for East.

An hour later, as Jeff sat beside his wife's hospital bed quietly talking to her, the door to her cubicle slid open and East stood there, filling the doorway. Jeff stood, blinking back a sudden rush of emotion, and walked over to hug his father. He felt East grip him hard, his big hands patting his back. Jeff held on, absorbing East's boundless strength for several moments, then finally eased back.

East held him at arm's length, his dark eyes sweeping over his son's face, missing nothing, studying intently. "How are you holding up, son?"

Jeff was glad he'd gotten cleaned up. Outwardly he looked a lot better than he had a couple of hours ago. But he knew he wasn't fooling East. "I'm fine." He stepped back, moving to Tish's side, wanting to talk about her, but the words clogged in his throat.

East followed him over, looking down at Tish for a long time. Finally, he squeezed Jeff's shoulder. "I know how hard it is to wait and worry, Jeff. I—"

The cubicle door sliding open had both men turning around. Dr. Edmund O'Neill stood in the doorway. "Mr. Kirby, I'm Dr. O'Neill. You paged me?"

"Yes, Doctor." East went over and shook hands as all three of them left the cubicle, closing the door. "Thank you for seeing me. I know how busy you are." They followed O'Neill to an alcove near the ICU entrance. "What's my daughter-in-law's updated prognosis?"

O'Neill thrust both hands into the pockets of his lab coat. "I wish I could give you some very hopeful news, but basically, not much has changed. Comas are difficult to predict. As I told Dr. Kirby here," he said, drawing Jeff into the conversation, "she could come out of it within the hour or tomorrow or next week. We simply can't predict."

"Her injuries are healing?" East asked.

"Yes, absolutely. We have every reason to believe that her body will recover with no permanent damage. The concussion, however, was severe. According to our most recent findings, the swelling of the brain is receding, but slowly. Anything further is impossible to project at this time."

East's tall, powerful body seemed to dominate the area as the doctor looked up at him. "And there's no way to tell if she'll be able to speak when she wakes up, or what she'll remember?"

O'Neill shook his head. "I've had patients in a coma for weeks suddenly awaken and begin talking as if nothing had happened. Others have had trouble remembering events, especially the one that caused their injury, but were otherwise fine. A few needed speech therapy, but that's not the norm. If there is a norm in these cases." He saw the disappointment on their faces and pulled in a frustrated breath. "I understand how you feel and I wish I could be more encouraging. But I wouldn't want to give you false hope."

"No, of course not." East held out his hand. "Thank you, Doctor. And thanks for being so good to my son."

O'Neill glanced at Jeff as he shook hands with East. "Professional courtesy. I told him to stay with her as long as he likes." He checked his watch. "Now, if you'll excuse me…"

"Certainly. Thanks, again." East watched the doctor rush off, then turned to his son. "Have you eaten? I'm starved. What do you say we go grab some breakfast?'' It was not yet 8:00 a.m., but it had been a long flight from California.

''Right away.'' Jeff walked to the circular desk and told Thelma where he was going, that he had his cell phone with him and she could call him if there was the slightest change. She agreed and he went back to his father. ''We can go downstairs to the cafeteria or we can leave the hospital and find a place. What time are you meeting with the bomb squad?''

''Not till noon.'' East said. ''Let's go out. The cab driver on the way in from the airport told me about an eatery near the hospital called Johnny's Place. Said it had terrific food.''

''Fine with me,'' Jeff answered, moving to the elevators.

Faux red leather booths lined both sides of the storefront restaurant with a half dozen tables down the center and a counter near the back. Broadway caricatures were drawn on the beige walls and the floor was black-and-white checkered-tile squares. The smell of coffee and bacon frying permeated the smoky air as Jeff and East walked in.

A waitress with a limp wearing a pink nylon uniform and a badge that read Elaine pinned to her left shoulder met them at the door and asked if they wanted smoking or nonsmoking. Jeff gazed at the smoke curling all the way up to the ceiling and couldn't resist asking her where the nonsmoking section was. She pointed to two occupied tables way in the back by the kitchen near the back door, which stood open. Hiding a smile behind his fist, he indicated an empty booth on the left and told her that would do. She marched over in her Minnie Mouse tennis shoes and plopped two plastic-coated menus on the table before hurrying off to answer the ding of a bell at the short-order window.

Sliding in, East smiled. "I'm starved."

"I bet." Jeff opened the menu, realizing he was feeling a little hungry. "So, what did the cab driver recommend?"

"The blue plate special, of course." East scanned the menu and found the item. "No wonder. One English muffin, two eggs, three pancakes, four bacon strips, and the bottomless cup of coffee." He glanced up. "How's that sound?"

"Like a breakfast for a lumberjack, but I'm game."

Elaine carried a groaning tray of food to the next booth, then stopped at theirs. "What'll it be?"

"Two blue plate specials," Jeff told her.

"Good choice." She graced him with a toothy smile and rushed off.

East leaned forward, his elbows on the Formica table. "Did you check into a hotel nearby?"

Jeff shook his head. "Not yet. O'Neill told me I could use the doctor's lounge to shower and change, which is what I've been doing. I catch a catnap in the chair." He sighed and all the discouragement he felt came huffing out. "See, I thought she'd wake up any minute, that I wouldn't need a room. I know it's crazy, but I feel if I just stay there by her side, she'll hear me talking to her and fight to come back."

"That's not crazy. I'm sure she *can* hear you and that she's struggling to come back. But until the swelling goes down, she won't surface." He placed a hand on Jeff's as it rested on the table. "But you need to be rested and ready and in good shape when she comes to."

Jeff nodded. "Yeah, I know. It's just that, each time I leave her, I start to panic. Like what if she needs me and I'm not there?"

East leaned back. "Believe me, I know. When you were kidnapped, I felt the same. I didn't leave the house, unreasonably afraid I'd miss the call telling me where you were.

I even showered with the door open so I could hear the phone. And when I did catch a little sleep, I dreamed of you, of the past.''

''Yeah, it's like that with me, too. I've been thinking back to when Tish and I first met. I talk to her about that time, how I felt then and now. And sometimes I fall asleep next to her bed and I dream about those early days.'' He scrubbed a hand over his face. ''I just want this to be over, to have her back with me.''

Elaine brought their coffee, set down a dish of little creamers and scooted off. Across from them, an elderly man was meticulously setting out his pills for the day and swallowing them down with water. Behind Jeff, a young couple were discussing a trip they were about to take, making plans to take the kids to Disney World. In a booth across the room, four tough-looking guys were pouring syrup on mountains of pancakes and laughing loudly.

A normal morning in a typical New York restaurant, Jeff thought as he looked around. Funny how everyday things he usually never noticed suddenly looked so good to him, so normal.

Only there was nothing normal about his life right now. He was in limbo, waiting, waiting.

Noticing his son's silent restlessness, East spoke. ''I hope you haven't given up hope, Jeff. Sometimes, hope is all we have to cling to. I never once thought for a moment that I wouldn't find you, that I wouldn't get you back well and whole.'' He paused. ''You're not alone when you're sitting by her bedside, Jeff. Everyone you know, Ally and me, all the people Tish knows, they're all there, hoping and praying with you.''

Eyes downcast, Jeff nodded. ''I know, Dad. I'm trying.''

''The only time we're truly forced to stand by and watch and wait is when someone we love is in jeopardy. It's out of our hands and nothing we do can change the outcome. Except we can pray.''

''Oh, I've been doing a lot of that,'' Jeff said, sitting back. ''I've reintroduced myself to the Man Upstairs and made every promise possible to Him if only He'll bring her back to me.''

East nodded, smiling. ''Bargaining with God. Yeah, I'm familiar with that.''

Just then, Elaine hurried over and placed a huge platter of food in front of both of them, topped off their coffee and left them alone.

Jeff inhaled the delicious aromas and dug in. Some fifteen minutes later, as he pushed his empty plate aside, he grinned. ''I sure didn't think I'd eat all that, but I did.''

East also had eaten every morsel. ''You needed the fuel. It takes a lot of energy to stand by.'' He signaled for the check, paid the bill and they left, stepping out into the bright glare of morning sunshine.

A street-cleaner truck came lumbering by, its wet brushes washing the gutters. A city bus wheezed to a stop where half a dozen passengers squeezed aboard. A New York cab wove in and out of traffic in a yellow blur. And a woman pushing twins in a double stroller walked by them, groceries bundled in the rear basket.

The city was hustling and bustling as always. Life went on, Jeff thought as East stepped off the curb to hail a cab, even while someone in intensive care struggled to rejoin the living. His stomach full, he felt better than before. And seeing East, aware of his solid support, had helped enormously.

As they stood at the hospital entrance, Jeff told him so.

''I feel better, too,'' East told him. ''She's got a fighting chance, Jeff. You go back in there and tell her again that you're right there, waiting for her.''

''I will, Dad, and thanks.'' Jeff hugged him fiercely one

last time, then watched him climb back into the cab and drive off. His steps lighter than when he left, he hurried back inside to ICU.

He'd been talking to her for over an hour, telling Tish about East's visit, all the good wishes of everyone they knew. Finally, tiring, he leaned back in the chair alongside her bed and sighed.

"I was thinking earlier about our wedding, that crazy day, and about the wonderful night. Remember, Tish?" He stared at her face, so serene even in this unnatural sleep. "We had quite a few lovely nights afterward when we moved into that apartment in Los Angeles near the hospital, right? The place was small, but we both agreed we wouldn't get a bigger one until the baby was born."

Jeff felt a smile form as he recalled the early days of their marriage. "I worked such long hours that I was bone tired most of the time. But just the thought of having you to come home to would make me forget my fatigue. And you were so wonderful. You put in for a leave of absence until after the baby was born. I know you said that when the baby was old enough to leave with a sitter, you'd return to SPEAR in some sort of office job. But I secretly hoped you'd be too happy staying home with the baby and me and not want to go back to work. At least not until our child was in school.

"I wouldn't have mentioned it to you because I'd hate to hold you back. But you know how I grew up, never a parent around to meet any of even my most basic needs. I wanted our child to have more, to have it all. I would, of course, be gone a lot at first, but later, I could arrange my hours so I'd spend more time with both of you. And I didn't want to miss all those great firsts, like first word, first step."

Slowly, his face sobered as he sat thinking, remembering. "We were happy, weren't we, Tish? Or was I living in a dream world? Was I so engrossed in my work and so in love with you that I didn't notice that you missed your friends in SPEAR, missed being in the field? Lord, I hope not.

"You *seemed* to be happy. We laughed a lot, like the time you made that stew dish and put in some kind of seasoning and the peas turned black? And the time you went to the laundromat and didn't notice that someone had left a bright-green sock in the washer and the whole load of whites came out a pale green? I didn't mind wearing green underwear. You were so upset and I remember I just laughed and tackled you onto the bed. We wound up making love, the green-tinted clothes forgotten."

Bracing his elbows on the arms of the chair, Jeff steepled his fingers and stared into middle distance. "When did it all begin to fall apart, Tish? Did it start way back and I didn't notice? Because of your upbringing, with servants and all, you didn't know how to boil water or clean a house or wash clothes. Yet we laughed at the few mistakes, like I said. I helped as much as I could and you learned. Pretty soon, you were making dinners that I used to fantasize about all the way home.

"There was Swiss steak and fried chicken to die for and this crab dish baked in the oven. And you did it on a pretty small budget, because we agreed I wouldn't tap into my trust fund unless we needed to buy something big. And, of course, you wouldn't take a penny of money from your father, which was fine with me. But we got by.

"We hardly ever quarreled. I'd get upset about small things, but I couldn't stay angry with you. I tried so hard not to disappoint you, to make you glad you'd married me. I did pretty well, except maybe for that one time, the day when you arranged for a surprise outing. I hadn't had a day off in ages and you wanted the day to be special. Only it didn't quite work out, remember?"

Los Angeles, early December

"Wake up, sleepyhead." Playfully, Tish pulled off the covers. "You've been sleeping for ten straight hours." She sat down on the bed, leaning forward to stroke his morning beard. "If I leave you here much longer, you'll wind up with bedsores."

"Mmm," Jeff murmured, trying to rouse himself. "Then you can play nurse."

"Come on, lazybones." She stood up. "I've got breakfast almost ready. You have time for a quick shower."

Jeff yawned expansively, trying to remember what plans if any they'd made the night before. He'd been working so many shifts that the few hours he had off were a hazy blur. "Why are you rushing me? Are we going somewhere?"

"You bet we are. It's a surprise."

Slowly, he sat up, his feet hitting the floor as he ran a hand through his hair. "A surprise, eh?" Truth be known, he'd love to spend the rest of his day off right here in this bed. It seemed he never caught up on his sleep. However, it wasn't that often they could spend time together and it was good to see Tish excited.

He gave her a smile. "Okay, boss. I'll be there in ten." He paddled into the bathroom.

It was more like fifteen minutes later that he made it into the kitchen, following his nose to the wonderful aroma of bacon. "I thought these cooking smells made you sick, babe?" he commented as he sat down at the table.

Tish carried over a plateful of bacon, eggs and toast and set it down in front of him before going back for her own. "It's funny. Some days the smell of something as mild as chicken soup makes me queasy and other times I'm just fine." She poured coffee for Jeff. "But coffee I can't manage at all."

He patted her still-flat belly as she stood alongside him.

"Looks like junior's going to dictate your menu for a while yet."

"That's all right," Tish answered, sitting down. "She'll be worth it, I'm sure." She smiled at Jeff across the table.

This was one of their running jokes. "*He'll* be worth it, you mean."

"We'll just see." Tish glanced up at the clock on the wall alongside the phone, then began eating.

"Are we on a time schedule?" Jeff asked, digging in.

"No, not really. I'm just anxious to get going."

And they did, stacking the dishes and grabbing their jackets. At the car, Tish held out her hand. "I have to drive. It wouldn't be a surprise if I told you which way to go."

Going along with her, he handed over the keys and got into the passenger seat. "Do I have to close my eyes?" he asked as she started the car.

"It wouldn't hurt. Otherwise, you'll be trying to guess and you'll distract me." L.A. traffic was still so confusing.

"Okay." Leaning back, he closed his eyes.

They'd been riding about ten minutes when Jeff's beeper went off. As he straightened to check the number, he heard Tish groan.

"Oh, no! I forgot about the beeper."

Jeff checked the number and recognized it immediately.

Slowing, Tish looked both annoyed and frustrated. "They can't leave you alone, not even for a day. We got away from the phone, but they found you anyhow." She pulled over to the curb. "I suppose you have to go to the hospital."

Jeff turned to face her. "Honey, I'm a doctor. You know I can't be completely out of touch."

Tish sighed. "I know. I just wanted us to have a nice day, just one day, away from phones and hospitals."

"We may be able to have that. It's not the hospital beeping me." Looking around, he spotted a phone booth up ahead. "Pull up over there, will you?"

Frowning, Tish did as he asked. "If it's not the hospital, then who's beeping you?"

"I'll explain in a minute," Jeff said, jumping out of the car and hurrying to the phone booth.

Tish watched him through the window, hoping it was just some little something he could straighten out on the phone. It wouldn't have been East calling or Jeff would have told her. Impatiently, she drummed her fingers on the steering wheel until at last, he came jogging back. There was a worried expression on his face as he opened the driver's door.

"Honey, I hate to spoil your surprise, but I've got to go see someone. I hope it won't take long. Scoot over so I can drive."

Easing herself over the divider, Tish didn't bother to hide her disappointment. "But you said the call wasn't from the hospital."

"It wasn't." Quickly, Jeff checked the traffic then executed a neat U-turn before stepping heavily on the gas. "There's this kid, only fifteen years old. Danny. He came into the ER one night when I was working there. His face was all beat up, a gash in his leg and he had a broken rib. He just hobbled in, bleeding, doubled over in pain. No money, no insurance, no one with him. I fixed him up and X rays showed several old healed fractures. I asked him what happened but he was reluctant to talk. After a while, I got him to trust me enough to tell me his stepfather beat him regularly and his mother was a drunk so he'd taken off last year, mostly living on the streets since, getting by on odd jobs."

"Oh, that's terrible." Her disappointment momentarily forgotten, Tish was all sympathy.

"Yeah, it is, and boy, could I relate. So I gave him a

few bucks and a hot meal, then got him into a homeless shelter that night.'' Jeff sighed wearily. ''The next morning when I got to work, Danny was waiting for me, all bruised up again. Some older guy at the shelter had robbed him and beat on him because he thought he was holding out on him, that he'd hidden more money.''

''What a terrible life.'' She looked at her husband's profile, the way his jaw tightened. ''Did you go through some of that?''

''Oh, yeah. Street people, especially the kids, are always scared. They're prey to everyone and everything—older homeless guys, the police, the weather, or dogs on the loose. There is no one to help them if they get sick or comfort them if they are lonely and afraid.'' He paused. ''Anyhow, I talked to this woman I knew from a while back who took in teenagers, tried to give them another start. She agreed to take Danny in. I thought he was finally on the right track, but I just talked to her. Danny took off a couple of days ago and now this grocer called her, said he caught Danny stealing and he was going to call the cops if she didn't go see him.''

''So instead, you're going to go see him, right?''

''Honey,'' he glanced over at her, placing his hand over hers, ''I have to. I hope you understand. I promise not to take too long, but—''

''But you just can't abandon Danny like almost everyone in his life has abandoned him. Of course, I understand.''

Jeff smiled and squeezed her hand. ''I'll make it up to you, I swear.''

He had to go. Tish understood because he was who he was and couldn't stand to ignore anyone in need. There'd be other days they'd share. ''Don't worry, Jeff. The surprise can wait.''

She watched as he turned into a neighborhood that had seen better days. There was a shabby apartment building, a pawn shop on the corner, a dry cleaners with a ripped awning hanging precariously from a rod, and a mom-and-pop grocery with fruits and vegetables displayed in crates outside. Iron gates were shoved aside during business hours, but Tish was certain that at night, this block looked like a prison.

It was hard not to feel guilty for having grown up far differently. It hadn't been easy because of her father, but at least she hadn't had to steal to eat or run away from beatings.

"Maybe there's something I can do for Danny," she suggested, though she hadn't a clue what that might be. "I want to help you."

"You're helping me by being so understanding," Jeff said as he parked in front of the grocer's. "Why don't you wait here until I check things out?" He left the car, looking around.

A woman pushing a baby carriage with a crying infant somewhere under a pile of groceries passed by, not even glancing up. Two young men huddled together smoking in the doorway of the pawn shop. A few cars drove by, most hurrying, wanting out of this rundown section. Otherwise, it was quiet.

Stepping toward the open doorway of the market, Jeff saw Danny sitting near the front with his left wrist handcuffed to the arm of a wooden chair. A pudgy balding grocer wearing a stained apron tied around his ample middle stood waiting, his small, mean eyes watchful.

Jeff walked over to Danny, saw the anger and humiliation in his dark eyes. And something else. Fear. "Are you all right?" he asked the boy.

Danny nodded toward the grocer. "He said he was going to call the cops in another ten minutes." He lowered his voice, trying to keep out the trembling. "They'll put me in the system, Jeff. I—"

Jeff placed a hand on his shoulder. "Easy." He turned toward the grocer. "You do this a lot, handcuff kids?"

The eyes narrowed. "So what? I got a right to protect my property. That kid stole from me."

Jeff's voice was low, controlled. "What did he steal?"

"Two apples. But how do I know how many other times he stole? These kids around here, filth is what they are. They need to be locked up. Honest, hardworking people shouldn't have to deal with them."

Jeff glanced over his shoulder at the sign on the apples, then tossed a five-dollar bill at the man. "This is for the apples. Now unlock him."

"No, no. That's not enough. I lose business while I sit here and guard this thief. I'm going to call the cops. They know what to do with thieves."

Jeff had known men like this grocer, those without compassion. Some used to try to sell him their rotted fruit at the end of a day. Stepping closer, so close he could smell the man's stinking breath, he leaned down. "You ever been hungry, Pops? I mean so hungry your stomach almost caves in and you can't remember the last time you ate? This boy knows that feeling and so do I." Deliberately he let his eyes roam to the man's fat belly and back up to his eyes, looking a little worried now. "No, I don't suppose you ever have."

Over his shoulder, Jeff glanced at the handcuffs on Danny. "Where'd you get those?"

"None—none of your business. I got 'em, that's all."

Turning back, Jeff examined the cuffs, then turned back to the grocer. "Police issue. I don't suppose you're a cop. How'd you get those, Pops?"

"I—I found 'em. You can't prove no different."

"Oh, sure. Police handcuffs, with the key and all, and you just found them. If you did, it was your duty as a citizen to turn them in. And by the way, it's against the

law for a civilian to handcuff someone.'' Jeff drew in a
breath and straightened, nodding to the phone on the wall.
''So, you still want to call the cops?''

The grocer studied Jeff's eyes, then turned away. ''All
right, just get him out of here.'' He handed the key over.

Jeff unlocked Danny's wrist. ''I'll just take these and
give them to the nearest cop so you don't get tempted to
break the law again.''

Needing to have the last word, to save face, the grocer
waved a fist at Danny. ''I ever see you around here again,
I call the cops for sure.''

Sliding his arm around Danny's slim shoulders, Jeff led
him over to the car, opened the back door and waited until
Danny slipped in, then got behind the wheel. ''Danny, this
is my wife, Tish. Honey, this is the boy I've been telling
you about.''

Tish turned and smiled at Danny who was looking
clearly uncomfortable. ''Hello, Danny.''

Not meeting her eyes, he mumbled a ''H'lo.''

Jeff drove away from the market where the grocer stood
glaring at them. ''He didn't hit you, did he?''

''Nah. I can handle guys like him.''

''I'm sure you can.'' Jeff let that hang in the air a few
minutes, until it sunk in to Danny that he hadn't handled
anyone.

''Jeff,'' the kid began, ''I'm sorry. I let you down. But
that lady, she has so many kids in that tiny house. We're
sleeping on the floor, in chairs. This one kid kept coughing
in my face all night, another was throwing up.''

''It's okay. But stealing's not the answer, either.''

They were in a much better neighborhood now and Jeff
spotted a restaurant up ahead. Stopping there, he and Tish
took Danny inside and fed him. The boy could really eat,
but then, he probably hadn't had a decent meal in days,
Jeff knew. He noticed that Tish, much to her credit, chatted

with Danny, not by asking probing questions, but just talking. She drew the boy out and they both could see the longing in his eyes for someone to just listen, to care about what he thought.

Jeff finished his coffee and came to a decision. He wanted to help the boy, but it would be up to Danny. "Listen, Danny, yesterday I was talking to our caretaker, the woman who looks after our apartment building. Her husband died last year and her son's away at college. She needs help running things. You know, yard work around the place, keeping the swimming pool up, some minor repairs and occasional paint touch-ups. She told me she was going to run an ad for someone. Does that sound like something you'd be interested in doing?

"Before you answer, understand that she couldn't pay much, but if she meets you and likes you, she'd let you stay in her spare room. Maria's a great little lady, but she's got arthritis and can't keep the place up anymore. I'd help you out when I can, but you have to enroll in school, keep good attendance, try. You're probably behind, but you can catch up. I did."

Danny was obviously remembering the talk they'd had where Jeff had told him his story of living on the streets and how he'd had to work really hard to overcome his past. But it was possible. The boy looked skeptical. "You'd do that for me? Why?"

"Because someone did it for me once. The thing about good deeds is that usually they multiply. Kind of neat, eh? I see potential in you, Danny. When you get through school and then college… No! Don't look like that. I said I'd help you and college certainly is a very real possibility. But you have to do your part. No more running, no stealing. If you have a problem, you come to me." Jeff turned to Tish, a question in his eyes. She nodded and he took her hand. "Both my wife and I will help you. What do you say?"

Jeff had never seen Danny smile, but he was smiling now even though his eyes were suspiciously bright. "I can't believe you're giving me this chance, but yes, I say yes. I won't let you down, Doctor."

"I know you won't."

Later, after they'd introduced Danny to Maria and she started fussing over him, settling him in, Jeff checked his watch and saw that it was already three in the afternoon. "Well, honey," he said to Tish, "I guess it's too late for your surprise."

"Yes, but I'm so proud of you, Jeff. You're making a real difference in that boy's life."

"We both are. Mind telling me what I missed?"

She shrugged and moved into his arms. "Nothing much. Just a trip to Disneyland. We'll get there one day."

"But we never did get to Disneyland yet, did we, honey? Never mind. You just get well and I'll take you there, I promise." He held Tish's hand and planted a tender kiss on her forehead.

"I think that was the only time I disappointed you for a whole day. Of course, there were other small disappointments, like when I had one emergency after another at the hospital and you'd worked so hard to make a special dinner that dried up by the time I finally made it home. Or even worse, I guess, when I got home too tired to eat or talk or do most anything, except to drop into bed for eight hours or so, then get up and start the routine all over again. I wasn't home much, but I kept telling you this wouldn't last, that it wouldn't be forever. I don't know if you believed me or not."

He ran a hand over his head, upset by his own thoughts, his memories. "I left you alone too much, didn't I? And it seemed that everyone in the building worked. You had no one to talk to, no friend nearby. Then there was all the morning sickness. It was especially hard on you because you'd always been so healthy. And here you were, throwing up, unable to eat, all alone.'' He sat up, angry at himself. ''Damn! I'm a doctor. I should have seen the signs of trouble ahead.'' He leaned forward, dropping his head in his hands. ''But, God help me, I didn't. I let you down, Tish.''

For several long minutes, he sat that way, eyes closed, beating himself up mentally for past mistakes. He knew better, knew you couldn't change the past. Yet he wallowed in his guilt, wishing with all his might he could turn back the clock.

Finally, with a heartfelt sigh, he sat up and took Tish's hand in his. ''I hope you forgive me for all that. I could blame it on being young, on simply wanting to get that period of my life over and done with so I could get to the good part. I know now that you can't do that, that we should savor each and every day because we never know how many we have left. I should have known that after the ordeal in Idaho, but I guess I forgot.'' Gently he kissed her hand. ''Forgive me, sweetheart, please?

''I was lonely, too. Your morning sickness and my fatigue drove a wedge between us. When I had a rare day off, you were so sick you spent it in bed. When you felt good and wanted to go out, I had to work. Man, if ever there was a catch-22, that was us.

''But, honey, you have to know, through it all, I loved you. Even on the rough days, all I wanted was to be with you. When I was away, I counted the hours until I could hurry home and hold you. One good thing we always had between us was that overwhelming attraction. No matter how tired either of us was, just a touch, a look, and we were ready to climb in bed and make love. I believe it's what held us together all those difficult weeks. And I believe you loved me through all that time, too.''

''Then the worst thing imaginable happened.'' Looking

at his wife, Jeff's vision suddenly went blurry, the tears hitting him unexpectedly. "If I live to a hundred, I'll never forget one moment of that terrible morning when I came home after being on duty eighteen hours. It was the second shift like that I'd pulled in as many days. I don't know how I drove home, tired as I was.

"The moment I opened our apartment door, I knew something was terribly wrong. It was so quiet. You usually had the radio or TV on. You said it didn't seem so lonely with noise in the apartment. I called out your name, but you didn't answer. Then I walked into the kitchen and I nearly lost it.

"You were lying there on the floor, so still, unconscious, a pool of blood next to you. I bent down and felt for your pulse and, thank God, it was thready but beating. Then I saw a heavy clot and I knew.

"Our baby was lost."

Chapter 11

Swiping at his eyes, Jeff leaned back in the chair, reliving the horror of that dreadful morning when Tish had miscarried. He felt as if he were right there, in that small apartment in L.A., experiencing it all over again….

His heart thudding, Jeff swallowed hard and rushed to the wall phone. It was off the hook, dangling by its cord. Obviously, she'd been about to call for help before she passed out, probably from the sudden loss of blood, the shock. He dialed 911 and they answered almost immediately. "I need an ambulance, quick. My wife, she's miscarrying. She's on the floor in a pool of blood and…and please tell the ambulance to hurry." He recited their address. "Tell them third floor, apartment 311." He listened to the operator who made him repeat the address. "Yes, yes, of course, I'm going to stay right here with her." He hung up.

Moving to Tish, he sat down and cradled her upper body

in his arms, unwilling to pick her up because she might bleed even more. "Oh, God, Tish, I'm so sorry. So sorry I wasn't here." He kissed her hair, felt her damp cheeks, so very pale. "What happened, honey? Was it just spontaneous?"

Had she just fainted? Had she hurt herself in the fall, even though he couldn't see any injuries? From his training, he knew that sometimes without provocation, these things happened. But it shouldn't have happened to them.

She'd been so happy lately, the morning sickness pretty much gone now that she was in her fifth month. She'd taken a sewing course afternoons at the local college and he'd bought her a portable sewing machine. She'd started small, making receiving blankets, tiny washcloths, hooded towels. Just yesterday, they'd talked about looking for a bigger place soon, one with a spare bedroom they could turn into a nursery. Tish was excited about her plans to decorate it, make the curtains, paint cute animals on the walls.

Rocking with her in his arms, Jeff felt his heart break. Why did this have to happen now?

He heard the heavy footsteps in the hallway moments before the two Emergency Medical Service men rolling the gurney came in through the door he'd left unlocked. "In here," he called out, his voice trembling.

"Okay, buddy," the taller one said, "we'll take it from here."

Jeff didn't want to let Tish go, but he knew he had to. Gently, he eased out from her and let the men check her vitals. "Be careful, okay?"

"Sure thing." The shorter man was struggling to make room for the gurney in the small kitchen. "Do you mind stepping into the next room, sir? We need to hook her up to an IV."

Feeling dazed, Jeff backed into the living room, but stayed in the doorway, watching. When they picked Tish up and eased her onto the gurney, she moaned and he winced. "Watch it, eh? Be careful with her."

They ignored him, hooked her up and strapped her on before maneuvering the gurney through the apartment and out into the hallway.

Grabbing his keys, Jeff followed them. He waited until they had Tish well anchored in the ambulance, then hurried to his car. He followed them to the hospital, quickly parked and dashed into ER where he ran into a fellow resident, Nigel Frost who was from England.

"Nigel, they're bringing my wife in," he said, grabbing the man's sleeve. "Miscarriage. She's lost a lot of blood." The EMS men were rolling her in through the double doors.

"I'll take her, Jeff," Nigel told him. "Go sit down."

"I want to go in with you," Jeff said, trailing after the gurney the men were pushing down the hallway with Nigel walking alongside, listening to the medics rattle off her vitals. As they entered trauma room 4, Nigel stopped by the door, blocking Jeff.

"Look, chum," he said in his clipped British accent, "you're to wait over there. I don't want you in with me, okay? I mean it." Two trauma nurses pushed inside.

"I'll be quiet, really. You won't know I'm there, but I've got to—"

Nigel's bony hand pressed on Jeff's shoulder. "For the last time, no. I'll come get you as soon as I can. Now go sit down." He turned, went inside, closed the door and pulled the curtain.

Damn! Jeff was annoyed, yet he knew Nigel was following procedure. Relatives in any trauma room could mess things up greatly. As a doctor himself, he could disagree with Nigel's call and there'd be trouble. Grumbling, Jeff paced the hallway, scarcely aware that his scrubs were splattered with his wife's blood.

Several fellow doctors came by and two nurses he knew

by name, all wanting to know what happened, offering encouragement. Emotions close to the surface, Jeff knew that hospital personnel looked out for one another, and their concern touched him.

In what seemed like hours later but had actually been less than thirty minutes, Nigel stepped through the door. Jeff pounced on him.

"How is she?"

"She's fine, Jeff. She didn't lose all that much blood. As I'm sure you know, the baby's gone."

"Yes…I know. Can I go in now?"

"Yeah, they're just finishing cleaning her up. We called her OB doctor. I gave her a shot so she's pretty groggy. She's asking for you."

"Thanks, buddy."

"No problem. I'm sure she doesn't want to hear it now, but she's young. Another time, eh?"

"Yeah, right." Jeff pulled himself together, hoping Tish would be too fuzzy to see how disappointed he was. Another time, Nigel had said. No, that wasn't what he wanted to hear nor would he say that to Tish. They'd just lost a baby.

Squaring his shoulders, he went into the trauma room just as a nurse he recognized as Debbie finished tucking in the clean sheet.

"Hi, Jeff. She's asking for you." She turned to Tish, her blond ponytail swishing. "Here he is, Mrs. Kirby." She walked toward the door, stopping to touch Jeff's arm. "I'm so sorry."

He whispered his thanks, but his eyes were on Tish. She looked so very pale, like the blood had seeped out of her face. Her skin was always a golden tan. It was a shock, but he tried not to react as he bent over her. "Hi, honey."

She blinked, tears leaking and tracking into her ears.

"The baby's gone, Jeff. I didn't do anything, yet it's gone."

He took her cold hands between his and tried to rub some warmth into them. "I know, honey. I know." He reached up to brush away her tears. "The main thing is, you're okay. I'm so sorry I wasn't there."

"I got up from the chair where I was sewing this little kimono and suddenly, I felt this strong cramp and warm liquid flowed down my legs. I looked down and it was blood. I went into the kitchen to call you, but then this sharp pain caught me and I doubled over. I—I think I passed out."

"Shh, honey, you don't have to go over it. It's going to be all right. You just rest now."

Her hand curled around his and held on tightly. "It wasn't my fault, was it, Jeff? I didn't do anything to—"

"No, sweetheart, you didn't do a thing. It was spontaneous. These things happen sometimes without warning and nothing you do or don't do can prevent them." He kissed her forehead, her cheeks.

"I let you down, Jeff. I know how much you wanted this baby."

"No, this was not your fault. Please, honey, you need to rest." Hadn't Nigel said he'd given her a shot? Why wasn't she drifting off? Maybe because she was too agitated. "They're going to take you up to a room so you can rest and recover."

"No, I want to go home, please, Jeff."

"You've got to stay in at least twenty-four hours, babe, to make sure there's no more bleeding." How could he take her home when he was due back here in another six hours? Who'd watch her if she needed something? "After you're well again, I'll take you home. I promise."

Resigned finally, her eyes fluttered closed just as Debbie came back in.

"If she's ready, I'll take her to her room. Dr. Delaney will see her there shortly."

"Fine. I'll go with you." Unhappily, as empty inside as he knew Tish must feel, he helped guide the gurney out of ER.

For days afterward, Jeff had relived that dreadful scene awake or asleep. He'd see Tish on the kitchen floor lying in a pool of blood, looking so pale, so helpless. Then he'd see her lying in the hospital bed on the stiff white sheets, no longer crying, her eyes open and haunted.

If he'd thought his nightmares were bad, the reality of their life afterward scared him even more. In preparation for her homecoming, he'd given up precious sleep and washed up all the blood and cleaned each room, vacuuming, dusting, polishing, scrubbing, until the place fairly sparkled. It was January and the weather was cool and fresh, so he opened the windows and aired out the place. He put fresh linens on the bed, did the wash and grocery shopped for her favorite foods. And he carefully packed away all the baby things Tish had made or bought so there'd be no tangible reminders.

He insisted on carrying her up the three flights of stairs, telling her she weighed scarcely more than a child, which was the truth. In the apartment, he wanted to put her in bed, but she chose the easy chair in the living room where she'd been doing her sewing. Her eyes were suspiciously bright when he gently set her down, but she didn't cry. He told her there was plenty to eat, but she said she wasn't hungry. He stayed with her awhile, but the one-way conversation was getting to both of them and he was getting nervous about his hospital obligations.

"I know you need to get back to work, Jeff," she said in a flat voice. "Don't worry, please. I'll be fine."

He hated leaving her, yet he felt so helpless because he

didn't know what to do for her, how to bring back the contented, smiling woman she'd been before.

She must have seen the indecision on his face for she took his hand. "Really, I'll be okay. I know you have to leave."

Hating the resignation in her voice and the requirements of his job just then, he bent to kiss her cheek, found her skin cool and dry. "I'll be wearing my beeper. If you need me for anything, *anything,* call me. And I'll check in with you."

She managed a small smile that didn't reach her eyes. As he headed for the door, he saw her lean back and close her eyes.

The next couple of weeks put an enormous strain on their fragile relationship. Although Jeff knew Tish loved him and he certainly loved her, they'd gotten married mainly because of the baby, at least on her part. And now there was no baby. It seemed to Jeff at times when he came home and found her sitting in the chair much as he'd left her that morning that the reason for their being together had vanished with the baby that never had a chance.

He tried. God knows he tried. He rushed home, weary and worried, but he'd go into the kitchen and put together one of Tish's favorite meals only to have her nibble around the edges before apologizing, saying she simply wasn't hungry.

He slept fitfully, despite his fatigue. And every time he awoke, she was lying there, pretending to be asleep but he knew she wasn't. He was so worried that finally he talked with Robert Delaney, the OB doctor she'd been seeing before the miscarriage, and told him everything.

A tall man with red hair and the freckled skin that went with it, Robert heard him out before speaking. "It's called postpartum blues, Jeff. I'm sure you studied it."

"Well, yes, but I honestly didn't think it would happen

with a miscarriage. And it's lasting so long. Over a month now and counting. She has no interest in anything. Christmas came and went and she scarcely noticed." Frustrated, he ran his hand through his shaggy hair, realizing he needed a haircut and hadn't had the time to get one.

"Miscarriage or delivery, her hormones react. Then there's the grief of losing a child. With a normal birth, at least you have a baby to snap you out of your depression. But with a miscarriage, there's nothing. It takes a while to bounce back. Do you talk to her about the loss?"

"I've tried, but she's not very responsive. Like she wants to put the whole experience out of mind. But she just sits and stares. She doesn't read or sew or watch TV. Rob, I'm worried."

"I can prescribe something that might help her. If she'll take it. You need to treat her normal, like you did before. Don't treat her with kid gloves." He paused.

Jeff cleared his throat. "Does that mean it's okay for us to…make love?"

"Yes. Physically, she's healed."

"But I'm afraid she's not ready for it emotionally."

"Every case is different, but making love to her, making her feel you still love her and want her, might do the trick. See, many women with spontaneous miscarriages feel a certain amount of guilt, as if they did something to abort the child. No amount of reassurance seems to take away that feeling. Except maybe letting her know that you still care."

"Okay. Maybe you're right."

Dr. Delaney wrote out a prescription and handed it to Jeff. "These are a mild antidepressants. Might help."

"Thanks, Robert." Jeff shook hands and left.

He planned the event like a seduction. He arranged to have a couple of extra hours off so he wouldn't be exhausted. He bought a special bottle of wine and half a dozen yellow roses, which was all he could afford. And a quart of peach ice cream, Tish's favorite.

Entering their apartment, he found her sitting in the same chair as usual staring out the window. Jeff drew in a deep breath. Now or never, he told himself. "Hi, honey," he said, walking over to kiss her. "For you." He handed her the flowers.

Tish looked up, surprised. She took the roses, smelled them. "They're lovely. Thank you." But she didn't smile.

"And this is for us." Jeff held up the bottle of wine to show her before going into the kitchen for two glasses. When he'd poured the wine, he came back to her and saw she was holding the roses to her and gazing out the window, a sad expression on her face. This wasn't going to be easy, he realized.

He put the flowers in water, then coaxed her into sipping her wine, all the while talking to her, bringing up stories from the hospital that were funny, not upsetting. She began to respond with a comment or two, even smiled a little, which encouraged him to continue. Apparently the wine was loosening her up somewhat.

He left to take a quick shower and returned wearing clean sweats, then poured more wine. "I've got your favorite ice cream for later. I thought I'd grill those two steaks I bought yesterday, make a salad. Are you hungry?"

"A little," she answered. She sipped more wine.

Jeff decided not to introduce the antidepressants while she was drinking. Maybe if he got her to relax, made love to her and all, she wouldn't need the pills. Maybe she'd go back to being the Tish he remembered, the one who laughed easily and often.

He put the radio on, an oldies station. Andy Williams was singing "Moon River" so he took her hand and tugged her out of the chair. "May I have this dance, pretty lady?"

he asked, smiling down at her. Her pale cheeks had spots of color from the wine and her eyes didn't seem quite so sad today.

Tish rose into his arms and he danced her around the small room while Andy serenaded them. She, too, was wearing sweats and white socks on her shoeless feet. In moments, he had her laughing as he sang along, his voice deliberately off-key. As the song ended, Jeff bent his head to kiss her.

The kiss started out as a soft brushing of lips, then he increased the pressure until he felt her draw in a breath and go on tiptoe, pressing herself against him. He deepened the kiss, sending his tongue into the sweetness of her mouth, tasting wine mingled with a rising desire. They swayed to the music that way a while until, his mouth still on hers, he guided them into the bedroom and backed her up until her legs bumped the bed. Holding her, he eased her down onto the mattress, the kiss escalating now, heating his blood and building a fire in hers.

But he kept the brakes on, calling forth all the gentleness he could, his hands lightly roaming her arms and rib cage while his mouth made love to hers. When he felt she was yearning, reaching, he slipped off her clothes and knelt to pull off his before returning to her side. Her eyes were bright and shining and her hands were seeking. For the first time since the miscarriage, Jeff knew she was thinking only of him, of fulfillment, of their love.

He made love to her slowly, taking exquisite care, his hands featherlight on her satin skin, his lips kissing everywhere until she was no longer able to lie still. Finally he braced himself above her and entered her, then lowered to take her mouth in a mind-blowing kiss. Slowly he moved within her and she kept up with him, then he quickened the pace, and still she followed him thrust for thrust.

Jeff raised his head so he could watch her beautiful face

as she climbed with him, her breath coming out in short puffs now, her hands at his back shifting restlessly. He withdrew almost completely, then plunged deep and long, hearing her gasp of pleasure as he stroked her. Seconds later, she arched and quivered, closing her eyes as she strained, then finally let go as the waves engulfed her.

Watching her, Jeff felt his heart soar at the beauty of their joining, then let himself follow as his own release stunned him. Breathing hard, he let her take his weight as he struggled to return to the real world. His eyes open and on hers, he saw the hazy passion cloud her vision.

"I love you, Tish," he whispered. "So very much."

Her hands at his back tightened. "I love you, too, Jeff," she said, her voice husky.

Knowing he was heavy on her, he rolled to the side, taking her with him, settling her against his heated body, her head cradled on his chest. They lay that way for several minutes, letting their damp skin cool.

Jeff was filled with hope, with love. At last, he had his wife back. It was going to be all right. He caressed her back, her shoulders, letting his fingers wander into her hair, massaging her scalp.

After a while, he eased back to look at her. "What do you say we go make dinner?"

She raised troubled eyes to his. "Jeff, what we just shared was incredible. But…this isn't working. I called my SPEAR office this morning. I'm going back into the field."

In the hospital bedside chair, Jeff straightened, glancing at his wife, still sleeping peacefully. "You'll never know how greatly your decision to return to work disappointed me, Tish. How much you hurt me that day."

He took her hand in his, studying the frail skin, turning it over in both of his. "Oh, I know all the reasons you gave me, that the pain of losing our baby made you feel as if you were losing your mind as you sat there in that tiny apartment day after day. But there were other choices. You could have gotten a job there in L.A. and stayed with me until I finished at the hospital. Then we could have both reported to SPEAR.''

He sighed deeply. ''I guess you were hurting so much that you didn't understand how much I was grieving for the baby, too. I realize you had the physical aspect of a miscarriage to get over as well as the emotional pain, but you didn't realize I was in pain, too.''

Jeff placed her hand back on the sheet and sat back again. ''I guess I can't blame you, although I wanted to, for abandoning me when I needed you so much. I've seen other women go through what you did and a lot of the time, they seem to feel as if they're the only ones experiencing pain. That baby was real to me, Tish. I lost a child that day, too. And then, I lost you.''

He sat for some time, elbows on his knees, staring down at the floor. Finally, he drew in a breath and looked at her again. ''I want you to know I've let that go. I know now that hormonal changes had a lot to do with what you were feeling. I've forgiven you for leaving like that, but I still didn't understand why you had to go just then.

''I didn't understand until months later when we saw each other again in Australia....''

Australian Outback, late March

The only thing that kept him going was work, Jeff realized. He threw himself into the hospital routine, working double shifts, overtime, often until he was too tired to drive the short distance to the small apartment that was a constant reminder of the wife who'd left him. More often than not, he'd crash in one of the hospital rooms, wake and shower in the doctor's lounge, pull on fresh scrubs and start all over again.

He heard about Tish from time to time from East and other agents, knew she was taking one assignment after the other, working long hours just like he was. To forget. To purge the memories.

Lord knew he tried to accept her decision, to get on with his life, but it wasn't easy. He wanted Tish back.

But that woman didn't want him.

In late March, SPEAR informed him that they'd made arrangements for him to go to Australia for more field training for his medevac specialty. Naturally, they'd cleared it with the hospital. So he packed his bags and went, hoping a change of scene would lift his spirits. Over the past couple of months, he'd lost weight and lost heart. He had to get both back or he'd be no good to anyone.

He'd slept most of the way on the fourteen-hour flight from Los Angeles to Sydney. Deplaning, he wandered around the airport, impressed with its size and newness. Since he'd slept through most of the meals they'd served, he grabbed a sandwich and washed it down with a beer before boarding a smaller aircraft to Adelaide, the city that had the closest airport to the outback station chosen for his assignment.

Another two hours and ten minutes in the air and he climbed down the ramp onto the tarmac, feeling the mild weather of an autumn morning, recalling that the seasons were reversed in Australia from the United States. Yawning, he realized he'd crossed the International Date Line and lost a day or two in transit. Which was probably why he felt so rung out despite the sleep.

In the baggage area, Jeff spotted a man holding up a sign with his name on it. Ron Hooper was the driver of the ATV who was going to take him to meet up with the other agents already gathered at the outback station. A forty-something, lean, tall man wearing faded jeans and a denim shirt, Ron was a friendly guy who'd lived in Australia for twenty-some years and loved it.

"You'll not find nicer people in the world than right here," Ron told Jeff as they started out. "Or better cattle," he added with a grin.

It was a rough ride over roads often incomplete, many unpaved and some that would be classified as a mere path. The southeast plains looked to be a lot of barren desert, Jeff decided. Ron kept up an interesting conversation for the nearly three-hour ride, telling Jeff all about the cattle station. He seemed pleased that Jeff had some experience working with cattle on SPEAR's Arizona ranch and asked intelligent questions. Still, by the time they reached Pear Tree Station, Jeff's bottom was more than a little numb from all the hours of sitting.

With the many time zones he'd traveled through, he found himself yawning as they pulled up to the main ranch house. Grabbing his one bag, since he'd learned to travel light, Jeff followed Ron inside and was introduced to the other SPEAR agents who'd been summoned. Fighting a lethargy that dragged him down despite all the coffee he'd had, he shook hands with four men who were sitting around a table strategizing.

As Ken, the spokesperson, explained to Jeff, a crisis had developed and Lise Meldrum—the station manager and daughter of Art Meldrum, the mostly absentee owner of Pear Tree—had escaped into the bush on horseback, along with SPEAR agent Russell Devane. Russell had been masquerading as Steve Trace, trying to capture Art Meldrum who, in fact, was really Simon, the traitor they'd all been chasing for months.

"You with me so far?" Ken asked Jeff who he could see was ready to drop. At Jeff's nod, he continued. "So when Russell found out the enemy was almost here, he called for backup, but Simon was hot on their trail so he and Lise had to hightail it out of here.''

Jeff's hours of learning to think on his feet at the hospital finally brought him up to speed. ''But wait a minute,'' he said, stopping Ken. ''Didn't you say that Lise is Art Meldrum's daughter, but Art is really Simon?''

''Yes, that's right. He was never around when she was growing up, although he adored her mother. I guess Simon has some sentiment in him because he named this place after a pear tree his wife planted years ago. But she was killed in a riding accident and Simon was too busy to pay attention to his daughter. She didn't learn how traitorous he's been until recently. She didn't want to believe it, but Russell proved it to her. However some of Simon's stockmen still believe he's a good guy and they've gone after Lise and Russell.''

Jeff shook his head. ''Kind of a confusing mess.''

''Yeah, it is,'' Ralph, another agent spoke up. ''We think that Simon left them and came through here, but we arrived too late to nail the wily fox. Now orders are we're to stick around here and wait for Lise and Russell to come back.''

''Why don't we go after them?'' Jeff wanted to know.

''Hey, man,'' Fred, a third agent, broke in, ''this is one damn big country and we haven't a clue where they went. So, we wait until they come back or we hear word of where they are.''

Ken nodded to Jeff. ''We have a heliport on the property and a helicopter in working order. If we find where they are and someone's hurt, which is entirely possible, that's where you come in. Your medical training, that is.''

''All right.'' Jeff stifled another yawn. ''Maybe I'd better get some shut-eye in case I'm needed. I'm pretty wiped out. Jet lag, you know.''

''Sure thing,'' Ron told him, pointing to a long hall. ''Go down that way. Your room's on the left, last one, right across from our other new arrival. I picked her up yesterday. Tish Buckner.''

Jeff had picked up his bag and started walking, but the name stopped him. Turning, he stared at Ron. ''Did you say Tish Buckner?''

''That's right. You know her?''

''Yeah, you could say that.'' Jeff headed for his room, his emotions suddenly in a turmoil. Since January when they'd parted, he hadn't left L.A. nor had he heard exactly where Tish had been assigned. He'd figured their paths would cross again one day, but certainly not on his first assignment since they separated.

Stopping in front of his room, he paused, looking at the door opposite his. Like at Red Rock, her room was directly across from his. Some would call it kismet. Others would tell him to ignore it, ignore her and get on with things.

Jeff went inside, kicked off his shoes and lay down on the bunk-style bed. In minutes, he was fast asleep.

He slept the clock around, a true luxury for Jeff, finally awakening at six. After getting a shower and putting on some clean clothes, Jeff walked out to the dining hall in the bunkhouse, stopping in the archway. The men he'd met yesterday were almost as he'd left them, still seated around the big oak table, coffee cups at hand, some still finishing breakfast, except for Ken who was in the sitting area on the phone. The only difference was that this time a woman occupied a chair, a woman with short dark hair and eyes that refused to meet his.

Several called out morning greetings to Jeff as he walked over to where Ron, who apparently doubled as short-order cook, was frying up bacon and eggs. Jeff picked up a mug and saw that his hand wasn't quite steady as he poured himself a cup of coffee.

''You ready for breakfast?'' Ron asked Jeff.

"I could eat, if you're cooking." Taking a bracing sip, he strolled to the table and took one of two empty chairs directly across from Tish.

"Seems you know Jeff Kirby, eh, Tish?" Ralph asked, watching the two of them, perhaps picking up on the sudden tension.

"Yes," Tish answered, looking strained as she finally looked up. "Hello, Jeff."

"How are you, Tish?" he asked quietly.

"Fine, thanks." She was saved from more stilted conversation by Ken who'd hung up the phone and rejoined them.

"Here's the story. We know that Simon stopped here after encountering Russell and Lise farther north. We also know he sent some of his stockmen after them, probably making up a lie to get them to hunt them down. We believe that Simon took off for parts unknown just before we got here.

"What we don't know yet is where the others are. I've tried to reach them on Russell's secured line and there's no pickup. If only he'd call, we could go get them."

"It doesn't look good," Fred volunteered.

"No, it doesn't." Ken wore a worried frown.

"Could we split up, send two agents in each direction, try to locate them that way?" Ralph suggested.

"Let's wait awhile yet, then we'll see." Ken took his mug and went back to the phone.

Jeff's breakfast arrived. The other men, finished eating, carried their plates into the kitchen and drifted into the sitting area. Tish remained seated, both hands curled around her coffee mug, watching Jeff eat.

Three eggs, bacon, hash browns and toast—a man-size breakfast. Jeff had been hungry when he'd walked in, but under Tish's quiet gaze, he wasn't sure he could swallow a bite. Annoyed with himself, he picked up his fork. Why should he be nervous? he asked himself. *She'd* walked out on *him*.

Focusing his eyes on his plate as he ate, he was nearly finished when she finally spoke. "I was always impressed by how much you could put away and never gain a pound," she commented in a soft voice.

Wiping his mouth, Jeff looked up. She'd gained back some of the weight she'd lost, he noticed as his eyes devoured her. "You're looking good, Tish," he said, his spurt of anger discarded just as quickly as it had come.

"Not half as good as you look," she said slowly, as if the observation hurt.

He wanted to keep her talking so he searched around for a neutral topic. "I hear you've been busy."

"They keep me hopping." She removed her hands from the mug, saw that they were trembling, and gripped it again.

"That's good. Keeping busy means you don't have time to think about the past." Rising, he carried his plate and mug to the kitchen, then walked over to join the men.

By seven that evening, the men were worried, impatient and restless. Where were Lise and Russell? Had they outmaneuvered Simon's stockmen, the ones who'd been working under Lise all the while and had seemingly changed after Simon egged them on? Or had the stockmen realized their error and changed sides yet again?

Dinner was over and done with and Jeff was tired of listening to first one agent conjecture, then another. Grabbing his jacket, he strolled outside. The night was clear and chilly, the sky darkening but a half moon fully visible. A couple of the remaining stockmen were over by the corral, smoking. The low moan of cattle in the distance could be heard, the earthy smell of animals drifting on a light breeze. He strolled over to the horse barn and paused at the first stall. A dark chestnut mare bobbed her head at him.

"Hello, girl," he said, stroking her long nose.

"Her name is Daisy," a soft, feminine voice behind him said.

Surprised, Jeff turned and saw that Tish had followed him out. She was wearing jeans, a white cotton shirt and a rust-colored suede jacket he recognized.

She wasn't smiling, but her brown eyes were steady on his. "Silly name for a horse, Daisy," she said, walking closer to the stall.

"Yeah, it is," he said absently.

For a long moment, she stood looking into his eyes, as if trying to read his thoughts. Finally, she spoke. "Do you want to go for a ride with me?"

They'd ridden many times on Red Rock Ranch and although he was unfamiliar with the Australian outback, he wouldn't mind exploring it a bit. Although, if he was honest, that wasn't the real reason he agreed to go. "Sure."

Quickly, they saddled Daisy and another mare named Queenie, then rode off. Jeff let Tish lead the way since she'd been here a day longer and probably had checked out the area. She urged Queenie into a trot and he followed easily. Some fifteen minutes later, they reached a rugged outcropping of rocks and a small pool of water. They dismounted to let the horses drink, looping the reins around the branch of a scraggly eucalyptus tree.

It was eerily quiet except for the rustle of a few night birds and a skittering furry little animal.

Tish walked down the barren plains, the moonlight showing the way. Silently Jeff followed. She'd created this scenario and he very much wanted to know where it would lead. After a few minutes, she stopped and turned, leaning against a tall rock. She waited until he came up to her. Again she looked long and hard in his eyes. "I've missed you, Jeff."

"I've missed you, too." Maybe this wasn't smart, maybe he'd get hurt all over again, but he had to tell her the truth.

"I owe you an explanation." She paused, as if waiting for him to contradict her, but when he didn't, she went on. "I had to leave, Jeff. I was in such a depression. I felt as if I'd let you down, let myself down, the—the baby. Everything. I was going crazy in that apartment, day after day, never anything to look forward to except a couple of hours with you when you so obviously needed sleep. Better women than me have seen their husbands through a hospital residency, but apparently I couldn't handle the stress, especially after losing the baby."

He didn't know how to answer that, so he kept still.

Tish stared at the buttons of his shirt visible in the open folds of his jacket rather than at his face as she drew in a breath. "I don't know if you can understand, but Jeff, I felt as if I were losing *me,* the person I was, and the one I wanted to be. You had your work, the hospital, people there you knew well. I had no one to talk to who would understand. I—I maybe should have talked more to you, but I felt so damn guilty." There was a catch in her voice.

Jeff slipped his arms around her waist. "It's all right. I should have been more understanding."

"No, it wasn't you. It was me." She paused a moment, her hands on his shirt, moving restlessly. "I never stopped loving you, Jeff. Not one day. I—"

Her words were cut off by his mouth capturing hers. The kiss carried so much pent-up emotion, trying to erase the pain of the past. He felt like he'd come home, like she was once more his, like a man who'd found a vital missing part of his being.

"Tish, I love you, too. So very much."

"Show me, Jeff. I've missed you every day, every night."

He backed her up to the boulder behind her, then he

lowered his head to her breast, drawing deeply, savagely, through the material of her blouse. The wild heat spread downward until he had her writhing and twisting under his relentless onslaught.

Jeff was driven, beyond slow loving, moving beyond gentle. He wanted to convince her they belonged together despite their differences. He wanted to brand her, make her his forever. Needs pounded at him fiercely as he ripped her blouse down the front, felt the buttons scatter, and then he feasted on her. He heard her cry out, her breath coming in ragged spurts, and he recognized not fear, not pain, but shocked pleasure.

His fingers fumbled to open his jeans, then shoved her slacks down and off her trembling legs. Her chest was heaving now and her hands gripped his shoulders. His blood swam hot and tormented as he struggled to free himself. His fingers found her and he heard her cry out, a strangled sound.

He was on the verge of exploding, but he paused, breathing hard. This was Tish, the woman he loved more than his life, the one he needed more than his next breath. He looked at her in the moonlight, a question in his eyes.

The expression on her damp face was utterly female. "I want you inside me, *now*."

The words he'd been waiting to hear. With one fierce thrust, he was inside her, anchoring her legs around his body, feeling her heels dig in. He closed his eyes on the sheer pleasure of it, the incredible beauty of it. She was exactly where he'd been wanting her, where he'd been dreaming of her, here with him.

He began to move, wildly, ruthlessly. In a frenzy of need, he pounded into her, his body braced against hers. Her breathing was as ragged as his own as she climbed with him. Her release came quickly, fueled by her emotions, driven by an urgency like neither had known before.

Finally, she shuddered and she relaxed against him. Only then did Jeff allow himself to follow.

Chapter 12

Jeff took a long swallow of water from the bottle he'd brought into Tish's ICU room earlier. Mentally recalling their time together in Australia had drained him.

Yet it had also energized him. "Remember how we'd snuck back to the ranch house with your jacket zipped up to your chin because of the buttons you'd lost from your blouse when I'd ripped it open, honey? Good thing the agents in the sitting room couldn't see a thing when we walked in, because your face was flushed and probably mine was, too. It would have been a dead giveaway." He smiled at the memory.

"I was so happy and I think you were, too. We spent the next whole day together, remember? I do, every minute. I think we fell in love all over again that day. I can picture us laughing as we fixed a thermos of hot coffee, then we grabbed our jackets, borrowed one of the four-wheel drives and headed out to explore. What a day that was...."

* * *

Tish gazed up at the cloudless sky, the sun just peeking over the dry, sparse plains. She shivered a little because it was quite cool, but the nip in the air felt good. Turning her head, she smiled at Jeff. "This was a good idea."

"Yeah, I have one once in a while." He grinned at her, glad to be here with her, glad to be alive. The memory of their lovemaking last night in the moonlight danced in his mind and had his eyes warming. He reached over and took her hand, wishing the Jeep had a bench seat instead of buckets so he could draw her closer.

"More than one, I'd say," Tish answered, a blush coloring her cheeks as she, too, recalled last evening. "I couldn't go to sleep for hours. I kept thinking about you, reliving our...horseback ride."

He laughed at her choice of words. "Me, too." Jeff turned down a deserted road. "I have no idea where this leads since I've never been in Australia before."

"Me, either, but I feel adventurous. Let's explore, go where the road takes us."

He squeezed her fingers, then let go to hold the wheel with both hands as they bumped along the rutted path. They rode for some time in silence. Now that they'd left the outback behind, the landscape here was lovely with lush hills and the occasional farmhouse and barn nestled in a valley. It was all so different from home.

Tish was different, too, Jeff couldn't help thinking. The quiet, sad woman who'd sat staring at the four walls for days after the miscarriage had been replaced by the mischievous, bold lover who'd been as hungry for him as he'd been for her. Maybe there was a chance that they could overcome the past and start all over again.

"Oh, Jeff, look over there," she said excitedly, pointing off to the right as they rounded a bend. "Aren't they adorable?"

There were sheep, not just a few but what looked like fifty or more sprinkled over the green, green hillside. Some were grazing, others lying down, and still more just standing along the fence line and staring at them as they passed by. With the blue sky backdrop, the scene looked like a painting.

"I'm not sure I'd call them adorable," Jeff said, slowing down, "but they are picturesque." He pulled off the dirt path close to the fence and almost before he'd come to a full stop, Tish was out. He watched her climb onto the first rung of the short fence and heard her call to the nearest sheep as he got out.

Propping one booted foot next to hers, he leaned on the top of the fence. "I don't think sheep come when you call them. I've read they're not the brightest of farm animals."

No sooner had he said that than a sheep that looked to be quite young ambled over closer to where Tish held out her hand. "I wish I had something to offer him. What do sheep eat?"

"Grass and they have plenty of that all around them," Jeff answered drily.

As they watched, a lively dog came bounding over, a brownish blur looking to be a cross between a small collie and a terrier, certainly an odd mix. Quickly, he got between the wandering sheep and the intruders on the fence and shooed his young charge back to the herd, but not before tossing them a look that seemed to say, get back. Running again, he raced up the nearest hill and guided another meandering sheep back to join the others.

"Busy little guy, isn't he?" Jeff commented.

"He sure told me," Tish said, smiling as she climbed back down. "Hands off, clear as day." Frowning, she studied the sheep nearest them. "What do you suppose those marking on their rump mean?"

Jeff saw that some sheep had a bright spot of blue tinted on the gray-white of their coat in the vicinity of the rump and others had pink. A very few had yellow markings. "I imagine the obvious answer would be that blue is for boys and pink for girls, eh?"

"And yellow is for…?" she asked, turning to him.

"The undecided." He pointed to where six or seven sheep seemed to huddle together. "See those with blue markings? All guys, probably secretly smoking cigars. No pink butts allowed."

"Chauvinistic sheep. I love it."

Tish laughed as she gazed about. "It's so lovely here, so quiet and peaceful. It seems a world apart from New York or even smaller cities. Not even at Red Rock did you get this feeling of tranquility."

"I agree. It's like I imagine rural areas of the States were back in the forties." Jeff gazed down the road where a large, two-story farmhouse sat, painted white with a picket fence that looked to be more for show than to keep anyone out, plus the obligatory barn painted red nearby. A farmer in blue jeans and plaid shirt was walking toward the field.

As they watched, the farmer put his fingers to his mouth and let out a series of whistles that echoed through the quiet hills. Suddenly the little dog went into action, running this way and that, shepherding the sheep toward the corral where the farmer stood.

"Look at that, will you?" Jeff commented as the farmer changed his tune and the dog ran to the far side where a stray had wandered and in moments had that sheep headed toward the rest. Running from side to side and back, in no time the dog had the sheep slowly trailing into captivity. "Remarkable."

"Could we go down and talk to that man?" Tish asked. "I'm dying to know what those colored markings are."

"I don't see why not," Jeff answered, getting back in the Jeep. "The people here seem really friendly."

In minutes, they'd pulled into the wide drive and walked over to the man who held open the gate as the last of the sheep mosied in. He glanced toward the young couple, a mildly curious expression on his round face.

"'G'day," the man said before Jeff could speak. "Nice weather, eh?"

"Yes, it sure is. I'm Jeff and this is Tish. We were out for a drive when we saw your sheep." He shifted his gaze to the dog who stood next to the farmer as the gate swung shut. "That's quite a talented dog you have there."

"That he is. Jimbo's the best sheep dog I ever had." The man stuck out his hand. "I'm Cyrus."

Jeff shook his hand as Tish stepped closer. "I've been wondering, what do the colorful markings on the sheep mean, Cyrus?" she asked.

Cyrus chuckled and tipped back his large brimmed hat. "Them's grading marks. Early on, we separate sheep as to what type they are, whether we'll use 'em for sheering, the ones with good thick coats year after year. Or the ones who'll be best for market. Mutton, you know."

"I see. But you've got three different colors."

"Yup, we do. Yellow's for the older sheep. Their coats aren't good for selling any more and they're too tough for table meat. Trouble is, I can't bring myself to butcher 'em, you know. Sentimental old fool, the wife calls me."

"I think you're very kind," Tish said and reached to shake his hand.

"Would you like to come in, have some tea? We've always got a pot steeping."

"That's very nice of you, but we'd best be on our way. Thanks, Cyrus." His hand at her back, Jeff led Tish back to the Jeep. Waving at the farmer, they drove off, noticing that the dog was resting now that his work was done for the morning.

"I think I could live here in this quiet village," Jeff said some time later as the Jeep rambled down the dry plains. More farms and sheep lay before them on both sides of the road for miles ahead. "Except that I'm an American through and through, I'd like this life one day. When I'm older, of course." He glanced over at Tish who had her eyes straight ahead, looking pensive. "What do you think?"

"Could I live here, you mean? I think I could, if not here then someplace similar. In retirement, perhaps." She turned to study Jeff's profile. "You'd be content being a small-town doctor?"

He twined his fingers with hers. "If you were with me." She'd been ready to give up SPEAR when she'd learned she was pregnant. Maybe they would be better off somewhere away from the madding crowd. Tish was more relaxed in a country atmosphere, as she'd been at Red Rock. But what about East and all he owed him? And SPEAR, the people who'd invested in his education expecting to be paid back by his becoming a medvac specialist?

Jeff sighed. Why was life so damned complicated?

"Sometimes I feel like those sheep," Tish said quietly, "being herded here, then guided elsewhere, at the whim of others. Then again I feel like that busy little dog, the fate of others resting on my shoulders, responsible for so many." She ran a hand through her short hair. "It's a dilemma, isn't it?"

Jeff couldn't have agreed more. "Maybe we're all torn by forces outside ourselves, tugging us to do one thing while our hearts want us to do another. That's man for you—and woman—never quite satisfied."

"Want to stop and have some coffee?" Jeff asked.

"Sure."

He pulled the Jeep under a somewhat scraggly bush of

indeterminate origin and age and parked. Reaching for the thermos and cups, he also grabbed the blanket.

Once they were seated, Tish let him pour the coffee while she immersed herself in the lovely peace of the morning. Squinting, she gazed toward a small shanty not far from them. "What do you suppose that is?"

Glancing over his shoulder first, Jeff handed her a steaming cup. "That, my dear, is an outhouse. Or a privy. Take your pick." He sipped the hot brew, welcoming the warmth, the caffeine kick.

"You're joking! Out here, in the middle of a desert?"

"Not joking. Ron, the agent who picked me up at the airport, told me that tour buses come out this way to show the city folk what it's like in the outback. They bring box lunches and set up tables, the whole bit. Naturally, they need a potty sooner or later. Tourists love to 'go native,' don't you know."

She smiled at his attempt at an Australian accent. "And do they sit around singing 'Waltzing Matilda,' too?"

"Probably." Setting down and anchoring his cup, Jeff lay back and propped his hands under his head. With one tug on the sleeve of her jacket, he had Tish down and leaning over him, nearly spilling her coffee.

He didn't care. He wanted her mouth on his, her heart beating against his. The kiss was at once tender and fierce, the longing on both sides very evident.

"Last night wasn't enough for me," Jeff told her, his hand sliding beneath her jacket, searching for and finding her breast. "I want you again. Now."

"We can't, not out here where anyone could come by." But she wanted him just as much.

"Okay, how about the outhouse?" he suggested, tongue-in-cheek.

She made a face. "Thanks, but no thanks." She snuggled down, placing her cheek on the spot over his heart. It was chilly, but Tish didn't mind. She was always warm when she was with Jeff.

"Mmm," he murmured, "I could stay like this forever."

"Just a moment ago, you wanted to jump my bones."

"Oh, I'd rise to the occasion now and then, but a man has to rest, you know."

Tish was quiet a long while, contented. "I wonder what the rest of the world, those who have no one special, are doing now?"

"Wishing they were us."

Tish raised her head. "Do you think that…" Startled at a movement that caught her eye just past her line of vision, she sat up to look. "Oh, Jeff," she said in a stage whisper, "look who's found us."

Jeff rose and saw three young kangaroos no more than a hundred feet from them. Scrambling up slowly so as not to spook them, both of them just stared. Two kangaroos were sort of wrestling or shadowboxing while the third kept trying to join in.

Suddenly, a much larger kangaroo appeared and, without a sound, herded the youngsters away.

"Let's go see," Tish said, creeping up quietly to get a closer look. Her eyes went wide and she couldn't say a word. None was necessary as Jeff joined her, as awestruck as she.

There were maybe a dozen and a half kangaroos, hopping about just like they'd seen in the movies. A few were young but most were older and larger. They seemed to be interacting with one another without a sound being made between them. A rambunctious pair really got into it, but the friendly bout was broken up by a third one who seemed to be a sort of leader.

They paid scant attention to the two humans watching them, so Jeff and Tish stood still, taking it all in. "Darn, I wish I had a camera," Tish whispered.

Later, neither could have said just how long they watched the hijinx. Then, as if to an unheard signal, the kangaroos started going farther away, until they disappeared from sight in the landscape.

"That was something to see," Tish said as they gathered their things and made their way back to the Jeep. "I'm surprised they're so tame. They didn't seem a bit afraid of us."

"Oh, I imagine the tour companies have put restrictions on the groups they bring up here so no one's ever really bothered them," Jeff said, getting behind the wheel.

They spent hours more driving rural roads, finally stopping at a small village, strolling to gaze into the windows of a few shops—a butcher, a pharmacy, a book store. Then they ate a hearty lamb stew served with chunky black bread in a friendly tavern, chasing it down with a dark ale.

By the time they returned to the cattle station, the sun was slowly sinking. They got some inquisitive looks which they studiously ignored. Not to be put off, Jeff stopped in front of their rooms across from one another and came to a decision.

"You're coming with me tonight," he said, and pulled Tish into his room before locking the door. She did not protest.

Remembering that happy time in Australia softened Jeff's features. "Oh, I know we hadn't worked out all the problems between us—the age thing which still bugged you, my time-consuming residency with months to go yet, you going back into the field which I wasn't in favor of. But there, in the vast plains of Australia, we both knew without a doubt that we loved each other and we belonged together. We promised we'd work things out no matter what.

"And I believe we would have if only the next morning, just after dawn, all hell hadn't broken loose."

Jeff leaned back in the chair, his mind back in Australia. "That was when Russell and the stockmen finally got Lise back to the station with the gunshot wound in her shoulder. I got a little worried that I might not be able to help her. The bullet had just missed one of her lungs. Russell was breathing down my neck every second, but I fixed her up. Finally, I felt as if I were earning my keep in SPEAR.

"The shock afterward was when we learned that Simon, who Lise had known all her life as her father, Art Meldrum, was the one who'd shot her when he'd realized that she'd told his stockmen the truth and they'd turned against him. Unbelievable. He shot his own daughter, then took off like the coward he is. Damn, I'd like to see us get him."

Again, Jeff leaned forward and took her hand, his voice once more low, but with an underlying anger. "He's the one responsible for you being here, Tish, the one responsible for that bomb." He felt his free hand curl into a fist. "I'd like a few minutes alone with him, but I think I'd have to get in line."

He forced himself to relax, worried she'd pick up on his anxiety. "Anyhow, a short time after I'd patched up Lise, we got the call and you were ordered to New York." Jeff sighed deeply. "If only your name hadn't been on the list of agents needed here." Letting go of her hand, he scrubbed his fingers over his ravaged face. "If not then, maybe you'd have been hurt another time. This is very dangerous work, Tish. I wish with all my heart I could talk you into taking a desk job in SPEAR and leaving the field. I know you like the work and that you're good at it. But honey, I need you as much as SPEAR does. More, I think."

Suddenly, their shaky future overwhelmed him. "Listen to me, talking as if you could climb out of this bed tomorrow. Lord, but I wish you could. I wish you'd come back to me, move back with me. To hell with the age difference, Tish. You *have* to live, babe, because I have to show you that we can make our relationship work. East taught me that family is what you create when you love someone and that age doesn't matter. Love is all that matters, and my love for you will never change.''

Emotions flared up inside him and he wished he could control them better, but he couldn't. Jeff bent his head, laying his cheek onto the side of her bed. "Please, Tish, come back to me. I need you so much."

Choking back tears, he sat like that a long, long time. Finally, emotionally and physically drained, he fell into a restless sleep.

She felt as if she were walking down a long tunnel. Her footsteps were slow, hesitant, indecisive. There was no one to lead the way, to help her along.

Her feet felt so heavy, as if each step took monumental effort. The wispy walls that surrounded her were white and filmy, the air hazy, as if she were in a foggy place. Something kept tugging her backward, but she struggled to go forward. She needed to get somewhere, but she wasn't sure where.

As she moved slowly along, she heard a voice as if from a great distance. She tried moving faster, toward the sound. The voice grew slightly louder and finally, she recognized it.

Jeff! *Jeff was calling to her. She listened hard, cocking her head, trying to make out the words.* Please, Tish, come back to me. I need you so much. *She felt tears slipping down her cheeks. She needed him, too, so very much. She wanted to tell him, but she was having trouble speaking. There was a heaviness in her chest.*

Slowly, she moved down the tunnel toward the light glow-

ing at the end. One step after another, seeing more clearly now. The heaviness lifted and she struggled to open her eyes....

Tish blinked once, then twice more. The haziness slowly drifted away and she looked around. A hospital room, tubes in her nose, her arm, a heavy bandage just below her throat. Why was she here?

Then it came back to her. New York, the bomb going off, people screaming, the sound of a building shattering so loud, so terrible. Glass breaking, steel falling, bricks hurtling. And something heavy hit her, something sharply painful, and she fell, fell down and down, a long way. She blinked rapidly to rid herself of the memory.

Gingerly, she tried to move her arms and felt no pain. Then she shifted her head and that's when she saw him.

Jeff was there, seated in a chair alongside her hospital bed, his head resting near her hand. His eyes were closed and he looked like he hadn't slept in days.

A sudden memory returned and fear leaped into her heart as her hand flew to her stomach and gently pressed down. The baby. Was it all right? How extensive were her injuries? Was the baby still there, still okay? Oh, Lord, she couldn't lose another child. She just couldn't.

Tish felt her cheeks grow damp. Was that why Jeff had been upset, because they'd told him she'd lost their second baby? Just when they'd found their way back to one another in Australia, rediscovered a love that had at first frightened Tish, then filled her with joy. Would he still love her if she lost his child yet again?

She hadn't had a chance to tell him about the baby she was carrying, the child that had been conceived on their last night together in that small apartment in L.A. She'd only just realized it herself on her way to the New York assignment, thinking she'd been late only as a result of the miscarriage.

Jeff hadn't wanted her to return to the field, yet she'd felt she needed some distance. Then in Australia, when they'd found their way back to one another finally, he'd again asked her not to go to New York on this new assignment. But she'd gone, certain she could handle herself. And now, what if she'd lost the baby as a result of the blast, as a result of her insistence on working in the field? Jeff would have every reason to stop loving her.

Her eyes stayed on him, his wonderful face. Even asleep, he wore a frown, one she'd undoubtedly put there. He was such a good man, so loving and caring. Yet she'd given him nothing but grief. She should probably walk away, let him find someone who wouldn't be constantly hurting him.

But how could she when she loved him so much, when just a touch from him could set her on fire? It had been like that since the first day they'd met. She hadn't trusted those feelings, thinking her passion for Jeff was merely physical and would grow cold with time. She'd been wrong. Instead, her desire for him had grown with each encounter.

Tish decided she couldn't wait any longer. She had to know.

Gently, she touched his hair, drawing her fingers through the thick blond strands, willing him to wake up.

He'd been dreaming of a day filled with sunshine at Red Rock Ranch in Arizona. He and Tish were riding Domino and Belladonna side by side, on their way to their favorite spot by the stream, in the saddlebag a lunch packed for later, after they'd made love in the shade of the old cottonwood tree. He was happy, gazing at her beautiful, smiling face. As he rode, a branch brushed at his head, snaring his hair. He reached up a hand to push it away and…and his hand touched flesh.

Jeff's eyes flew open and he saw that Tish's hand was

in his hair. Lifting his head, he saw her eyes were open and on his, that a gentle smile was forming on her lovely face. "Tish! Oh, thank God, you're awake."

"Hello, Jeff." How good it felt to see him so clearly.

Easing a hip onto her bed, he leaned down to her. "How are you feeling?"

She moved her head around, testing, then frowned. "I have a headache, but that's all. How badly am I hurt?"

"You're coming along just fine. But you had a severe concussion and you've been in a coma for three days now...."

"Three days!" Her hand flew to her stomach. "The baby! Is the baby all right?"

Jeff's face registered his stunned surprise. "What baby?" Was she back in time, remembering the days before the miscarriage?

Tish licked her dry lips. "I was on my way to New York on the last leg of the trip from Australia when I figured out that I was pregnant. I didn't have a chance to tell you and—"

His mind busily did the math. "But we'd only made love a few weeks ago in Australia. You couldn't know so soon."

She shook her head. "No, it had to have happened back in the apartment in Los Angeles before I left, that last night. Don't you remember?"

He did then, their poignant farewell. "Then you're about three months along! That's wonderful, honey." He leaned to hug her awkwardly around all the tubes.

But Tish was still concerned. "Wait, Jeff. What if I—I lost the baby in the bomb blast? What if my injuries caused..." She couldn't say any more, the words clogging in her throat.

Why hadn't Dr. O'Neill mentioned her pregnancy? Jeff wondered. But it didn't matter. He smiled down into her worried eyes. "It doesn't matter. I don't care, not as long as you're alive and okay. You're the most important thing in my life. Baby or no baby, our marriage is what matters, our love is the important thing.''

As he pulled her into his arms, Tish felt tears of joy slip from beneath her closed eyelids. He loved her still, no matter what had happened. And she would spend the rest of her life trying to make him happy.

Finally, gone were her fears that someone wouldn't love her for herself alone. She was the most important thing in his life he'd said, and she was overjoyed to hear the words.

''I love you, Jeff, more than you'll ever know,'' she whispered.

Epilogue

Some time later, Jeff sat in the chair alongside Tish's bed holding her hand. He couldn't stop smiling, thrilled that she was going to be all right. Her fingers wrapped in his, she clung to him, too, fearful of letting him go.

The nurse had been in, pleased that Tish had awakened. She'd taken her vital signs, marked her charts, examined her briefly and cranked up her hospital bed so she'd be more comfortable. Before leaving, she'd told them that she'd paged Dr. O'Neill who was in surgery and he'd be in as soon as he was finished.

"My wife tells me she might be pregnant," Jeff told Thelma. "Is that so?"

"I'd rather Dr. O'Neill discuss that with you, Doctor." She left them alone.

Tish looked crestfallen. "That doesn't sound good. Why wouldn't she tell us? Surely that information has to be on my chart. I mean, what kind of doctor would examine a patient and not pick up on a pregnancy?"

Jeff was more optimistic. Her awakening had buoyed him, had made him believe that more miracles could happen. "A busy one, maybe. His main concern was saving your life. He might not have checked for a pregnancy." Although he doubted that. In most patients of child-bearing years, an automatic pregnancy test was usually taken to prevent administering a medication that might harm or terminate the pregnancy. The thing that struck Jeff as odd was that Dr. O'Neill hadn't mentioned the baby to him, a medical colleague. However, he wasn't going to worry Tish with that just now.

Trying to control her impatience, Tish let her eyes roam over Jeff instead, admiring his strong, masculine face that needed a shave. He also had acquired some worry lines that she hated having put there. She squeezed his hand. "You look so good to me."

"Not half as good as you do to me. In my entire life, not even during the episode in Idaho when I was buried alive, have I ever been as scared as I've been these last three days. Promise me you won't do this to me again, Tish."

Blinking back an emotional rush of tears, she nodded.

"Do you remember what happened before the blast, or don't you want to talk about it?" Jeff asked.

Before she could respond, a tall man with brown hair gave one quick knock on the ICU door and walked in, his amber eyes on Tish, his handsome face forming a smile. "Hey, lady, it's about time you woke up!"

Tish smiled back as Jeff got to his feet. "Del! I'm so glad you're okay."

"It takes more than a little old bomb to take us out, right?" he said, walking over.

"Jeff, this is Del Rogers, the SPEAR agent who saved my life."

"Oh, I wouldn't go that far," Del said modestly.

"Of course, you did. You pulled me to safety after the blast. That's my last memory of that day."

Impressed and grateful, Jeff turned to the man. "I sure want to shake your hand," he said. "I can't begin to thank you."

"You're very welcome." Del shook Jeff's hand, then turned to Tish. "I heard you were in a coma and I wanted to come over sooner, but I'm on assignment. Finally found the time and they told me at the desk that you'd just come to." He reached to touch her hand. "I'm so glad you're going to be all right."

"Me, too. Thanks, Del, for everything."

Seemingly uncomfortable with being thanked so emotionally, Del stepped back. "I've got to get going." He nodded to Jeff. "Nice meeting you." He took a last look at Tish. "I'll see you later."

Tish watched him walk away. "What a great guy."

"I'm grateful he was around to help you." Just as he glanced at his watch, the cubicle door slid open again and finally Dr. O'Neill walked in, still in his operating scrubs. "Doctor," Jeff greeted him, "we have a surprise for you. She's awake at last."

"So I've been hearing," he answered, moving to the bed and removing his stethoscope from around his neck. "How do you feel, young lady?"

"A little headachy but otherwise all right." Tish impatiently held still while he listened to her heart and lungs, waiting for him to tell her his findings.

Finally, Dr. O'Neill straightened, a smile on his thin face. "You're doing just fine and, to answer the question you haven't asked, your baby's fine, too."

"Oh!" Tish's hands flew to her mouth and her eyes filled with tears. "Thank you," she whispered.

O'Neill turned to Jeff. "I debated about telling you, but I didn't want to add to your worries in case something went wrong." He smiled then. "You'll be able to take her home soon."

Jeff felt his heart swell. Tish alive and well, the baby okay. He couldn't have asked for more.

"I'd take it easy for a while if I were you, young lady," the doctor said. "No climbing around bomb sites."

"I'll keep close tabs on her, Doctor," Jeff promised. "I think we're overdue a trip to Disneyland, right, honey?"

"That's right," Tish answered. "Don't worry, Doctor," she added, happiness lighting up her pale face and adding color, "my days of playing secret agent are over." She reached for Jeff's hand. "From now on, I'll leave all that to my husband."

* * * * *

Chapter 1

Agent Del Rogers was a hunter. For now his prey had eluded him, but a hunter has patience. He has self-control. And above all, a good hunter never takes the hunt personally.

Turning away from the hospital, Del forced his fists to relax. The reddened skin on the back of his hands twinged and the patches on his arms where the hair had been singed off were beginning to itch, reminders of his last encounter with the man known as Simon. Yet Del had gotten off lightly compared to the agent he had just seen in the intensive care ward. The bomb in the warehouse last week had caught everyone off guard. The next meeting with Simon would be different. Next time, SPEAR would be ready.

He strode along the sidewalk, stretching his legs to work out the lingering aches in his muscles. Out of habit, he scanned his surroundings, yet he knew he wouldn't spot his quarry here. Yellow cabs shouldered through the late afternoon traffic; car horns and sirens mingled with the background hum of Manhattan. A warm puff of air scented with yeast and oregano wafted briefly from the doorway of a pizzeria before it was swallowed by the pervasive metallic tang of exhaust.

It was April. The hunt for Simon had been going on for almost a year, but it was bound to end soon. SPEAR was gradually closing the net. The best operatives in the top-secret government agency had taken their turn at running Simon to ground. Despite the traitor's uncanny ability to elude them, his hiding places were dwindling. Now it was only a matter of time before he walked into their trap.

On the corner beside the subway entrance, a splash of color against the iron railing caught Del's eye. A flower vendor was sitting on an overturned bucket, hawking bunches of fresh daffodils. Del dug into his pocket and tossed a coin to the weathered old man.

"Thanks, sport," the man muttered. He turned the coin over in his grimy hand. "Hey, what is this?"

"It's a double eagle."

"Ain't got change for that," he said, squinting at Del.

"Didn't think you would. The last time I had one of those coins was three years ago in Juneau."

As soon as Del said the prearranged code words, the flower seller shrugged and picked up a handful of daffodils. "You must have some hot date."

"Uh-huh." Del took the bouquet, running his fingertips of the stems until he felt the small plastic rectangle that was concealed there. He headed down the stairs to the subway, slipping the microcassette tape out of the flowers and into his pocket. He would have to wait until he met his partner Bill Grimes at the surveillance site before he could listen to the briefing on this tape—like all the SPEAR briefing cassettes, it would erase as it played.

He was pulling the graveyard shift with Bill tonight. Del wasn't being given any consideration for his burns and bruises, and he wasn't asking for any. At this stage of the chase, every available operative was needed to ensure Simon didn't slip away again.

The subway train squealed to a halt at Del's stop, jarring his swollen knee. He ignored the discomfort and blended into the crowd that spilled onto the street. He walked a block east, crossed Third Avenue, then paused in front of a shoe store, using the reflection in the glass to check out the passersby. Satisfied that he hadn't been followed, he glanced at the daffodils he still held. His lips quirked as he remembered the flower seller's comment.

Being holed up in an apartment all night with Bill, staring through a sniper's scope, wasn't Del's idea of a hot date. And he was certain Bill wouldn't like the flowers.

But Del knew someone who would. He lifted his head, his gaze going to the coffee shop on the other side of the street. Maggie was the kind of woman who would love flowers. She would be thrilled to get these daffodils. He could picture how she would smile and stick them in a sundae glass and chatter about how yellow is such a happy color....

No. A bouquet of flowers could carry a message in more than one way. And Del couldn't afford to give any woman the wrong message, especially a woman like Maggie. She deserved better than that. Life hadn't dealt her a good hand, yet she was making the best of it, facing her problems with a good-natured determination that he had to admire.

If things had been different, if he had known her eight

years ago, he might have considered giving her more than just a bouquet.

Del wavered for an instant, then tossed the daffodils into the trash can.

It was better this way.

Silhouette®

INTIMATE MOMENTS™

presents a riveting 12-book continuity series:

A Year of loving dangerously

Where passion rules and nothing is what it seems...

When dishonor threatens a top-secret agency, the brave men and women of SPEAR are prepared to risk it all as they put their lives—and their hearts—on the line.

Available May 2001:

CINDERELLA'S SECRET AGENT
by Ingrid Weaver

As a sharpshooter for the SPEAR agency, Del Rogers was determined to capture an arch villain named Simon. Love and family did not factor into his mission. *Until* he found the Cinderella of his dreams in the form of a pretty, pregnant waitress. Helping to deliver Maggie Rice's baby girl was all in a day's work. But keeping his heart neutral was an entirely different matter. Did this chivalrous secret agent dare indulge in fantasies of happily ever after?

Available only from Silhouette Intimate Moments
at your favorite retail outlet.

Silhouette®
Where love comes alive™

a Year of loving dangerously

If you missed the first 9 riveting,
romantic Intimate Moments stories
from *A Year of Loving Dangerously*,
here's a chance to order your copies today!

#1016	**MISSION: IRRESISTIBLE** by Sharon Sala	$4.50 U.S. ☐ $5.25 CAN. ☐
#1022	**UNDERCOVER BRIDE** by Kylie Brant	$4.50 U.S. ☐ $5.25 CAN. ☐
#1028	**NIGHT OF NO RETURN** by Eileen Wilks	$4.50 U.S. ☐ $5.25 CAN. ☐
#1034	**HER SECRET WEAPON** by Beverly Barton	$4.50 U.S. ☐ $5.25 CAN. ☐
#1040	**HERO AT LARGE** by Robyn Amos	$4.50 U.S. ☐ $5.25 CAN. ☐
#1046	**STRANGERS WHEN WE MARRIED**	
	by Carla Cassidy	$4.50 U.S. ☐ $5.25 CAN. ☐
#1052	**THE SPY WHO LOVED HIM**	
	by Merline Lovelace	$4.50 U.S. ☐ $5.25 CAN. ☐
#1058	**SOMEONE TO WATCH OVER HER**	
	by Margaret Watson	$4.50 U.S. ☐ $5.25 CAN. ☐
#1064	**THE ENEMY'S DAUGHTER** by Linda Turner	$4.50 U.S. ☐ $5.25 CAN. ☐

(limited quantities available)

TOTAL AMOUNT	$ _____
POSTAGE & HANDLING	
($1.00 each book, 50¢ each additional book)	$ _____
APPLICABLE TAXES*	$ _____
TOTAL PAYABLE	$ _____
(check or money order—please do not send cash)	

To order, send the completed form, along with a check or money order for the total above,
payable to **A YEAR OF LOVING DANGEROUSLY** to: **In the U.S.:** 3010 Walden Avenue,
P.O. Box 9077, Buffalo, NY 14269-9077 **In Canada:** P.O. Box 636, Fort Erie, Ontario L2A 5X3.

Name: _____

Address: _____ City: _____

State/Prov.: _____ Zip/Postal Code: _____

Account # (if applicable): _____   075 CSAS

*New York residents remit applicable sales taxes.
 Canadian residents remit applicable
 GST and provincial taxes.

Silhouette®

Visit Silhouette at www.eHarlequin.com   AYOLD-BL9

HARLEQUIN®

bestselling authors

Merline Lovelace
Deborah Simmons
Julia Justiss

cordially invite you to enjoy three
brand-new stories of unexpected love

The
Officer's
Bride

Available April 2001

HARLEQUIN®

Makes any time special ®

PHOFFICER

Look in the back pages of
all June Silhouette series books to find an
exciting new contest with fabulous prizes!
Available exclusively through Silhouette.

Don't miss it!

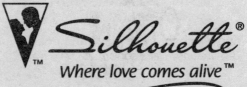

*P.S. Watch for details on how you can meet
your favorite Silhouette author.*